THE GODKILLER

THE GODKILLER

SKHARR DEATHEATER™ SERIES BOOK 04

MICHAEL ANDERLE

DISRUPTIVE IMAGINATION

LMBPN Publishing
PMB 196, 2540 South Maryland Pkwy
Las Vegas, NV 89109

First US edition, January 2021
ebook ISBN: 978-1-64971-409-1
Paperback ISBN: 978-1-64971-410-7

THE GODKILLER TEAM

Thanks to our JIT Team:

Wendy L Bonell
Rachel Beckford
Diane L. Smith
Peter Manis
Jeff Eaton
John Ashmore
Jeff Goode
Kelly O'Donnell
Angel LaVey

If I've missed anyone, please let me know!

Editor
SkyHunter Editing Team

To Family, Friends and
Those Who Love
To Read.
May We All Enjoy Grace
To Live The Life We Are
Called.

*— **Michael***

CHAPTER ONE

"You'll need to understand that not all clothes are made equally. Even once you get past the differences in the skill, one must consider differences in style. For example, the seamstress I'm looking for might be skilled in one form but not another. And you need to think about all the many differences in fabric and how well they are suited to the various styles."

Skharr nodded politely as the woman continued her somewhat lengthy and convoluted explanation. He could understand missing good companionship during a long journey more than most, although he more than made up for it with Horse's presence. His present travel companion appeared to enjoy talking, and he wondered if she would continue to do so even if he weren't present.

In fact, he had a feeling that she wouldn't stop even if she never saw another person for a month. The horses that dragged the wagon she lived in would be enough company if she proceeded alone, but she seemed inclined to talk about her interest in making clothes. From the way she was dressed, he could tell that she made her own and had some skill in it.

She lived on the road but was not quite a vagrant, as she was more than able to make her living making garments for the folks in the towns where she stopped for food and supplies.

Her outfits flowed, looked a little worn, and complemented the long-brimmed straw hat she wore to keep the sun out of her eyes. The clothes matched her tanned skin, and her large, green eyes flicked her gaze to him whenever she paused for breath.

He couldn't pinpoint her accent in the common tongue, although he assumed that was because it seemed to be an amalgam of at least seven different dialects he had come across in the past—with possibly even more mixed in.

"Would you say you're looking for a change in garb?" Ytrea asked and drew the barbarian back from his reverie. "I would not wish to make you feel uncomfortable, but your clothes are painful for me to see."

Skharr looked at the admittedly drab coloring of his clothes. "Clothes are worn. No care if others dislike."

She grunted and nodded. "Well then, consider it an open invitation. I know some folk prefer that their clothes be functional over nice-to-see, but for myself, I prefer for them to be seen."

His gaze slid quickly to her. "When fighting, what clothes look like matters little."

"I've not needed to fight much. Fashion has always been about lookin' good, which makes the wearer feel good, see? They don't need to be easy to wear for that, understand?"

He did not understand. The color and fit of his clothes never made him feel better and they sometimes made him feel worse, especially if they demanded that he strut about like a peacock. The single most important matter to him was if they would prevent him from being able to defend himself.

Then again, folk who didn't spend as much time fighting as he did would have other priorities.

"Make clothes fashionable, fit well?" Skharr asked and tilted his head.

"It's hard to make them both. Expensive too."

"Your clothes?"

"They are comfortable to sit in but I can't run very well in them, which is best for me. I don't like to do much runnin' and take life at a slower pace."

"Sometimes running from something."

"If I need to run from something, the chances are I shouldn't have been involved with it in the first place."

Sometimes circumstances changed in that regard, but Skharr had a feeling that she wouldn't budge on the issue. She liked her clothes to make a statement so she didn't need to. It made sense for a traveling seamstress but less so for a warrior.

"I can show you my clothes if you like and explain what it means," she continued.

"Your clothes?"

"These, if you like. Or I have others in the back. You would know that if you didn't always sleep on the ground outside. If you were traveling closer to Ryngold, I could show you where I get all my fabrics and you'd see exactly what I'm talkin' about."

Skharr shook his head. "Destination is Skepsis. Won't travel alone when possible. Better to travel with company."

She laughed and brushed the long, thick curls from her face. "Well, I always have the company of my horses. They don't seem to mind my stories and my ideas on clothing and fashion. Of course, it's always more interesting when someone talks in response, but I'm not too fussy about that. You never did say why you were heading out of the Capital city, of course, but that's fine."

Ytrea truly didn't need his help to keep the conversation going as she had proven often during the time they had spent together. It had been fortuitous for him when he'd left the capital and found someone who was traveling in more or less the same direction that he was headed.

He couldn't help but enjoy the company himself and from what he could tell, Horse rather enjoyed it as well. Of course, that was likely because of the added company of the two mares that drew Ytrea's wagon.

"We do find along the way that most of the civilizations have a few good ideas when it comes to their clothing, but they hold onto the bad ideas as well." She pulled a dried piece of fruit from a pouch at her side and chewed it pensively. "Even the drow have a few good ideas, but they tend to choose the colors that fade into the hues of the trees, and I don't like those. Even the horses all have their preferences."

He looked at Horse, who snorted and shook his mane.

"See, your horse knows what I mean. He wants his coat fresh and gleaming. What is his name again?"

It wasn't the first time she had asked and it wouldn't be the last time he explained it either.

"Horse."

"Yes, the horse. What is his name?"

"Horse is his name."

"Interesting. And easy to remember, I suppose. Horses are noble creatures and therefore the name is noble, although I've heard that the elves have a word for horses—Roksa. Or...Rokko. I can't remember which one means horses. Oh, and the dwarf word for the beasts is Dervald, so perhaps a name like that would suit him best."

Horse snorted and whinnied softly.

"Do not think your name will change now," Skharr assured the beast before he turned his attention to his companion. "Horse is his name."

"I know. I was merely thinking about what name would suit a future horse of mine best. I wouldn't want to name him the same as yours."

Skharr narrowed his eyes but shook his head and chose not to pursue it. It did appear as though she had picked up on it the last time he had explained his reasoning for naming Horse the way he had and she was merely trying to push past it.

Ytrea would, he knew, continue to talk until he stopped her, but the odd lilt of her accent along with the musical quality of her voice made him not want to stop her. She certainly showed no sign of slowing on her own.

Horse froze in mid-step. His eyes widened and his ears flattened toward the back of his skull as he looked around the road they currently traversed. The warrior stopped abruptly as well, narrowed his eyes, and tried to peer through the tall grass that surrounded the road.

He patted the stallion on the neck and moved cautiously to the back of the saddle. The wagon proceeded at a slow pace ahead of them while he retrieved the sword he had hidden among the saddlebags. What would be best for this situation would be to have his bow ready, but he would have no time to string it once the ambush was sprung.

"Is all good with you back there?" Ytrea asked and drew her horses to a halt.

Skharr did not reply. He was entirely focused on the grass around them until he discerned telltale movements.

The would-be ambushers made no effort to cover their approach well and it seemed their sole intention was simply to make sure that the wagon didn't move forward. They jumped onto the road and a few tried to grasp Ytrea's horses by their bridles to ensure that they didn't run off.

All they accomplished was that they had to back away quickly to avoid being bitten or knocked back when one of the beasts, still attached to the wagon, reared awkwardly in response.

"Ho, ho, see our luck here, lads," one of the men shouted. "A lady in need of company falls into our lap. We can help her with that, can't we?"

All five wore ragged clothes, with disheveled hair and no armor to speak of, although one had fashioned a crude breastplate for himself from what Skharr guessed were broken pans.

One carried a club, another a short staff, and the other three held rusty knives in their hands.

Locals, if Skharr had to guess, turned to banditry not because they were used to the violence but more likely because they knew the roads were not too often patrolled by imperial forces.

From the way they presented their weapons, it was easy to tell that they were most certainly not deserters or former soldiers. They waved them forward somewhat awkwardly like they hoped that anyone who saw them would be sufficiently intimidated.

Desperate folk, the warrior decided and moved his hand away from his sword. He wouldn't need it, not for this.

"I am sure we are willin' to welcome new company to join us for the trip," Ytrea said and smiled at the motley group. "Where are you headin'? I'm off to Ryngold."

"We're heading into the back of the wagon," the leader with the improvised breastplate answered as he approached. "You're welcome to join us back there if you like."

"That won't be necessary I don't think," she said and looked around. "We can stop and make camp out here."

"I'd be more than happy to ruin your dress out in the open, but I'd prefer some time alone with you in the tall grass before my boys have their turn at you."

"Why would you want to ruin my dress?" she asked.

The barbarian couldn't tell if she truly didn't realize what they wanted or if she tried to ignore the obvious. The best part was that the group hadn't paid him any attention, as interested as they were in her.

It was all for the best—both for him and for them.

He moved around the wagon to the side where four of the brigands now circled and tried to sneak behind the woman as she spoke to the apparent leader. They most likely planned to drag her from the wagon by force.

Leaving them alive was probably not the best course of action to take. These were not men driven to lawlessness purely by desperation but it seemed they'd also discovered the pleasure they derived from it.

Only one of the four realized that he was coming and shouted a warning to the others a moment before the barbarian pounced.

It had been a long time since he'd been in a proper fight. Spending time in the palace had been relaxing but had allowed few opportunities for a fight. The word was that he was a favorite of the new emperor, which meant those who were not intimidated by his size were afraid to anger the ruler if there was a fight.

There were few simple pleasures in the world quite like the rush that came when he saw the fear suddenly appear in the eyes of men who realized how thoroughly destructive their miscalculation had been.

It was the same look he could see in the first brigand's eyes a moment before his fist crashed into the man's jaw.

The loud crack of the bandit's jaw snapping was enough to alert the rest of the group that they were under attack, but Skharr doubted that it would do them any good or change the outcome of the skirmish in any way.

His elbow snapped around to drive into the skull of the man to his right as one of the knives was thrust toward his stomach. It was wielded by the smallest of the group, although the man had reacted the fastest and at least tried to land a blow.

"There's no need to be bad about this," he heard Ytrea shout behind him.

The warrior couldn't disagree with her but as committed as he was, he could do little other than step out of the way of the clumsy thrust. His evasion accomplished, he grasped the smaller man's arm with both hands and twisted until he felt his opponent's elbow pop out of its socket. With a grunt, he dragged the man around to position him between him and the last man standing of those who were on his side of the wagon.

He could see it coming almost before the man surged forward

and raised the knobbed club over his head for a powerful but uncoordinated strike.

The blow struck the younger, smaller member of the band of brigands. Skharr heard a soft crunch and the youth's eyes rolled to the back of his head and his whole body went limp.

A look of surprise crossed the face of the final man as the barbarian tossed the unconscious or possibly dead bandit to the side and closed on him as well.

The ruffian swung his weapon half-heartedly but Skharr caught it before it reached anywhere near the speed it would require to crack skulls and shoved it back into the bandit's unprotected face.

His nose was very clearly broken and blood spouted as he clutched it with agonized groans, which left the warrior holding the club alone. He shifted his hold to the bottom and hammered the weapon first into the other man's knee, then followed with a hasty reverse into his jaw. The strikes damaged both and the ruffian collapsed into a whimpering pile at his feet.

Skharr turned, expecting to see Ytrea already dragged from the wagon by the sole marauder who remained. He was surprised to see her leaning over on her seat atop the wagon while an odd, choking sound issued from her would-be assailant.

The man still held his knife but the widened state of his eyes said he was in no position to use it. The woman had produced a blade that the barbarian hadn't seen before, and it was buried deep in the man's neck.

It was an awkward position to attack anyone from, but she appeared perfectly comfortable as she adjusted her hold and drew the blade savagely across the rest of the brigand's throat. Blood splashed over her hand but she continued to slice until she had almost decapitated him.

It was a little odd to see a young woman whom he had regarded as little more than flippant and perhaps a little naive savagely executing a man. It forced him to restructure the picture he had of her in his head.

The bandit crumpled and she yanked a small kerchief from her dress with which she deftly cleaned her weapon and her hands.

"Did you truly think I could not protect myself?" she asked, and Skharr realized that he was watching her closely. "I may not look vicious but there have been many opportunities where I needed to teach a few lessons at the point of a blade. I would say the same about you, yes?"

"Hmm." He grunted a neutral response and looked at the club he still held before he released it. "Interesting."

She leaned to the side of the wagon and watched as he began to search the four men who were in varying states of consciousness. One groaned as he rifled through his pockets, but Skharr pushed him down with little sympathy.

"Do you truly expect any of them to carry anything of value or worth?" she asked.

"As you just taught the dead shit, it is better to verify and not be surprised," he retorted. He knew that she was probably right. Men such as these would not carry anything of worth on their persons. It was more likely that they would have spent anything as quickly as possible on drink, food, and pleasurable company and only emerged to steal again when their pockets were empty.

"Interesting," she whispered as Skharr finished his search and kicked the last man to the side of the road. He clicked his tongue for Horse to join him as he had a mind to continue their journey.

"What is?" he asked but paid attention to her. It was possible that the dead and wounded had left a rearguard in place—likely one with a bow—to ensure that no stragglers managed to escape.

But not very likely, he decided. The marauders didn't seem the type to think that far ahead.

"You've grunted at me all through our time together," Ytrea said in response to his offhand question. "Is that a ploy?"

He shrugged. "Could be. Keep moving. Dark soon."

She laughed and shook her head as she snapped the reins. Skharr paused to pull his long hair back into the strap that held it in place.

"I suppose I'm not the only one keeping secrets," he said finally as they continued at a slow pace.

"No indeed," she said and a small smile touched her lips. "I would like to share if ye are willin'."

The barbarian shook his head. "Best to keep some mystery between us, no?"

Still, it was good to know what she was capable of. At least the dagger hadn't come out when he had been asleep and she seemed to know how to use it effectively.

But still, some questions were not worth knowing the answers to.

"If you say so," Ytrea muttered. "But where were we? Ah, yes, the benefits of using fashion to say what you mean. Too many think clothes are merely clothes, but like your armor—where you wish to have function as well as protection—clothes can also serve two purposes."

Yes, he decided with an inward smile, he was better off not knowing the answers.

CHAPTER TWO

The sun would not set for another few hours when he turned away from the road to the more distant city he had selected as his next destination. Skharr knew there would be no point in continuing with Ytrea and she seemed perfectly capable of protecting herself. Besides, she'd told him that she would remain in Ryngold for a while and he had no desire to kick his heels while waiting a travel acquaintance to complete her business.

The fact that she had asked him to travel with her for her protection felt like the oddest kind of deception and all told, he only felt lucky to have left with his purse and throat intact.

Too many folk like her would have tried to gut him, and from the way she handled her blade, if she had caught him by surprise, she might have been successful.

Still, perhaps it was best to leave those thoughts on the road where they belonged.

"Come on, Horse," he muttered and the stallion fell into step behind him. They had already covered a fair distance by the time he decided to backtrack and spend the night in comfort. He could resume his journey well rested and fed in the morning.

One of the guards at the gate of Ryngold told him that most of the better inns of the city were housed across the bridge and in the streets leading to the main keep. Skharr nodded. Now that he'd arrived in the large town, it certainly seemed a night spent in relative comfort after almost a week of pulling rocks out from under his blankets was deserved.

"And you'll sleep somewhere warm and with a good supply of fresh, sweet hay," he noted and patted his four-legged companion on the neck. "And maybe some apples. We cannot assume that all places have them—especially at this time of year—but if they do, I'll be sure that you enjoy a taste of them."

Horse snorted and nudged his arm as they continued in comfortable silence.

A few people turned and stared as he walked at a leisurely pace, although he doubted that it was only because he was a madman who spoke to his horse. Barbarians were not seen regularly in these parts, and one such as him—with head and shoulders taller than the rest and scars to show that he was not the peaceable type—always tended to attract attention.

Although one look from his gleaming green eyes—made all the more menacing with the scar over his right eyebrow—turned even the most curious gaze away.

The attention had never been a problem as he simply ignored it. What made his life difficult was the fact that his appearance, as distinctive as it was, made it easy for folk to recognize him as well—and not as a simple oafish-brute barbarian.

He needed to travel far from these parts, but it would be a few years before he could afford it, which meant he would have to find work. Not only that, it needed to be the kind that paid well.

It was considerably less difficult now that he was better known among the mercenary guilds of the region.

After a fair walk, he stopped in front of a small inn positioned next to the river, where he could already smell the mouthwatering aroma of the evening meal being prepared inside.

"What say you, Horse?" Skharr asked.

The beast tossed his mane and continued to move into the small courtyard in front of the inn itself.

"Good afternoon, traveler." A stout man with a thick grizzled beard growled a greeting from around a pipe. "If you'se looking for a place to lay your head for the evening for ye and yer beast, you'll find none better than the Riverbed—not for the same prices, mind ye."

"Place in the stables, fresh hay for Horse?" the warrior asked. "And apples, if possible. Meal for me, and room."

The man nodded and pushed up from his seat. "All that'll cost ye a silver for the night, good master. If'n you'se got an extra copper on ye, I'll send a lad down to the market to gather some apples for the beast 'fore it closes for the evening."

Without even a second's hesitation, Skharr took the silver and copper from his coin purse and handed both to the man.

"A bargain well-struck then." His new host laughed heartily before he turned to one of the young lads playing with sticks in front of the stable. "Boy! Get off yer lazy bum and see the beast to a stable. Have a care that the hay is fresh. Then head on to the market—old hag Jenny's—and get a basket of her apples for the creature as well."

The youngster jumped at the shouted orders and rushed to where Horse stood and extended his hand toward the bridle.

The stallion snorted and jerked his head to keep the reins out of the lad's reach.

"He'll follow," Skharr rumbled in explanation. "Won't you?"

The beast nodded and sure enough, as the boy moved tentatively forward, Horse followed him without any reluctance.

"You got you a fine horse in that'un," the innkeeper muttered as he puffed on his pipe. "A bit older but smarter from the looks of it. Will ye have a hot meal and a bed right away then, master?"

The barbarian shook his head. "Theros Temple. Guild. Where?"

The innkeeper seemed unfazed by his large patron's speaking mannerisms and pointed in the direction from which Skharr and Horse had come.

"You follow the river down east a ways. Ye can't miss it. The statue of the god himself will be right on the riverfront. If you see that, you know you've arrived there. A mercenary, then, are ye?"

He nodded. "Leave saddle on Horse. I return."

"I'll let the boy know."

Skharr followed the man's instructions and strode along the river while the sun began to set behind the walls of the city.

Sure enough, the statue of Theros was a clear indicator that he had arrived at the right location. The almost twelve feet tall marble statue of the god had been positioned as if it somewhat arrogantly watched over the city.

"Not quite the way I remember him," the barbarian muttered and narrowed his eyes. "Perhaps that is what he looks like when he isn't an old man."

That did present the question of whether a god would grow younger or older as time passed.

"He probably created that himself," he mumbled and shook his head. "It would explain the bulge."

With a smirk of amusement, he started up the marble steps leading to the Theros temple. In most locations, the guildhall and temples to the gods they served were kept separate, but not in Ryngold. In fact, it seemed as though the temples themselves spread out from the hall to make it look like a seven-pointed star.

From what he could see, priests mingled with the mercenaries still spread through the large space and the scent of incense hung over everything. It was a little too sweet, and he wished fervently for fresh air as he hurried through the temple and entered the guildhall.

It was an active and noisy environment. Blacksmith hammers rang on anvils as they made and repaired weapons and armor for the men and women who used them, while the guildmasters shouted orders to the mercenaries around them.

Skharr found the Theros guildmaster easily, a lean man with a crooked nose and a handful of battle scars carved along his arms. His long, deft fingers pushed coins quickly across the table while he counted them under his breath.

"We're not looking for any more open requests." He paused in his counting as the warrior approached. "Unless you have a contract, we won't take an application to the Theros guild. Good day."

"Too many requests then, yes?" Skharr asked and studied his surroundings with vague interest.

The man didn't answer immediately and instead, finished counting the coins before he scooped them into a small purse and handed it to an aide after he'd sealed it with the guild's mark.

"Too many after folk heard about some barbarian giant fighting in the name of Theros," the man grumbled. He looked up and froze as a hint of recognition touched him, then grimaced. "Ah. I just made a fool of meself then. Unless there be a sudden uptick of giants in our region, I'll take the liberty of assuming that you are Skharr the DeathEater."

"Skharr DeathEater. Nothing between."

"Right, then. I apologize. It's been a long few days. Word has begun to spread of the imperial succession and there is a great deal of business in it for the mercenary guilds."

"Speaking on that topic, I have a contract for which I owe the guild's due." Skharr retrieved the scroll written up for him when the boy was still a prince and not an emperor. The final price had risen a great deal but he had accounted for it. Still, fifteen gold pieces were all that was required, and the guildmaster counted it quickly before he handed another purse to an aide.

"You are quite the interesting character among the mercenaries," the man said once he sealed the scroll of the completed contract away. "Your legend appears to be spreading and from what I hear, a few dozen rich contracts are waiting in which nobles asked for you specifically. More than a few ladies of high repute also wished to know if you were available for private contracts. I am not entirely sure what they mean by that—"

"And you do not want to," the barbarian said hastily and shook his head.

"Well, then. Are you looking only to pay your dues to the guild, or are you looking for work?"

"Only the kind of work that does not involve nobles looking to secure my services," he replied. "Something local and preferably simple."

"It's not often that I hear that request," the guildmaster admitted. "You should know there is a dungeon not far from here near the coast. It was cleared decades ago, but there is talk among those who live nearby that the power is showing itself once more in the region. It was built by the old gods, according to the local legend, and considerable treasures still remained to be looted by anyone who might set their minds to doing so. A sound bounty has been placed for those willing to clear the place again and set the minds of the farmers to rest."

Skharr shook his head quickly. "Nothing like that."

"Truly? I would have thought—with your reputation—that it was the kind of thing you took on regularly."

"A little too regularly of late. No nobles, ladies, dungeons, or gods."

A few of those who stood nearby chuckled at his words, but they returned hastily to their business when he glared a warning at them.

"There is a contract on a group of ne'er-do-wells who have taken up residence in a mine in the highlands after forcibly removing the dwarves who were working in it. So far, they have not sent any raids from their position so the viscount has not taken it upon himself to deal with them, but the dwarves have assembled the coin themselves. Ten gold pieces to clear the vagrants out. All the others I've spoken to think that it is too little coin for too much trouble, as it'll need to be spread amongst a group, but if you'll take it on your own, it might be worth it."

That did sound a little more appealing. Skharr nodded.

"It does interest me. Do you have the contract?"

The guildmaster reached under his desk and pulled it out for him. "About...I'd say fifteen miles beyond the gates, you'll find yourself at the foot of the mountains, where dwarves like doing their work."

"Didn't they have any fighters among them?"

"Those they had were killed when the vagrants arrived, so the assumption is that they have numbers on their side. The count by the survivors was a little over twenty."

The warrior pocketed the scroll.

"Most folk would blanch at the possibility of facing twenty armed bandits alone," the guildmaster commented.

"Most folk are not Skharr DeathEater."

His travels to Skepsis would have to wait for the moment. Not that he had any pressing business in the region. It had simply been a location where, he'd been told, there would be more than sufficient work for a man of his skills. It would wait while he found himself work in Ryngold.

It was best to stay away from the larger cities for the moment anyway. He had made too many enemies of late, and with the kind of work that hounded him from the higher classes of the empire, he would find himself with a dagger in his back or poisoned in an alley sooner rather than later.

Simple work was best, even if it didn't pay quite what he'd hoped.

Horse trudged behind him, and the barbarian patted the

beast's neck gently as they followed the slightly uphill road. They now walked directly into the foot of the mountains that rose into peaks above them like snowcapped daggers into the pale blue sky.

"From what the guildmaster said, we have a few more miles to go," he said. "You had your fill of apples and rest in the town. It's time to earn those, my friend."

Horse tossed his mane and Skharr could feel the beast glare at him.

"Well then, maybe you do all the fighting when we arrive at the damn mine and I'll carry the weight and eat apples all day. How does that appeal to your sensibilities?"

The creature had no answer to that—not that he expected him to—and they continued their ascent to the point where he could see signs of the mining that had taken place. Most of the trees had been cleared from around the area, which made it easier for large teams of horses to drag what had been mined away. The ground was disturbed from where the dwarves had searched for the rich veins of whatever they had mined for in the region.

They were the best at finding those veins, of course, but even they needed to probe and explore in order to locate them.

"What are we looking for?" Skharr asked as he brought himself and his companion to a halt. They were close enough to the mines now that he knew he would encounter the ruffians soon. The sun had begun its descent too, although that was not a terrible thing.

If he had to fight the shits out in the open, having the advantage of darkness would be preferable.

He searched the landscape ahead and when he spied the smoke that rose from a handful of campfires, he decided this was close enough.

Horse stood patiently while the warrior donned his armor—provided to him as a gesture of thanks by the newly crowned emperor—and retrieved his weapons from the saddlebags. His bow was easily his weapon of choice, and he strung it deftly and shouldered the quiver of arrows.

It was always possible that things might turn out badly for him and he didn't want to be without quality weapons, so he also drew the silver-inlaid sword he was growing more and more accustomed to. Even the sight of the two serpents with emerald eyes had grown a little less uncomfortable, despite their association with the dagger forged of similar design.

The elf who had given the small blade to him had said it would grant wishes provided he was willing to pierce himself in the heart with it. With the passing of time, however, he had begun to feel a little less confident that she had told him the truth.

Then again, he wasn't about to stab himself in the chest merely to prove her right or wrong.

"Keep out of the forest," Skharr advised Horse. "I thought I heard a wolf or two in the area, and where there is one, there will be more. Stay close, but if I don't return...well, you know what to do."

The stallion nudged him gently in the chest and he smirked before he turned and strode purposefully up the final slight ascent. He made good time as he advanced on the campfires that had now begun to throw more smoke into the air.

The sun would set behind him in a few minutes, which gave him the advantage of being able to see the men without them seeing him very clearly.

His line of approach meant they would have to look directly into the sun. All of them appeared to be more engaged in the food that was being prepared for their evening meal than in any real effort to watch their surroundings.

Skharr settled on one knee and studied the group. He counted more than twenty of them, although he had expected as much from the beginning. The dwarves had likely only met the advance party, and he was willing to guess that the group had added to their numbers after their success and in anticipation of sending raiding parties out into the region.

They looked surprisingly well-organized. There was most likely a leader among them whom he would have to kill to break their spirit, but none stood out immediately from the group he could see in front of him.

That would change as things unfolded.

Skharr laid his sword and shield on the ground beside him and felt for an arrow in his quiver. There were enough ways to break the group up into smaller ones that would be easier to deal with.

An arrow with wrapping around the head was the one that he wanted and he reminded himself that he would need to make a few more when he had a little time. He held it in his bow hand, nocked a regular arrow to the bowstring, and took a slow, deep breath. His final push up the road to the mines with his weapons and armor on had been enough to coax a sheen of sweat from his skin, but the cool wind from the coast helped.

The barbarian resumed his surveillance of his quarry and after a few moments, identified one man who seemed to have the ears of the rest. He carried a heavy cast iron pot of soup and used a ladle to distribute the food among the group. Although he spoke fairly loudly, the distance was such that Skharr couldn't hear precisely what he said. It seemed to be light-hearted— perhaps he'd related an amusing anecdote—as eruptions of laughter issued from the different clusters of his comrades.

Perhaps not a leader, the barbarian decided, but certainly a man the group listened to. He drew the bowstring back and felt the strain of the bow in his hand as he tracked his target's movements until he found another group and stopped to serve them from the pot.

It was necessary but still a crime to waste what he was sure was good food. He released the arrow and it arced with a soft whistle toward its intended target.

The arrow punched easily into the man's back, continued cleanly through, and emerged from his chest. The impact was hard enough to thrust him into one of the campfires and spill the food he had been serving over the men closest to him.

The group bolted from their seats and looked around amidst frantic shouts that indicated their confusion as to what had happened. No one seemed to be able to grasp why their comrade was sprawled in the fire.

Skharr used the modified arrow next. It required a great deal less in terms of aim and he simply selected one of the fires and loosed the projectile almost immediately. He took another three arrows from the quiver, planted them in the soil at his feet, and drew another in readiness.

The camp had begun to descend into chaos. Among the dozens gathered in their smaller groups, some continued to question the death of their cook while others stumbled away from the fire that had suddenly begun to spew a noxious smoke.

Skharr took a deep breath and settled his aim on one of the men. He seemed to have recovered a little and now shouted orders, trying to organize the group to put the fires out and to alert them to the fact that they were being attacked. It was too soon in the skirmish for that kind of coherence and something had to be done before the brigands regrouped.

The man was hurled back and almost completely pinned to a wooden beam behind him by the arrow that ripped through his chest. Blood sprayed across the group around him.

In that moment, it finally dawned on all of them that someone beyond their camp was firing the arrows.

Before they could react, another of their comrades died when an arrow pierced through his throat and shuddered in place as it lodged inside another beam of wood. Again, the spray of blood drew a series of curses from the hapless man's comrades.

The group, in their smaller clusters of men and women, turned their attention toward the outside. They moved away from where the smoke blocked their visibility and tried to locate their attacker as the setting sun blazed behind his back.

A woman pushed out into the open ahead of all the others but dropped back with an arrow jutting from her chest. The light leather armor she wore provided no protection against the onslaught.

Skharr recognized that there was no more time for him to remain where he was and hold his position. He straightened quickly and turned to stride purposefully in a line parallel to the mountain to put distance between himself and the group that was mobilizing quickly to go in pursuit.

It was an odd sensation. He knew that any other mercenary in his position would feel a little more panicked about almost two dozen bandits hunting him. A few arrows were loosed when anyone caught sight of him, although they fell well short. That wouldn't last, however. Not if what he planned came to fruition.

With calm deliberation, he circled to guide the group on a chase around the area but never let them approach him close enough to shoot him.

The sun set fully, and the darkness mixed with the smoke that had begun to seep the whole area provided him with enough cover to circle to where their camp waited for them. Burning the bandits out would be the only way to make sure they did not return once he had killed enough to scare them off and allow the dwarves time to reclaim what was rightfully theirs.

As he approached the tunnels into the mine, however, he slowed instinctively and eventually stopped completely. The smoke in the air was enough to remove any signs of any other scents or smells—except for one that was pungent enough to penetrate anything. Skharr narrowed his eyes and grimaced in distaste when a low rumble issued from inside the tunnels. It turned gradually into a powerful roar, which only made the pungent smell worse.

"Ah, no. By the flea-infested whelps of Janus' poxy whore..." He grunted, backed slowly away from the tunnel entrance, and after a few steps, increased his speed a little. "They have a cave troll."

CHAPTER THREE

Contrary to most myths, Skharr had found that trolls were generally intelligent creatures. Those legends of them being dim-witted and easily outsmarted by the average human were generally due to the fact that while they could speak the common tongue, their oddly-shaped jaws and elongated tongues made it difficult and they spoke slowly.

Even so, those who spoke of them being quick to anger, quick to violence, and generally sadistic creatures had been proven true —at least in his experience–as well as the claims that the creatures hated the sunlight.

He remembered fighting one of the monsters in the past. It had only been once but he had barely escaped that particular event with his life. He often thought that leaving the troll and the bridge it was guarding alone was one of the wisest choices he'd ever made, even if he'd had to travel for miles until he found another place to cross the river.

If he had to guess, this particular troll was likely the leader of the group, which explained why all the bandits spent their time outside of the mine it had claimed for itself.

The brigands were approaching but they paused as well when

another roar issued from inside the cave. With muttered oaths and whispered exchanges of orders, they inched away and seemed to have forgotten that they were trying to kill him.

They were likely thinking about surviving what was to come and he couldn't blame them. As intelligent as trolls could be, when they were angry, there wasn't much short of another troll that could bring them to a stop.

Shadows cast from inside announced the creature's arrival at the entrance and heavy steps made the ground shake before it stepped fully into view.

It was large at a little over twelve feet tall, and from the sight of the horns growing from its shoulders, easily one of the oldest that Skharr had ever seen. Its thick gray skin was covered in large, pebble-like scales, and the pale red eyes scanned the outside before it unleashed a thunderous roar of rage again.

It grasped a massive, crude falchion about as long as the barbarian was tall and dragged it over the packed earth behind it. Sparks kicked up with every step the creature took.

"I take it you know how to handle this one?" Skharr asked, but the way they continued to back away from the beast answered his question.

He smirked and shook his head as a few of the men rushed forward, waved their arms at Skharr, and shouted at the creature to attack him. They didn't appear to realize the danger they were in while their comrades retreated and all but ran away and abandoned them to the results of their stupidity.

The troll snorted and growled, took a step forward, and brought its falchion into a heavy swing. Skharr flinched when the blunt weapon powered into all three, hacked into them, and hurled the trio across the camp. They were dead almost before they realized that their so-called ally had attacked them.

"It is best for me to move," the warrior whispered when the pale red eyes shifted to look across the camp to where he stood.

It was a little daunting to have to look up that high to meet the creature's eyes, and the ground shook with every step that it took in his direction.

The barbarian had no issues with simply turning his back and running the other way. If there was one thing he had over the troll, it was that he had more stamina, and if he could stay ahead and away from it, he could outlast it. Besides, it would not want to be caught out in the open when the sun rose.

The ground shuddered beneath his feet and Skharr turned when he realized that not all the bandits had chosen to run away from the monster. A few thought they could fight it, evidently, and they stood their ground and fired arrows at it. The projectiles buried themselves in its tough hide but did nothing but anger the creature. There didn't even appear to be any blood flowing from the wounds.

As it drove into them, the troll ignored most of the strikes from their weapons, ducked its head, and swung the sword. The vicious swipe carved into two of the men who were closest to it while the creature simply trampled a third.

Despite the seriousness of the situation, Skharr allowed himself a small smile. The troll was doing his work for him and very effectively too.

He stopped with his bow in hand and reached for one of the arrows from his quiver. More of the bandits were returning, either to help their friends or because they didn't want to leave their little camp to be demolished by the rampage.

The wiser members of the group started to run away, back into the cover of the trees. He doubted that they would return, not with the smoke that rose unrelentingly and would ensure the attention of the local patrols.

He could simply backtrack to where Horse was spending the evening. If he returned to the city, he could tell the guildmaster that the job was done. By then, the bandits would either be dead or fled, and the pay of fifteen gold pieces was nowhere near what he would have charged to kill a troll. Besides, he'd not been told about it and found it hard to believe that no one had known of its existence.

Perhaps he would be willing if they negotiated for more gold, although he doubted they would pay his price.

But the more he thought about it, the more he realized that he wouldn't go anywhere. Instead, he would allow the troll to continue to tear through the bandits like they were rotting wood.

That would make his work far easier, but he would deal with the troll. He would merely have to find a way to kill the creature.

Hopefully, he reminded himself somewhat gloomily, from beyond the reach of the massive falchion.

Tucked amongst the trees, he watched as a handful of the remaining bandits disappeared into the woods, no doubt wisely heading off to find themselves another line of work.

No, he reasoned, they would be in the same line of work but elsewhere. Certainly far away from the angry troll.

He shook his head to refocus and pressed the arrow to his bowstring. The creature snatched one of the bandits up, bit into his neck, and tore the head off, and blood spilled over its cracked lips.

Skharr's opening would close soon, and he drew the arrow back. Killing trolls was more than merely getting through the thick skin. They had two hearts and three livers, which complicated matters. There was even talk about how they had four testicles, but he had never been able to ascertain if that was true.

The most interesting part—and worrying, depending on whether you were a spectator or participant—was the fact that the monster would go into a deeper rage if one of the redundant organs was attacked, which left the head as the only possible way to kill it quickly.

Unfortunately, their heads were protected by hard bones, horns, and skin thick enough that it was used as armor in the southern regions where trolls were more numerous to the point of being a nuisance.

For now, the huge beast continued to bite into the bodies that were left with scant respect for the corpses of its fallen comrades. It did not seem to care that they had fought on the same side not long before, and he had no desire to ask it about its change of heart.

"Someday, living up to my reputation will be the end of me," he whispered.

With that assurance, he simply raised the bow and let the arrow fly.

It cut loudly toward its target but the troll didn't seem to notice that it drove deep into its skin until it looked at its stomach and the dark-green blood that seeped from the wound that was created.

The red-eyed gaze darted to him almost immediately and he drew another arrow from his quiver.

The monster was impossible to miss, especially since it rushed toward him at an impressive, terrifying speed.

One more arrow was loosed to catch his attacker on its shoulder before the barbarian dropped his bow and dove to the side. He scowled as the falchion glided over his head before he dragged himself to his feet, yanked the scabbard from where it hung from his back, and dragged the sword free.

There were no other options available to him now. If he tried to run, he would meet the same fate as those raiders who were half-eaten. All he could do was fight.

It would be a real fight this time. Skharr couldn't help a grin and he grasped his sword with both hands and stood his ground as the troll gathered itself, looked around for him, and roared again in fury. The rot in its mouth filled the air with a powerful stench that made his eyes water, but despite his instinctive recoil, he knew he had to get in closer.

At another sweep of the falchion, he jumped back to avoid having his body hewn in two and immediately lunged forward. He roared defiance at the monster as he pushed himself inside the range of his adversary's swing. It felt counterintuitive and every part of him said he needed to be as far away from it as he could. But running wasn't a viable option and certainly wouldn't kill the monster, which had to happen.

Skharr darted to the right as the creature swiped a grubby, three-fingered hand at him and tried to grab and drag him closer. It was a smooth evasion, and he slashed his blade across the massive arm. Despite the thickness of its skin, the blade cut through it with an impossibly smooth stroke to open a wide gash. Blood poured from the wound and drew another bellow from the monster, this time of pain as it stepped back and stared at its forearm with a hint of confusion.

The warrior had found the blade in a magical dungeon, and he knew it was sharper than many might have thought. The slight victory gave him a moment to gather his wits again as the troll poked at its wound while it yanked the arrows out of its skin.

Removing the longer arrows resulted in opening the wounds and more growling and grumbling from the beast.

"You should have left them in, eh?" Skharr asked.

"Don't tell what do!" the troll roared and shook his head.

The rage that trolls were famous for was now very much in evidence, and he stood his ground as he watched the falchion and waited as it began its swing to lop his head off.

Skharr remained in place for as long as he dared before he flung himself to the left, rolled over his shoulder, and used the momentum to regain his feet behind his opponent. With a grunt of effort, he slashed his blade across the back of the monster's thigh and felt the tendons sever with almost a snap beneath the strike of the razor-sharp sword.

His adversary roared in pain and twisted toward him. The barbarian had only a moment to glimpse a gargantuan arm power toward him like a club before it hammered into the side of his head.

He knew he hadn't been knocked unconscious but in one moment, he stood next to the troll and in the next, he sprawled on the earth a few yards away and scowled at the rocks that dug into his hip and chest.

"Fuck-ugly mug-brained cave-dwelling slime sack." He hissed a breath and pushed up quickly, half-surprised that he hadn't already been trampled by his irate opponent.

When his gaze located the troll, it limped toward him instead and peered continually at its leg with a hint of confusion. Skharr narrowed his eyes. It was good to know that cutting tendons worked as well with trolls as it did with humans, although he hoped he wouldn't have to draw on that knowledge too often.

Although the barbarian managed to remain standing, the world seemed to spin around him. The sensation made him feel nauseous as he struggled to keep his balance while his adversary inched toward him.

The monster raised the falchion again, and he forced himself sideways to avoid the blow. He stumbled clumsily away as his would-be assailant tripped and fell forward.

He needed to finish this, he told himself firmly. It simply wasn't an option to keep hacking at the monster in the hopes that he might manage to kill it. Eventually, one of the troll's swings would connect and when it did, he would be dead.

Skharr drew himself tall, shook his head in an effort to clear it, and looked at his hand, which felt uncomfortably empty. He realized to his horror that his weapon had been dislodged from his hold with the force of the blow to his head.

"Shit!"

He had no time to try to retrieve it and so reached instead for the dagger tucked into the back of his belt. His adversary rumbled belligerently as it lurched toward him again and swung its heavy sword, this time from above to chop him cleanly in half from shoulder to hip.

The barbarian pushed himself to the side and grimaced at the impact of the weapon as it pounded into the ground. He lashed out immediately before he could think about it and buried the dagger into the troll's forearm.

It screeched at a surprisingly high pitch and the arm lashed out hard enough to send him stumbling away. He was able to catch himself before he fell again and nausea surged as the beast tried to pry the dagger from his arm with fingers that were too thick and stubby to get a grip on the blood-soaked handle.

If there would ever be a chance, it was now.

Skharr looked around frantically and caught sight of his sword thanks to its gleam in the moonlight. He drove himself forward and grunted with the effort as his legs fought him with every step.

Fortunately, it was close enough that it required only a few steps to reach it, and he dropped to his knees and retrieved the weapon in a smooth motion as he regained his feet. The whole world swam through his vision again but he forced himself through it. He would have no other chance for this.

He had to finish it.

"Die, you slug-livered sack of shit," Skharr screamed and swept the blade into the back of the troll's other leg. The injury sapped it immediately of strength and with a howl, it dropped to its knees, although it continued to swing wildly and aggressively.

Its efforts would not work, not this time. He ducked under the strokes and almost heaved when the powerful stench threatened to overwhelm him. By pure force of will, he shook his head and thrust forward again. He only vaguely registered his scream of defiance as he drove the blade into the troll's throat.

The thick skin gave way easily and hot blood gushed from the wound to coat his hands with putrid muck and air from the monster's lungs. His teeth gritted, he pushed deeper still until his bone cracked on the other side of the thrust. The blade was buried to the hilt and he could see the silver of it gleaming on the other side.

The pale red eyes stared at him and the last remaining hint of a gleam of life faded in the few seconds that he stared into them.

Each eyeball was about the size of his fist, he realized as the lids closed over them and all power that remained in the troll suddenly disappeared. Its body slumped to leave him holding his green blood-soaked sword in hand, breathing deeply as he stared intently at the creature to make sure it truly was dead.

It was probably best if the surviving bandits had run away. He doubted that he would be able to offer much of a fight if they returned.

With that in mind, he turned, dropped suddenly to his knees, and was violently sick on the hard stone ground.

———

"You were sick?"

Skharr nodded. "That blow to the head had me. I would have died had the fight lasted any longer."

The innkeeper nodded. "Still, you did better than how most would fare against a troll. You brought the fucker's head back?"

He couldn't help a wince at the mention but the barbarian nodded slowly. "I doubt that the smell will ever wash out of my saddlebags but yes, I did. I assumed that the guilds would want to know there are trolls in the region although I doubt there are any more. It was old, likely driven from its tribe, and decided to live off of the deaths of humans for its twilight years. Still, there is no point in being too careful, I suppose. They'll probably put out a bounty on troll heads in the region."

"Will it work?"

"Not likely." Skharr grinned and sipped his mug of ale before he exhaled a satisfied sigh. "Some might attempt to pass the head of a bull off as that of a troll."

"Why a bull?"

"Well, they hear that trolls have horns but never consider that those might be on the shoulders."

The innkeeper nodded and refilled the mug. "Still, the Theros guild will pay you more for a fight against the troll?"

"They might, but I doubt it. I took the contract and fulfilled it. As far as anyone cares, how it happened or who I needed to kill for it to be accomplished matters little. I should have merely left the troll and come back for more coin."

"That would not be in accordance with the legend of Skharr the DeathEater."

"Legends do not pay for a night of sleep at an inn. They only rarely pay for a hot meal when I'm in need."

The innkeeper ran his fingers through his beard and nodded slowly. "I suppose that is true. Legends rarely survive their encounter with reality."

Skharr barked a laugh and raised his mug. "Here is to never encountering reality, then."

He leaned his head back and downed the contents of his mug quickly, leaned a little farther until the mug was empty, and straightened as he thumped it onto the countertop.

"Are those friends of yours?" the innkeeper asked as he collected another jug of ale.

The barbarian turned as two men entered the inn. Neither looked like they belonged in a small establishment next to the river. Both wore long, pristine white robes marked only by the rough outline of a man's bearded face in dark brown. Medallions hung from their necks with a similar marking, although those were covered by the long beards—one chestnut and the other a brilliant red—that contrasted sharply with their bald heads.

"Priests?" he asked.

"Indeed. Servants at the temple of Theros if those markings on their robes are of any significance."

The one with the red beard asked something of one of the

men near the door, who directed their attention to where Skharr was seated near the bar counter.

"This cannot be good, barbarian," the innkeeper muttered.

"Is that so?" He looked meaningfully at the man's full jug. "When do priests ever search for a barbarian?"

"They do not."

A succinct answer if there ever was one.

Skharr smirked and pushed another two coppers across the counter toward the man. "I think I'll need another beer."

His host nodded and refilled his mug, then filled another and left it next to the first.

"You'll need two or I miss my guess," the man said before he retreated to gather a few more full jugs from the basement.

CHAPTER FOUR

S kharr had a feeling the innkeeper was right. He took a long, slow sip from the mug in his hand and glanced lustfully at the second, although he doubted that he would have time to finish both before the priests reached him.

The problem with being a man of his size was that he required a substantial amount of ale to render him drunk. Still, he knew better than to start with the spirits that struck harder this early in the evening.

"Sir Skharr?"

He had certainly not drunk enough for this.

"I apologize for intruding on your evening of...celebration," the one with the red beard said and sat quickly on the one side while his comrade mirrored him on the other. "And we hope to only fill your evening with more cause for celebration, sir."

The barbarian narrowed his eyes, all his senses now alert. The two men approached him differently than he'd come to expect. They didn't treat him like a dim-witted barbarian. There was respect, a hint of fear, and the kind of reverence that made him uncomfortable.

The other nodded and leaned closer. "We come at the behest

of Theros himself. If it were not from his lips, we would not intrude."

"We need to ask if you can find it in your heart to fulfill this task, Sir Skharr."

Irritated, he shook his head. "A moratorium on that. My name is not Sir Skharr."

"Ah, of course, Sir DeathEater. Our apologies for the confusion."

"No. No." Interestingly, he was neither drunk nor sober enough to engage with the two and correct them. He needed to fix it immediately. "I...no. I assume there is a high priest waiting somewhere to pass the word of...Theros along?"

"Well, we would not want to intrude on your...celebration. There would be time for our high priest to share the word of the Lord High God Theros with you. He would not want you in a foul mood while you receive the word of the lord high god."

"That... Well, I am already in a foul mood. You have already intruded. So we might as well see what this is all about, yes?"

Both men exchanged a glance and tugged nervously at their beards. Neither seemed old enough to be real priests to any gods worth their salt. From the limp, weak appearance of their arms, it was clear that neither was used to using their hands for anything more intensive than sharpening their writing quills.

Still, they would continue to wait for him and they would ruin the slow, plodding progress he was making toward drinking himself into an oblivious state.

"Well, we hoped to catch you before you accepted any more work for the guild," the brown-bearded one said and the other nodded in agreement. "The high priest discovered too late that you were in Ryngold, and you had already left by the time we were dispatched to find you. So, when word reached us that you had returned, we needed to find you immediately Sir DeathEater."

"And may we say that your single-handed victory over a monstrous troll was most…inspiring, Sir DeathEater."

He rolled his eyes. They would continue to call him that until he either broke both their jaws and tossed them out or he went with them to meet their high priest. His present inclination notwithstanding, he had a feeling that beating a pair of curved-spined philosophers would bode poorly for him in the region. Folk tended to not appreciate hearing of their priests being beaten.

"Give me a moment." He sighed, took hold of both tankards, and raised first the one on the right, followed by the other on the left, and emptied both as quickly as he physically could.

Thankfully, the addition of the mugs' contents did make him feel a little warmer in the ears, which was a clear sign that he would feel a little drunker by the time he spoke to the high priest.

Skharr dragged in a deep breath as the pressure welled from his belly and he belched deeply and loudly enough for it to carry through the room.

He smirked when a few of the drunker men and women in the room cheered and clapped at the sound and he pushed out of his seat.

It still wasn't enough to make him feel any less secure in his balance on his feet, which truly was a pity, but he would work toward that eventually.

"We appreciate you taking the time to hear us in this, Sir DeathEater," the redbeard said and bolted out of his seat.

"I always make time to hear the word of the Lord High God Theros," he said. "I would merely hate to do so on an empty stomach."

He slipped the strap of his sword over his shoulder and checked to make sure he hadn't left anything else in the bar.

Most of his equipment and supplies were still in the stables with Horse, who was enjoying another bucket of apples that he had made sure the beast was provided with.

Skharr felt badly about dragging the old stallion all around the world with him and tried to make sure that Horse was well-compensated for itrang in the currency he enjoyed the most.

"We do not need to leave now," the brown-bearded noted as he stood from his seat as well. "You may enjoy more drinks or perhaps a meal. We will wait until you are ready to leave."

"I won't be able to enjoy either with the two of you perched on my shoulder," He replied. "I intended to go to the temple later in the day anyway."

He could see the innkeeper incline his head, his confused expression hosting the unasked question of what a barbarian would do at the temple of Theros.

"It's…a long story," Skharr offered as justification for his lack of an explanation.

"Excellent!" The second priest chortled. "We will accompany you to the Temple of Theros immediately."

The warrior rolled his eyes but moved toward the door with them.

As he pulled it open, a couple of the patrons approached the innkeeper.

"Why's the barbarian got to go to the Theros temple anyhow?" one asked.

"Assed if I know," the innkeeper replied.

The statue still seemed decidedly odd to him. Skharr had no idea why, but merely the sight of it made him scowl as he climbed the marble steps toward their destination.

Fewer people mingled through the temples and the guild now as the sun was about a quarter of the way down the sky. It was a reassuring reminder that he still had time to drink himself into an oblivious state before the sun vanished entirely, depending on how long it took for him to find out what exactly was wanted from him.

The large chambers of the temple already rang with foul language when Skharr stepped inside, although the lack of surprise from the two priests who escorted him suggested that this was not uncommon behavior. Still, his guides did not appear to want to be involved in what was happening.

Both stopped short of joining him as he moved forward into one of the larger chambers in the temple, where a woman yelled vociferously at a man he assumed was the high priest.

His robes were a deep-red velvet but covered in the same markings as the other priests. A shaved head was combined with a long beard, although it was a soft white and longer than the others, so much so that it almost reached below his stomach.

"What is the point of the laws speaking of sabbaticals if I can be called back in while in the middle of one?" the woman demanded, a little red in the face. "I am genuinely asking. If we can see our sabbaticals ground into dust at a moment's notice, why would we engage in one in the first place?"

"You know that we would not summon you if it were not the direst of circumstances," the high priest said as he lit a few of the incense staves. It looked like he attempted to move away from her, but she continued to follow him as he made his rounds. "It is your duty as a paladin to return in dire situations."

"The circumstances are always dire," she retorted belligerently. "That is why you have more than one paladin sworn to your temple. When one of them is in need of time away from all the dire circumstances, she takes a sabbatical!"

"It is different this time."

"It's never different!"

As she pulled her hair away from her face and tucked it behind her ear, Skharr realized that he recognized the woman. Her body language was different as well as her garb, which was why he had not recognized her at first, but seeing her face clearer and closer removed all doubt.

"Ytrea, is that you?" he asked and leaned against one of the pillars.

She snapped toward him, her hands closed in tight fists at her sides as if ready for a fight, until she realized who had spoken.

Suddenly, all the aggression in her body melted away—far too quickly, perhaps—and she grinned broadly at him.

"Skharr, the DeathEater! I thought you were moving on to Skepsis."

"I was delayed. And then delayed again. I almost didn't recognize you in…" He gestured to the clothes she wore.

Ytrea looked at the garment. Compared to the dress of many colors she had worn when they traveled together, it was practically drab, although the long, flowing purple robe was by no means an eyesore. The color was not one often found without ornaments and embellishments, but he decided that the simplicity of it wasn't a terrible thing.

She didn't look like she agreed and scowled at it like wearing it hurt her physically.

"Unfortunately, certain uniform dress requirements are demanded of paladins," she explained, lifted the dress a little, and inspected the fabric.

"Ah, excellent," the high priest called when he realized Skharr had joined them. "Welcome, Sir Skharr. We have been expecting you and I am so pleased that you are in the city to speak to me."

He shook his head quickly. "It… I am not Sir Skharr."

"Sir DeathEater, then?"

"No. No, sir. I am not a knight and have never taken any vows that would grant me that title."

"Ah. Well, no matter then. It is fortuitous that you find me while I am speaking to her, as the task I have encountered requires expertise from you both."

The barbarian narrowed his eyes, and he could see the anger

rise in Ytrea once more—although he now doubted that was her true name—as she turned her attention to the high priest.

"See? You have the skills of one giant of a barbarian. You have no need for any of your paladins. Simply send him off with his weight in gold and he'll deal with your issues without a problem if the legend surrounding the man is true."

"There is perhaps a seed of truth," Skharr corrected quickly. "But legends have a tendency to grow in my absence."

"I am aware of the truth surrounding your deeds, Si—Skharr," the high priest interjected. "And while they are quite impressive, I surmise that even you would not be able to accomplish this task alone."

As much as he appreciated the fact that not everyone assumed he could charge into the depths of hell to collect the heads of demons on his own, it still sounded as though the man tried to issue a challenge he expected him to rise to. Perhaps he should beat his chest and talk about how he could do anything on his own if he wanted to. It was patently not true, of course, but it would provide an opportunity to laugh.

Skharr knew better than to respond to that kind of prodding, and the silence that ensued turned their attention to the older man. Nervously, the priest dragged his hand over his bald head before he continued.

"There have been rumblings in the deep of late," he said finally and gestured for the two to walk with him. "The kind that will always be a cause for concern for those who know what to listen for. I have sent scouts to the coast, and they confirmed what I already feared was true in my heart."

"Enough with the babbling portents of doom, old man," Ytrea snapped. "Tell us what you need killed and be done with it."

The man's face twisted in annoyance but he maintained his composure. "I fear that this is one of the few creatures in this universe that none can kill, unfortunately. From the reports of my trusted advisors and the evidence of what I have felt for myself, I can say with a great deal of certainty that an Old God has awoken."

"Old God?" Skharr asked and raised an eyebrow. "I was under the impression that High Priests to the Elevated do not believe in the existence of the Old Gods."

"Only those who have not seen the evidence of them with their own eyes," the high priest commented. "Which means those living far from the seas. Do barbarians worship the Old Gods?"

"No gods are worshiped among my people," he stated firmly.

"Ah. Do you not believe in the gods?"

"We are aware of the existence of gods. We simply do not worship them."

The high priest seemed confused by the concept but shook his head and moved past what was certainly the kind of discussion that could last for days. The decision was a fortunate one as Skharr had no interest in engaging in a debate of that nature.

For the moment, it was best to leave it all unexplored. If the man wasn't insane, the concept of one of the old ones waking from the depths was certainly something that required their attention.

"I never did like the Old Gods," Ytrea commented and shook her head. "Especially those with tentacles coming from their faces."

The barbarian grinned as she mimicked the appearance of most of them by hanging her fingers over her mouth and wiggling them as though they were tentacles. It was an amusing image of something that was decidedly not funny, and he spared her a chuckle.

The high priest was not amused. "If we are finished mucking about, I think we have much to discuss."

"Yes," Ytrea agreed. "The question that immediately arises is what kind of group you will bring together? What good is a paladin who has no partner or partners to heal? Oh, and there are more than a few who I will not work with. Skharr is not among

those, although that might change. Reyan, that red-headed bastard, will never fight alongside me again, not after that stunt that he tried during the skirmish near the Trawar mountains. His comrade Gorran can follow him straight into the nearest entry into the Labyrinth, alongside Xera and that bitch Yaro."

Skharr tilted his head and studied her as she continued to list those mercenaries she would never work with again. He assumed the list grew with every quest she embarked on.

"Hmm, oh, Waahres can fuck himself," she continued. "Mortun can die and then fuck himself. Oh, and Jaxson. I'd rather work with a dozen smelly barbarians than work with that sick fuck again. I have no idea why he didn't follow Janus. He's close enough to the fucker's representation to make it work."

The barbarian knew a few of those she'd mentioned, although only one personally. He had only heard of the rest from other fighters and sure enough, the group were a collective bunch of bastards. He'd never heard of Jaxson, but he assumed the man fit right comfortably and appropriated with the bastards she'd named.

"I don't smell," he retorted finally when she paused, perhaps for air.

"I never said you did," Ytrea replied without so much as missing a beat. "If you are the type to charge head-first into a dungeon in the name of Theros, I would be glad to have you alongside me."

"Wait—am I to understand that the two of you know each other?" the high priest asked and studied both in turn.

"Not as one associated to Theros," the woman answered and again appeared as though she had anticipated the question. "Fortune had us traveling together from the capital all the way here, although he said he was on his way to Skepsis. He was well-behaved for a…well…"

Skharr narrowed his eyes at her pause and raised an eyebrow in response. "A barbarian?"

"Yes."

He chuckled. "Am I to understand that you are, in fact, a Paladin of Theros?"

She sniffed and glowered around the chamber they were in. "I am on sabbatical. I am allowed to let my hair down, both literally and metaphorically." She brushed her hair from side to side with a smirk. "And perhaps a little more, yes?"

The high priest shook his head and tried to press on with the topic at hand.

"Come, follow me."

They exchanged a glance but did as they were told and the man led them to one of the far wings of the temple. He made no effort to speak until they entered a smaller chamber, although it was still larger than the inn Skharr was housed in.

It looked like it was the high priest's personal living quarters, with shelves with hundreds of books and a handful of desks in place, heavily laden with papers, writing quills, and inkwells.

On the other side of the room, away from the desks, were a handful of divans, enough to comfortably seat five or more with small tables between them. Crystal carafes of wine as well as a selection of sweetmeats and dried fruits were provided.

"If you could wait here while I gather all my notes," the man asked and gestured for them to wait as he moved into the deeper chambers hidden from view by thick curtains.

"Well, while we are waiting..." Ytrea approached one of the tables and filled a small crystal glass with wine from one of the carafes. "Could I interest you in something to wet the tongue?"

Skharr shrugged. "I've never been one to decline a drink, although I do have the contents of four or five ale mugs in me already, and I would not want to be overly affected. Yet."

She grinned and poured him one of the glasses. "It would be interesting to see you...affected."

CHAPTER FIVE

The wine tasted like it had been touched with herbs and a trace of honey that dulled the heady taste most wines tended to have. Skharr tilted his head, inspected the dark red liquid inside his glass as he twirled it, and took a deep breath of the fumes that arose from inside.

"So you know something about wine, do you?" Ytrea asked and sipped from her glass before she sat on one of the divans.

"A little."

"If you aren't the most layered barbarian I've ever met."

"Met many barbarians, then, have you?"

"My fair share." She took another sip of wine to empty the glass and poured herself another.

"If we are to speak of layers…" He sat calmly beside her and inclined his head so he could keep her in view at all times. "Why did you not tell me you were a paladin during our travels together?"

She shrugged. "I also never told you that my name is Lady Cassandra, but I do not hear you complaining."

"Well then, Lady Cassandra, how is it that you find yourself on sabbatical?"

"I needed time away from my duties. It is written into the code that a sabbatical is a sound way to reestablish my confidence in my abilities and in my faith."

"I see. Then why—"

"Ah, ah!" She held a hand up to stop him. "It is my turn for a question. Which of the stories that I've heard about you are true?"

Skharr tilted his head. He couldn't be sure which stories she'd heard, but the chances were there weren't many songs written of his exploits in the wars before he abandoned it all to start a farm.

"Well…" He grunted and sipped his drink. "There was a dungeon not that far from here—a good three or four days' ride from Ryngold but comparatively close."

"I think I heard of that one. You fought a lich there, yes?"

He was genuinely surprised that she'd heard of it.

"Yes. Yes, I did. There was a situation with a noblewoman in Verenvan that proved difficult."

"I heard that story."

"About how I was poisoned?"

She tilted her head and after a moment, shook it emphatically. "No. It was certainly not about a poisoning."

Skharr opened his mouth to reply but shut it again. There would be nothing to gain over discussing that particular snippet of his history.

"Well, there was surviving the Ivehnshaw Tower."

"Ah, I believe I heard that too. How did you manage to survive?"

"Luck. And some help from the other two survivors. The tasks…well, they involved having those who entered kill each other to proceed deeper, to the point where even though hundreds went in, only a handful would be able to leave, even if they survived to the end."

"You know that dungeon is rumored to have been built by the Lord High God Janus, yes?" Cassandra asked and refilled his glass when she noticed it was almost empty.

"Really?" Skharr asked and tried not to show any sign of what he had learned while inside. "I hadn't thought of that. Why would a god build such a treacherous place?"

"Some say it is there to cull the weak warriors who would fight in his name. Others say that it is a test of some kind."

"It seems fairly sadistic and pointless to me," he mumbled around the lip of his glass.

"True, but everyone knows the Lord High God Janus is an absolute ass."

Skharr smirked and chuckled. "Now that I have certainly heard."

"You have? Who from?"

"The Lord High God Theros."

She paused in mid-sip and swallowed what she had in her mouth before she carefully brushed aside a few strands of hair that hung over her face. "Do you jest?"

"No. I did not know it at the time, but the god himself appeared to remove me from a farm I was working on to drive me to continue my work in the field of death and violence. I only found this out when he appeared to me in a dream while I was in the tower. He saved my life that day."

"Have you wondered why a god would want you to find yourself on the back of a horse again?" Cassandra asked.

"I never ride a horse," Skharr clarified quietly. "He is a brother."

"Wait." She paused to pop one of the dried apricots into her mouth and chewed pensively. "I should have asked about that when we were on the road together. I thought you were merely tired of riding or maybe wanted to appear stoic and strong in my presence."

"Why would I want to do that?" he asked.

"To impress me?"

"Would a man choosing to walk when he could ride impress you?"

"No," she admitted. "But menfolk have been known to act foolishly to try to find their way under my fringe."

He thought about it for a moment and finally nodded. She wasn't wrong about that, at least.

"I wouldn't do that," he replied simply.

"I see." Cassandra sighed. "Are you of a different preference, then?"

Skharr looked up from his glass. "What?"

"Do you prefer to stick it to the menfolk? I hear it is more common among the barbarian tribes for men to prefer bedding men, and women with women. Or at least less of an objection."

Again, most of that was true.

"There are fewer reasons to avoid it. In the end, we care not how folk enjoy themselves or who they enjoy themselves with. But no, I prefer to stick it to the ladyfolk, to use your words."

Cassandra nodded and looked down. "Ah."

He sipped from his glass before commenting, "You seem disappointed. Why?"

"No reason. I'm merely mourning that my fragile female ego is now shattered."

"You?" Skharr asked with a smirk. "You have a fragile female ego?"

"Not as Lady Cassandra, Paladin of Theros. But when the barbarian Skharr DeathEater met me, I was a flighty, ignorant female who men would try to protect and attempt to bed, although not necessarily in that order."

Skharr turned as the High Priest returned from his private quarters, his nose buried in a stack of books and papers that he carried closer to them.

"Are you to say he did not?" the man asked. He didn't look up from his study but adjusted his pince-nez with a fastidious gesture.

"Did not what?"

"Protect and bed you."

"He did the first. Not the second."

"I find it a rare occurrence that women who are threatened with rape would be interested in an energetic evening of fucking," Skharr noted. "I did not think to offer."

"It is not uncommon for women to be in the mood for energetic fucking after a good fight," she replied with a smirk. "Or, rather, not uncommon for this woman."

"It is not uncommon for paladins to find themselves a great many ways to enjoy themselves while on sabbatical," the high priest mentioned and arranged most of the books and papers on one of the desks, although he retained a scroll. "The rules of their orders are constraining, and when temporarily freed of those constraints, they do tend to enjoy all the pleasures usually denied them."

"Unlike the priests, who continue to enjoy all those pleasures since they are the ones that write the rules for all the different orders," Cassandra snarked.

"It's not like that."

"It is. Do not bother to deny it."

"It's—"

"I said don't," she snapped, and a hint of the dangerous creature she likely was while a proper paladin of good standing crept through.

"Very well."

"The sabbatical allows me to be anyone I might choose to be," she explained for Skharr's benefit. "I was offered to the order as a child and I had no choice in the matter. From my formative years, I have constantly traveled the world on one dutiful quest or another, and all I could do was focus on what others wanted from me. I enjoy making clothes and matching clothes and having them play together to make me look better than I ever did in this...this atrocity."

She pointed at her clothes and once again, the barbarian couldn't think of a single reason why the dress was an atrocity.

The belt that made it cling around her hips certainly enhanced her figure.

But she knew more about what clothes worked together than he did, and he had no desire to start her on the topic again.

"Well, as long as the paladin finds their way back to the order, there should be no issues with what they do for themselves," the high priest assured her absently, still reading through the scroll in front of him. "Although a few times, the sabbatical must be brought to an untimely albeit temporary end should the order require the paladin to return. Which, in this case, it does."

"I'll burn the code if you find a way to drag me back every time I try to enjoy myself."

"What were you doing in the capital city?" Skharr asked.

"That is not important," she replied and toyed with her hair.

"Indeed, it is not important in the light of our discussion and if you might both be facing what I suspect is true." He handed the warrior the scroll he had been reading.

"I thought you were sure," Cassandra reminded him.

"I am, but even so, such things cannot be rushed. Especially since no one has seen the Old God rising from the depths."

"And I assume that if we were to see an Old God rising, it will be altogether too late for all of us," Skharr muttered as he examined the contents of the scroll.

"Indeed. Whispers are all we can determine at the moment."

It did make for interesting reading, including a depiction of the Old God in question—possessing a name he would never be able to say aloud—rising from the depths. The question remained, however, of how the person had survived long enough to scribble a description of the being's appearance.

He could see it crush a house and a windmill with a single hand, while it called lightning from the sky with the other. It had hundreds of eyes spread over a bulbous head, and dozens of tentacles grew over the bottom of its skull and covered the mouth and a nose he could not make out.

"Who made this inscription?" he asked.

"It is said to have been written by the Lord High God Theros himself," the priest noted as he leaned closer to make sure they were talking about the same image. "However unlikely that may be."

"Skharr says he has met the Lord High God," Cassandra said and bit languidly into one of the pastries.

The old man looked confused and tugged his beard. "Truly? I would have thought—no."

"Thought what?"

"Well…no. I would have hoped, however, that he would have shown himself to one of his faithful instead of a…well, one of your—"

He pointed at Skharr, who understood immediately.

"Why would he show himself to a lowly barbarian when you are all trussed up to let him fuck you in the ass?"

"Well. It's not how I would describe it, but if you do…" The old man shrugged.

Cassandra snickered. "Have you considered that a Lord High God would want nothing to do with your pale, wrinkled ass? Perhaps he has a preference for the power in Skharr's."

"What?" the warrior asked.

"Do not think I haven't noticed," she replied with a wink.

He paused, his eyes narrowed, then shook his head and decided to move on. "What do you need to know to have this"—he gestured at the image—"possibility confirmed?"

"Certain rituals need to be performed to raise one of the Old Gods from the depths." The old man pointed at the inscriptions at the bottom of the scroll. "Rituals that must be stopped before it rises or we will all die a horrifying and painful death."

Skharr nodded, although the script was written in a language he didn't understand. There was no reason to tell them that, however.

"Well, if you do find out more, tell me, and I am sure a price can be arrived at." He rolled the scroll and handed it to the high priest. "For myself, I need to find work that pays now if I wish to continue living in this city."

He stood, feeling a surreal sense of impending doom as he moved away. If the priest learned more about what they had discussed, there would be numerous signs to follow. If he didn't, it was best to not involve himself with the cults that worshiped the Old Gods. They had a tendency to be violent.

"Will you honestly continue to look for work in the guild?"

Skharr almost jumped at the sound of Cassandra's voice so close to him. He hadn't even heard her footsteps approaching yet there she was, walking beside him.

He had too much ale and wine in him. It wasn't a bad thing, necessarily, but he wouldn't be at his sharpest until the drink wore off.

"Until the priest can pay me, I need to find work that does," he answered noncommittally.

"Might I join you?" she asked. "I have no intention to don my paladin uniform until it is needed and until then, there is no point in sharing my true identity with the other mercenaries."

"So I should call you Ytrea instead of Cassandra?"

"Yes." She nodded. "Cassandra is my name when I am in full armor and prepared for battle. Ytrea is my given name."

"I… All right. My reputation is confused as it stands and I am sure you will get all the rumors you would like out of it."

"What is that supposed to mean?" she asked. "Something along the lines of what you did for those noblewomen in Verenvan?"

Skharr shrugged. "I have no idea what you mean."

"I mean that those posh and prim ladies used you, and not only for your ability to fight."

"Is that what the rumors have been about me?"

She smirked. "Well, only if you know what to listen for. Most would simply say they wanted to use you to make sure that only the finest suiters came to their houses and to scare off the rest, but once one realizes that one of those suitors attempted to murder you—and ended up dead by your hand... Well, it is no mystery that you stuck the noblewomen with more than merely a well-padded contract invoice."

Skharr chuckled and nodded. There was no point in being modest now. The flighty and naive woman he met on the road was clearly an act and "Ytrea" certainly had a sound mind and a clever wit about her.

"Very well, then. It is possible that there is a hint of truth to these rumors."

"I already knew that," she asserted. "But it is interesting that you admit it so brazenly. No wonder the suiter wanted you dead."

"Perhaps you should ask him—oh. That will not be possible, I suppose."

That elicited a laugh from her. "Who knows what other truths we might uncover by conversing with the good men of the guild?"

CHAPTER SIX

She would play her role again and Skharr wasn't sure how he felt about wandering about with someone who carried on dishonestly like this.

Even so, he could understand why she would not want to be recognized as a paladin. All those he'd met in the past were sanctimonious, pompous asses—the kind who were generally "respected" to their faces but mocked and openly hated when out of earshot.

Most mercenaries were intelligent enough to not make enemies of paladins, but that didn't mean any of them had to like them.

Still, Cassandra—or Ytrea as he was supposed to refer to her from this point forward—was something of an oddity. Perhaps this was how all paladins acted when they weren't bound by whatever code they were held to.

The guildmaster looked up almost immediately, saw him approach the desk, and waved to catch the barbarian's attention. He narrowed his eyes at the woman at the warrior's side but proceeded to ignore her.

"I suppose we should not be surprised that you took the head of a troll when sent to deal with a handful of common bandits," the man said. He scratched his crooked nose and frowned deeply as Ytrea approached the table to carefully inspect the papers atop it. "The dwarves who sponsored the contract said that they were unaware that there was a troll present."

"Of course they weren't aware of it," Skharr retorted. "Exactly like they didn't know that the brigands numbered closer to thirty."

"Did you kill them all yourself?" Ytrea asked and stared at him with wide eyes.

"No, the troll turned on his comrades and killed more than I did," he answered.

"Well, killing the troll was the mightier feat," the guildmaster noted as he took a piece of paper from Ytrea's hand and placed it on the table and out of her reach. "The dwarves said they could offer you another five silvers for your efforts as that is all they can afford for the moment, but once they reclaim their mine, they would be willing to discuss an additional reward."

Skharr doubted that. He hadn't even expected them to offer five more silvers, which he pocketed quickly and without argument.

"Still, I suppose a troll would be no challenge compared to the dragon you killed," the guildmaster continued. "I've never seen a dragon myself, mind, but from the stories told, I can imagine that a troll would be paltry by comparison."

"He killed a dragon?" Ytrea asked and her eyes widened again. She truly was very good at her act. "You killed a dragon? When did this happen?"

"Not long ago," the man noted and hastily moved a few more papers away from where she stood now that she was distracted. "The tale of how the newly crowned emperor took his throne is beginning to spread, and it speaks about how the two of you killed a dragon together. I assume some creative license was taken as it was the emperor's bard who wrote the songs that will

55

take the stage of a few amphitheaters around the empire, but it makes for impressive listening nonetheless."

"I'll have to have a word with this bard." Skharr growled his irritation.

"You did kill a dragon then," Ytrea whispered and grinned. "How…arousing."

The guildmaster raised an eyebrow. "Well, if you want to try slumming amongst those of us who are not barbarians, you should know that I am more than willing to indulge you."

She turned to him, scrutinized him carelessly, and tilted her head as she asked, "Have you fought a dragon, then?"

His face turned a bright crimson but he met her gaze. "No."

"Damn."

The man laughed and shook his head. "Well, I had to try. Why did you kill the dragon?"

"If you had ever encountered a dragon yourself, you would know that one does not fight it so much as…run away from it," Skharr muttered. "Which means, I suppose, that I've not killed a dragon either."

"But if you can't kill dragons, why are there so few of them?" Ytrea asked.

Skharr had a feeling she already knew and that she was still playing the part of the somewhat vacuous scatterbrain, but the guildmaster was more than willing to indulge her.

"Find their nests in the trees or clifftops and break the eggs," the man said with a decisive shake of his head. "Or take the eggs and sell them if you can manage it, since there are mages out there who think the eggs have a great deal of magical value. That said, it's safer to simply destroy the eggs. The mother will pursue you for miles if you try to keep one, or so I've read. And once the eggs are smashed, the dragon moves away and becomes someone else's problem."

"It seems a little cowardly," Ytrea commented.

"When faced by an intelligent, winged creature that can spit fire or acid while protected by hard bones and armor-like scales?" the guildmaster retorted. "Sometimes, caution serves a man better than idiotic valor."

"And some folk would enjoy the nature of the challenge, fighting against the impossible odds," she countered.

"How many of those folk are alive?"

Ytrea paused and nodded. "You make a fair point. Still, I think charging into a dungeon with little to no chance of success might prove that valor does have its merits."

"It does, sometimes," Skharr noted. "Wisdom is displayed by knowing when to stand your ground, when to attack, and when to turn tail and run."

"Have you ever run from a dungeon?"

"Yes, I have. Although in that case, it was when I was pursued by a group of brigands and used their blood to summon a demon that brought the whole godsbedammed magic-riddled fucked-up place down on my head. That was when I decided that I would rather not fight a fucking mountain."

"Have I told you about the other dungeon that they say is becoming more active now?" the guildmaster asked.

"Aye." Skharr grunted dismissively.

"Tell me about it," Ytrea demanded.

"It's one of the older dungeons in these parts near the sea and said to be inhabited by one of the Old Gods—you know, those that live in the depths. Tripe, I know, but it was full of treasure when it was emptied some...I think seventy-five years ago, now. Still, talk about it increasing in activity again has begun to surface."

"Where did these rumors start?" Skharr asked.

"Believe it or not, folk thought it would be a fine idea to start a farm in the region. Can you imagine having an open farm out near a dungeon? Idiots like that needs them a lesson taught if you ask me, but that's no matter. The first ones killed was a group of children who found their way in there."

"Children?" Ytrea asked and shook her head. "Why would they be near somewhere like that?"

"Who is to say? Children enjoy exploring and they put themselves in trouble simply because they have nothing better to do."

"What happened?"

"The father approached the guild for help to clear the location again. It was assumed there was a handful of fledgling monsters inside that the original group missed. Another group was gathered and a bounty posted. Almost thirty warriors had joined the party before they left...six months past now."

"And there has been no sign of them since, I suppose," Ytrea whispered.

"There was sign all right—bodies. Three of the members were found a few miles from the dungeon, gnawed on by scavengers. The rest... Well, you know what the assumption is or there would not be talk of the dungeon becoming active again. There is a bounty for more information and any monsters killed that have spawned from the place."

"And how would one confirm the killings?" Skharr asked, his expression skeptical. "I doubt you could carry many heads while you are busy fighting to stay alive."

"You managed it," the guildmaster pointed out.

"I hewed the head from the troll after it was dead and after the whole group was dead or gone. I assume that would not be possible if they were running away from skeletons and the like."

"Skeletons are the bodies of the dead that are brought back into a state of living death by necromantic powers," the guildmaster explained for Ytrea, who nodded slowly. "Still, I suppose a truth potion would be needed, both to confirm the information as well as the killings, although I can imagine that the Barbarian of Theros would be disbelieved. None would think that you have any reason to lie."

"Aside from the bounty offered on the information?" Skharr asked.

"Well, the assumption is that you would be too scrupulous to lie. Others might, however. Not many who follow the Lord High God Janus would be believed on their word alone. He is an ass of a god and attracts his like."

"Agreed," Skharr and Ytrea said in unison and exchanged a quick look. She laughed.

"Another way to determine the veracity of claims would be for you to go to the offices of Henley A'Tar. He is the resident mage and he has a memory stone in his possession that would also help."

The barbarian narrowed his eyes and glanced at each of them. "A memory stone? I don't think I've ever heard of a talisman like that."

"He claims to have invented it himself." The guildmaster chuckled. "But we all know he copied it from the work that was found in a dungeon and left behind. Of course, he was the first one to decipher what the talisman was for, but it doesn't mean that he invented it."

"I would say the point is moot given that he has the only one," Ytrea interjected. "A memory stone brings out the memories of the person holding it and projects them onto the nearest reflective surface—a mirror, a plate, or even still water."

"That seems…dangerous," the warrior replied and shook his head dubiously. "What would happen if I did not want all of my memories remembered?"

The guildmaster glanced at Ytrea, who held her hands wide apart and mouthed the word "dragon" to him, which was quickly followed by a wink.

Skharr smirked. He did not want to think about how he barely escaped his encounter with a dragon alive, of course, but there were other memories too. These were the kind he kept down savagely and that only resurfaced in the form of dreams or the odd tremor when facing something that reminded him of them.

No, there were things he had no desire to see through a mirror, a plate, or still water. They were dangerous, even only as memories.

He tugged Ytrea's hands farther apart by almost four inches.

"It was a large dragon. "

"How thick was the dragon?" she asked.

"I...what?"

"You told me the length but left the crucial detail of the girth aside."

"I think we are no longer speaking of dragons," the guild-master muttered.

She grinned. "Perhaps not. More like snakes. Wait, did you call him the Barbarian of Theros? More of your legends, I suppose?"

"Not...quite. I would say the fact that I am a barbarian and fighting for Theros' guild would be enough to grant me the name."

"The word is that you are also quite pious as well," the man stated as his attention drifted to his papers again. "That you donate more than you owe in dues in thanks to the Lord High God for his help in battle. I would assume you had more to do with that than any god might, but who am I to question what the Lord High God is capable of?"

Skharr had no intention to fill him in on what the Lord High Gods were capable of and what they did to pass the time. There was no point in giving the man nightmares.

"Regarding the dungeon you mentioned," Ytrea continued. "What would it take to organize a group to head out there to deal with it?"

The guildmaster scratched his crooked nose and his brow furrowed in thought. "You wouldn't want to go in alone, even the two of you. At best, you will deal with dozens of crazed cultists who have no fear of death and are on a mission to raise the Old One. At worst...well, you might have the Old One to kill."

That sounded like what Skharr thought they would encounter.

"If you are interested in sharing the gold and loot, we would have to find a group of fighters who are well aware of the dangers that would be encountered therein," the man continued.

The warrior nodded. "If my knowledge of how dungeons are run is valid, we can expect there to be few survivors even if we achieve success."

"Well, I will spread the word." The guildmaster tapped the table. "If there is one thing I know about the mercenaries in this city, it's that they are crazier than the rest and more than willing to risk their lives to kill whatever pays the most. I am sure I could bring a group together, although I make no promises about their quality."

Skharr looked at Ytrea, who shrugged lightly.

"It is all we can ask for," he conceded. "The loot will be divided equally among all surviving parties. That should draw in those who know of the dangers."

"We all appreciate your optimism," Ytrea muttered and rolled her eyes.

It was unsettling to think that he had been dragged into another dungeon battle this soon after he promised he would keep to himself and to the smaller, shorter, easier fights for a while.

If he had to guess, it was the kind of thing that Theros had dragged him from his farm to do, and the damn god now drove all these different and complex, dangerous battles toward him. In the midst of this, all he could do was continue to fight desperately for his life until something claimed it.

He had no illusions. Eventually, a dagger, sword, claw, or horn would injure something that no potion could heal and it would be the end of him. And all those legends that now circulated about him would vanish like the morning mist.

It was an unsettling thought, to be sure, but one he had made his peace with many, many years before.

"Come," he said briskly to Ytrea, who still infuriated the guildmaster by inspecting his papers without permission. "I have a mind for food and drink—and much more drink."

"You are so much fun," she said with a laugh that drew the attention of the mercenaries around them momentarily, although they returned to their own business quickly.

The inn was a little fuller than Skharr would have liked, but they found a table with no difficulty. He suspected that the innkeeper had kept a table open for him should he need it.

Not that the barbarian was a special case. It appeared as though the proprietor kept a table reserved for those who slept under his roof, and Skharr found the one was set aside for him and an extra chair was brought for Ytrea, although he wasn't sure what to call her when they were alone.

Or as alone as they could be in a crowded inn full of folk who grew more and more drunk as the seconds ticked past.

"Did you mean what you said at the guild?"

He looked up from the mug of ale in his hand and realized that his companion was scrutinizing him intently.

"I said much at the guild. You'll have to be more specific."

"About most folk not returning from the trips into the dungeons you fought in?"

"From the perspectives of sheer numbers, yes." He took a long, slow sip from the mug and his gaze drifted to the platters of food that had already begun to be distributed through the room to the cheers of the men and women gathered there. "Of those I attacked in the past, some were mostly cleared already. Another had been cleared before I arrived and replaced by a Lich who tried to summon a demon. The other...well, I already told you."

She nodded slowly and sipped her beer. "What do you think our chances of surviving this one are?"

Skharr shrugged. "I've never fought one of the Old Gods before. If I remember the stories I was told as a child correctly, it took a mighty war of all the beings on the planet to subdue one and even then, he was sent to sleep in the depths, not killed. Of course, legends and stories have been twisted into myth over the millennia of retelling, so I can grant us some optimism."

"And what optimism is that?"

"The two of us are more likely to survive than those who will join us." He raised his mug.

Ytrea laughed and tapped hers against it. "Well, I suppose we can drink to that. You should know that if I am to join you on this mission, I will still be on sabbatical."

He tilted his head to the side and could feel the drink already starting to tell on his sense of balance. His head suddenly felt a little too heavy. "Is there…is that important? What is the difference? Will you fight differently?"

"No, nothing like that." She shook her head. "I will not lead this group. I will not be a Paladin of Theros in this fight, merely Ytrea."

"As I recall, Ytrea can kill a man as easily as Lady Cassandra, Paladin of Theros."

He laughed but stopped when he realized that she hadn't joined him.

"It is different," she explained and leaned forward. "Folk expect a great deal from a paladin in battle. If I am not one in a fight, I will not wear my formal plate and mail and I will not wield my weapons of power."

Skharr nodded and tried to keep his face as somber as he could. "I have a serious question for you."

"Yes?"

"Do I call you Ytrea or Cassandra?"

That did tease a laugh out of her and he grinned, feeling as though he had won. This battle at least.

"Either suits me," she answered and lifted her beer to her lips. "Although I do prefer Cassandra. It is what I am used to hearing when in the heat of battle, and I think it would suit me better. There are many who share my name, enough to make it fairly inconspicuous."

Skharr nodded his agreement. "What is the formal plate and mail like? Would it be something we should bring along anyway? Because I feel we could probably sneak it out of the temple as long as you were willing to distract the high priest."

"What?"

He chuckled. "You should know that a full suit of plate and mail are expensive and hard to find. I have never been able to find a full suit that matched my size, if you will."

"You don't understand. It was a suit of mail and plate that was given to me by Theros himself."

The barbarian stared at her for a long moment, unsure that he had heard her correctly but sure enough, it seemed as though she said Theros had given her a suit of armor.

"I feel you need to explain that. All Theros did for me was... well, save my life that one time, I suppose."

"It was part of my vows," she said and acquiesced to his request for an explanation. "The deal I took, if you will. I use the armor to move through the battlefield like an unstoppable creature, and he gives me the power to carry it without any loss in my usual speed or stamina."

"Stamina is important, although not always only for when you're wearing armor."

She smirked but failed to reach the laughter he had hoped for. He had a feeling she was taking the conversation a great deal more seriously than he was.

"Unfortunately, while he granted my request for the armor, he did not grant my request for a spell to make it cooler to wear."

"One moment." Skharr cautioned her with a wave of his hand as their plates of food were set out on the table for them. He waited until they were alone again before he spoke. "If I heard that correctly, you asked the High Lord God Theros for a suit of armor that would be comfortable to wear, easy to carry, and would keep you at a pleasant temperature in the heat of battle."

"I thought that since I was vowing my life to his service, he could provide me with something to make the service a little more tolerable," she answered. "And technically, I asked him for the armor to weigh almost nothing, but he reminded me that there would be a race to steal my armor at the earliest opportunity if it was itself blessed with absolutely no weight for eternity. You are a barbarian so you don't understand, yes? You only rarely wear armor."

"That is not correct," he countered. "I always wear as much armor as I can find, which is perhaps less armor than most fighters would prefer. There are few suits of any kind that fit me and those that do generally fail to account for the width of my shoulders. They tend to be constricting."

"They are...quite wide," she agreed and leaned closer to inspect them. "Does it not bother you?"

"The armor? I have always believed that the wounds they prevent would bother me more."

"No, no, not the armor." She shook her head. "All the art where all the artists do is cover your...ah..."

"Dragon?"

"If you say so. And, well..." She held her hands up about a foot apart. "You must be joking."

"Must I now?"

"I don't know of a normal woman who needs a foot of cock in her. I don't know any who would fit that much."

Skharr shrugged. "Some women are bigger and more...uh, demanding than others. One can always find ways to please them depending on how full they wish to be at that particular point in time."

"Like...who would need it?" she asked and shook her head.

"A giantess, maybe? Or one who has giantess blood in her, I suppose."

He looked at his food, bit into the warm bread, and dipped it quickly in the garlic and cream cheese that was provided beside the soup.

Cassandra leaned forward, her eyebrows raised in surprise. "You cannot be serious. A giantess? Are you suggesting that you survived fucking a giantess?"

"A barbarian does not...fuck and tell," he mumbled from around a mouthful of food.

"That is not remotely accurate," she argued. "That is precisely the kind of feat a barbarian would brag about until all who heard it were sick of listening to the retellings."

"Not a DeathEater," Skharr said quietly.

"I...huh." She grunted and leaned back in her seat. "I'll admit I do not know any others of your clan. They are not very well-documented and most of what was documented were half-truths and rumors based on what was left behind after your raids."

"Could that be due to the fact that we do not fuck and tell?" he asked and raised an eyebrow.

"Or it could be because you eat of your enemies," she retorted and sipped her beer.

"Not all. Some are too sinewy and chewy to properly prepare and would be an utter waste of our spices," he replied. "We use those to make our bows and spears or as the supports for our tents."

She coughed loudly, leaned forward, and tried to cover her mouth when her drink was suddenly aspirated up her nose.

"Oh, fuck you, DeathEater," she gasped and shook her head. "You will not hear the end of this."

"I am sure," he said and took a mouthful of the mutton in his soup. "We will need to start collecting supplies for our trip. I think we should start tomorrow."

"What kind of supplies will we need for a trip into a dungeon?" she asked and drained her mug of beer.

"There are those that would be required on any other journey to keep us fed and protected against the elements," he told her, knowing she had probably traveled far and wide enough to know the basics that were required for journeys that lasted longer than a few days. "For the dungeon itself, we will likely need torches and talismans."

"Talismans?"

Skharr nodded. "It is more than likely that magical protections will be in place, the kind we will not be able to traverse without magical help of our own."

"We'll need to talk to the mage about that."

"Yes, the mage. Henry…Adoor."

"Henley A'Tar," she corrected him with a laugh. "And I think we need more drinks for us to be able to continue this conversation. You are much more fun when you reach the edge of drunkenness."

He stood from his seat, feeling no attack on his balance as he collected the two empty mugs. "Agreed."

It was a short walk toward where the innkeeper was busy filling and refilling mugs for the other guests, although it seemed like he focused immediately on Skharr when he arrived at the counter.

"Are you enjoying your food and drink, Master DeathEater?" the man asked, collected a jug, and poured its contents into their mugs. "You and your guest?"

"Very much so," Skharr answered, not sure if he was slurring or not.

"You should know that the policy for this establishment is an extra silver piece if you intend to…entertain your lady guest on our premises."

The barbarian looked to where Cassandra was seated. He hadn't been gone a full minute and she was already being accosted by a handful of locals. He could tell that she had reverted to her role as the coy and flighty, talkative seamstress, smiling and looking away from the two men who reached out to pull her chair out.

His heart beat a little faster and ticked in the back of his mind as he retrieved his purse and removed two gold pieces.

"I said one piece," the innkeeper said loudly enough to cut over the noise that filled the common room. "One silver piece, not gold."

"I am aware."

"Then what are you paying me two pieces of gold for?"

He took a deep breath and the heat rushed across his body to push the warm drunkenness to the side as he rolled his neck.

"They are to cover the damage caused," he said casually.

CHAPTER SEVEN

It was generally part of the role of a paladin to stop frivolous fights and intervene when there was the possibility that innocents might be injured at the hand of drunken barbarians such as himself.

On some level, Skharr expected Cassandra to step in to stop things from escalating into violence. He had somehow ascribed an innate nature to her that would make her step into the role even though she had deliberately left it behind not long before.

Not that he truly expected her to try to stop the fight that was inevitable. That was purely supposition on his part, but his gaze fixed on her while he waited for her to act left him distracted. He barely noticed when a third assailant swung a massive fist toward his face.

The impact was startling but not altogether unpleasant. There was little force behind the blow and the drunken man fell back immediately, clutched his hand, and uttered a low wail of pain.

The barbarian was not even forced back a step, although he grimaced and felt his jaw instinctively to make sure nothing was broken and no teeth had been knocked out. He had been drinking a great deal and he could feel a numbness in his fingers.

Skharr knew himself well enough to know that it resulted in a lack of awareness of pain on his part.

The other two who had harassed Cassandra failed to learn from their comrade's mistake, rushed at the still-standing warrior, and attempted to bring him down with a cooperative tackle between them. He was forced back three or four steps and knocked into a nearby table, although the occupants were quick to make sure none of their drinks were spilled. They began to cheer the fighters on, while others gathered around to watch.

He had never minded having an audience, and if the truth be told, he certainly felt in the mood for a good fight.

A couple of fists were thrown into his gut, and two were tossed at his jaw, although like that of their predecessor, there was no force behind them. The warrior grinned and tasted a little blood in his mouth as he watched another punch aimed at his head. The two men had grown bold as if they thought the fact that he made no effort to fight back meant they had the advantage.

Without warning, he ducked his head and drove it forward into the fist that was aimed for his cheek. A sharp spike of pain rocked across his head with the impact but the sound of bones snapping in the man's hand made it more than worth it. A scream of pain echoed through the inn's common room and Skharr stepped in, grasped the man by his broken hand, and dragged him close in to punch his fist across the man's jaw.

More bones cracked and the man spun in place before he fell, his whole body immediately limp. The first drunkard was on his feet and his anger seemed to overcome the pain in his hand as he rushed forward to attack.

The barbarian would have suggested that he simply remain on the floor and let himself out of the fight with a mildly injured hand, but there was no way to tell what was going through the man's head in that moment.

Only what would connect with his head in the moment after that.

Skharr leaned back as the punch sailed past his face and almost struck his comrade, who still attempted to drag the barbarian to the floor. The warrior brought his knee up into the first man's gut, knocked the breath from his lungs in a single stroke, then caught him by the neck with a grunt and threw him down with a resounding thud. Glasses shook all across the room and a cheer followed from those whose mugs had been overturned.

He paused to make sure his opponent was well and truly unconscious before he turned his attention to the last of the three still standing. The man released him and took a step back when he realized that he was in a fight on his own against the large barbarian who had dealt with his two cronies so quickly and easily.

A step back revealed his hesitation, and Skharr could see that the decision to retreat soon became more and more inviting.

It didn't take much deliberation before he chose not to allow it.

"If you think it'll be that easy for you," he snapped, caught the man by the collar of his shirt, and dragged him closer, "you are mistaken."

The drunkard tried to pull away again, and Skharr yanked him in close and dropped his forehead abruptly to crunch into the front of his opponent's face.

It appeared that the man's nose was broken, but it was probably not the only thing broken in the mess that the unfortunate's face had turned into. He was still conscious, but barely, and sagged into the warrior's hold until the barbarian decided the fight was over, released his shirt, and simply let him fall.

Skharr straightened slowly as a cheer erupted from the group in the common area of the inn, and he marched to where the innkeeper had not bothered to watch the fight but seemed transfixed by the coins that had dropped on his counter instead.

The barbarian collected the two full tankards left for him and moved to rejoin Cassandra where the paladin remained seated.

"Your drink," he rasped and placed one of the tankards in front of her.

"That was…enlightening," she commented, shifted a little in her seat, and took a long draught from the tankard.

Skharr pulled a piece of cloth from his pocket and wiped the blood that had spattered onto his face. "What do you mean?"

"Your fighting prowess. And style. Very interesting. Powerful, aggressive, and yet able to take a strike when you are unable to avoid it."

"I could avoid some of them if I wanted to," he retorted as he slid into a seat across from her. He didn't meet her gaze, still focused on tidying himself up and using the back of a bronze spoon to help to find the places that needed cleaning on his face. "It honestly doesn't feel like a fight unless they manage to deliver a punch or two. Simply trampling them makes me feel like a mad bull. This way, it looks a little fairer and more like they initiated the fight and I finished it."

"Interesting. So you mean to say you took those strikes intentionally?"

He nodded. "Or rather, I failed to evade or block the blows intentionally. If there is a man or woman out there who is capable of stopping me with a single blow, they deserve victory."

"Even if they were…a troll? Or an orc chieftain?"

The warrior opened his mouth to reply but snapped it shut. He took a sip from his drink and tasted a trace of his blood in his mouth. "I draw the line when a single punch is capable of killing me instead of merely rendering me senseless."

Cassandra laughed. "Yes, I suppose that is a wise course of action to take. Have you ever been struck by a troll?"

"Yes." He nodded and regarded her curiously. "Have you?"

The paladin nodded slowly. "I cannot say that I cared for it. She did not hit me with the full power behind her blow, and it still felt like a small house was falling on me."

"There is...I don't remember much about the strike myself." Skharr shrugged his shoulders. "All I remember is seeing the arm coming toward me and in the next moment, I was on the ground a few yards away and trying to understand what had happened. It was hard to stay on my feet after that, but I gave as well as I was given, and the troll is dead while I am not. It proved to be a learning experience."

"What did you learn?"

"To avoid being struck by a troll."

"Ah." Cassandra grunted and took another long sip from her tankard. "I suppose that is a simple lesson and well-worth keeping in mind."

He nodded. "A wise paladin would learn from the mistakes of a foolish barbarian."

"It is a good thing I am not a wise paladin then," she answered smoothly with a small smirk. "And I look forward to killing monsters with you come the morning."

Skharr knew that meant she would take her leave in a moment, and he followed her to the door.

"I know the merchants we'll want to speak to before we leave on our quest," she told him once they were outside. Somehow, she instantly looked more sober and sure on her feet than she had been inside. "I can look into making sure we are well-supplied for the journey, but that will be the end of my leadership in this."

"You expect me to lead on this quest?"

"I expect you to charge forward and do what you do best." She patted him on the arm. "Do so knowing that I will support you along with a few others who have the courage to do so."

He nodded. There was little more that he could ask for. Despite his many years spent in battle, he had never had a mind for the tactics that went into engagements on a larger scale. As she said, he was generally placed at the front lines to career headfirst into the opposing force and break the bodies and the spirits of the men he was assaulting. It tended to work for him and he was forced to assume that it was a good way to start the battles.

Of course, being far into the front of the battle lines meant that fewer projectiles came down over his head. For his particular style of battle, it was the best place to be.

Still, as Cassandra made her way back through the town, he couldn't help but consider how much he relied on his physical power. He had never expected to fight into his waning years. The assumption had always been that he would be dead or back among his kin by the time he was no longer physically able to fight.

It would take only one misjudgment on his part and he would no longer be in a place to decide that he'd had enough. All he could hope for was that a few tales would be told of his passing—perhaps in a last stand atop a wall in the middle of a siege or in a duel against a powerful opponent.

He collected a few of the apples that had been requested from the innkeeper and headed into the stables to where Horse was stabled.

Night was falling and the beast was dozing when he slipped in, but Skharr was instantly forgiven when Horse saw the gifts the barbarian had brought for him.

"What think you?" he asked as he sat on a small stool and handed the stallion one of the apples. "A duel or a powerful last stand atop a wall, swinging an ax into wave after wave of monstrous hordes?"

Horse snorted and shook his mane.

"Agreed, survival is the better option, but if I were to end up dead on some battlefield, what do you think would prove to be the finer death?"

The beast stared at him as he handed him another apple.

"True, a duel would not be the most memorable way to die. Unless, of course, I was to win the duel and die of my injuries. Perhaps for some mighty cause or to end a battle that many a skald and bard would sing of."

That didn't appear to convince his companion, who stopped waiting for the barbarian to provide him with another apple and shoved his nose into the bucket he had brought to claim his own.

"Of course, I would come to you." Skharr grunted and leaned his back against the wall of the stable. "You are closer to seeing yourself at the end than I and therefore, with it looming over your head, you might have the insight I lack. Most of my folk fight well into their eighth decade and longer before their body proves too brittle to battle at the front lines. There is no reason to expect any different for myself. Of course, in the end, we might find ourselves in battle against the kind that does not care about age and will strike me anyway. One powerful enemy is all that is required to show me the error of my arrogant ways."

Horse nudged him gently in the shoulder.

"Well, far be it from me to complain. You are no chicken born in the spring but power and strength are still your allies. You have many years ahead of you. But I assume you'll then want to live out your twilight years in comfort and ease, not traveling the world behind a foolish barbarian too stupid to know when his time is at an end."

Skharr had enjoyed the company of a few horses in his time— all possessing the same regal name—but he had not been with any of them quite as long as he had been with Horse. He had acquired the beast from a knight who fell off the saddle and could ride no more. The man wanted to kill the beast for the perceived treachery, but the barbarian managed to make off with him. It had been no place for horses. Knights were supposed to treat their mounts better than that.

But then, he supposed, it turned out for the best in the end. He enjoyed having Horse beside him, even if the beast tended to complain more than the others had.

"Then again, there would be a great deal for us to see in the world," Skharr commented. He had already given up on feeding Horse the apples one at a time since the beast would likely bite him if he tried to interrupt his feeding now. "For example, I happened to meet a paladin who is not a sanctimonious prick."

Horse whinnied uproariously and tossed his mane as he knocked the empty bucket over.

"I know. I was surprised as you are. Do you recall the woman we journeyed with on the way here?"

Once again, Horse looked doubtful.

"Yes, the same one. I don't think even her horses knew or if they did, they were keeping it a secret. Horses generally aren't any good at keeping secrets, so you'll find me as surprised as you are. Her name isn't Ytrea either but rather Cassandra, and she is a Paladin on sabbatical. As she tells the tale, she was offered as tribute to her order and found that the lifestyle never quite agreed with her, which is why she chose a sabbatical. She interests me."

He looked up as Horse nickered loudly, seemingly amused.

"Not like that. Well, a little like that. I would have to be blind or utterly uninterested in human females to find myself uninterested. But the fact that it is not only a physical attraction might be the most interesting part. There is a...violence to her that I find interesting. And appealing. She will join us in our next venture, so I think you will see what I mean."

Horse looked curiously at him—like he didn't quite believe what he was saying.

"You will see for yourself. We'll leave sometime soon. The fact that we'll fight something that I don't think I've ever fought against or dreamed of fighting against in my wildest fantasies might be why I am a little more maudlin than usual. Old Gods were always tossed carelessly aside as the myth that even my kin never believed in. My initial response would be to disbelieve any mentions of creatures like that. Still, it would be unwise of me to be wholly skeptical at this point. I have met gods, spoken to them, and had them save my life."

It didn't look like Horse was very interested in the conversation, but that didn't mean Skharr would stop talking. His audience was probably more captive than any other he would enjoy.

"Old Gods...old myths of creatures capable of turning a man's mind on itself with a single thought." Skharr shook his head. "What is one man to do in the face of such...monsters?"

Horse turned to look at him with a pair of massive brown eyes.

"True, a man and a horse," he conceded. "But the point stands. What chance have we against creatures of legends like that?"

There was no answer from Horse aside from snuffling the empty bucket in the hopes of finding more apples. He snorted his disappointment.

"We can do nothing aside from pit ourselves against them and see what our measure is, eh, old friend?" Skharr grinned and patted the stallion's neck. "I do so enjoy our talks. For a four-legged beast, you hide a great deal of wisdom behind that placid appearance. I suppose that, like our friend Cassandra, you only keep up appearances for ulterior motives?"

Horse eyed him in a way that only confirmed his suspicions.

"I thought as much. Well, as long as we can be honest with each other, I think there will be no problems." He scratched the beast's forehead. "I'll make sure you get more apples in the morning but for now, rest. We'll soon not have much time for it, and we had better make the most of what we can have."

After a few more attempts at the empty bucket, Horse lowered his head as Skharr moved toward the door of the stable, closed it quietly, and let his friend slip into his much-needed rest.

The warrior smiled and shook his head as he exited the stable. He deliberately avoided the common room and instead, climbed the outside steps directly to the room that had been set aside for him. He would need to take his own advice.

CHAPTER EIGHT

There were a few things to be noted about the comfort of the hay-stuffed mattresses that the innkeeper used. The fact that he managed to keep them free of lice and other pests while close to the river was quite a feat.

The comfort was also understated, although Skharr woke with a discomfort about him that was difficult to shake.

He groaned softly as he pushed from the bed and rubbed his temples gently. His body was tender in a handful of different places, and as light filtered in through the window slats, he could see the places where he had been struck in the brawl the night before.

Bruises marked his skin all the way along his ribs and midsection, and the dark-blue coloring would turn a sickly yellow in a few days. It would take less time to heal if he still had the healing charm around his neck, but Horse was more deserving of its effects.

"Fucking godsbedammed—shit." He hissed a breath as he rubbed his fingers over the bruises. He had drunk enough to dull the pain in the moment, of course, but there was no telling how much damage had been done.

Thankfully, he could feel nothing broken and taking deep breaths told him that he hadn't pulled or torn anything that would prevent him from being able to engage in any quests. It would be painful but he would survive.

He shook his head and pulled his clothes on before he moved to the door and down the steps into the common room. It was a few hours after sunrise, and the establishment was considerably quieter now than it had been the night before.

Gods would be thanked for that individual piece of mercy, although he soon realized the room was not entirely empty. Two men and a woman were seated at a table, eating what appeared to be a morning repast although they didn't speak to each other as they ate.

The innkeeper was cleaning mugs and plates behind his counter, and when he saw Skharr, he nodded his head toward the strangers.

At least that message was clear enough. They were there for him. The proprietor already had a platter with a few thick cuts of beef, cheese, and two slices of bread ready for him as he slid into his seat, along with a bowl of steaming soup.

"A little apple juice," the innkeeper said quietly as he placed a mug down next to the platter. "To assuage the effects of a night of drinking."

He nodded. Even the soft speaking tone of the man was enough to make his pounding head a little more pronounced, and he waited for him to move away before he tried the fruit juice.

Sure enough, he felt a little better after a few sips. He could taste a hint of mint and other spices that he could not place, but they appeared to do some of the work as well.

None of the three strangers said a word, not even so much as to acknowledge his presence, although they all watched him out of the corners of their eyes.

One had orc blood in him, that much was made clear by the slightly elongated jaw and a few teeth that protruded a little.

They weren't quite long enough to make full tusks but it was still enough to make him distinctive. He was larger than the other two by quite a margin, with broad shoulders and arms as thick as Skharr's, although he was shorter and possessed a hint of a bulge over his belt.

The woman clearly had no human blood to her, although the barbarian needed the time it took to work through half of his meal to settle on her precise lineage. Half-dwarf, he decided, which accounted for her shorter, stockier stature and her thick brown hair that looked like it would spring up in a sphere around her head if it was released from the band that held it in place.

But her cheekbones and her eyes finally allowed him to reach the conclusion that the other half of her lineage could only be some kind of elf. He was certain that her ears would show the traditional points, although they were hidden by the thick hair. Her eyes were larger than a human's would be and perched on high cheekbones. One was a deep-red and the other a light yellow.

He'd never met any half-elves. It was known that they existed but as far as he knew, it was rare. The reasons for their rarity was the subject of much debate, and Skharr had a mind to ask her what the story was if and when it seemed appropriate.

The third seemed the closest to human among the three with an unruly head of bright orange hair, deep-green eyes, and a face that looked a little too young. Perhaps it was the lack of any sign of a beard.

"You're with the guild, then?" the barbarian finally asked to break the silence as he lifted the two slices of bread with the last remaining cut of beef and some cheese packed between them and took a bite.

"Aye," the man grunted. "And you're the Barbarian of Theros?"

Skharr nodded and took another bite of his food before he leaned back in his seat to chew pensively.

"You're an odd group," he noted and looked at each of them.

"You're human, I take it. I'd say this one has orc blood in him, and this one…half-dwarf, half-elf, yes? I feel this is the beginning of an odd tale with a hilarious punch-line."

The man laughed. "A barbarian, a man, an orc-spawn, and an elf walk into an inn…it does have an interesting ring to it. It would certainly have the attention of the listeners from the start."

"Half," the woman corrected, raising an eyebrow. "I believe that introductions are in order."

Skharr nodded and it took a moment for him to realize that they expected him to start.

"DeathEater. Skharr is my name."

"My name is Abirat," the human stated, rubbed his bare chin, and looked around the group.

"I am called Salis," the half-elf said.

"Dwarves I know many of," Skharr commented. "But not many elves who would consort with them. Your father was the elf, I would say. High Elf?"

She shook her head. "Drow. High elves do not mingle with dwarves by way of treaty. I am told I have my father's red eye."

It was a little unsettling, he decided when she turned both eyes on him. It felt like he was being watched by two separate entities but it was the kind of feeling he could shake off without too much difficulty.

"You should avoid calling anyone orc-spawn," the third member of the party remonstrated. His voice drawled and slurred gently, although not to the point of making his speech unintelligible. "At least if you don't mean to start a fight. Most orcs find the term offensive when used outside of the tribes."

"My apologies," Abirat said and lowered his head gently. Skharr could detect no hint of mockery in the man's apology.

"My name is Grakoor," he said with a firm nod. "I have been known to throw punches when provoked but not for offenses given me. I would prefer to settle a war of words with words of my own."

It was a little jarring to hear. Despite the difficulty he had with speaking the common tongue, he did so quite well. Even the accent almost made it easier to understand.

"As much as I enjoy the battle of wits, I've always been more partial to those involving swords myself," Abirat countered, and Skharr studied him more closely and registered the pair of short sabers he carried at his waist. "And we have a more pressing battle to deal with now. Dungeons can be considered battles, yes?"

"There is coordination in battles," the warrior answered smoothly. "Tactical assessments and sometimes, you can even count on chivalry between the parties involved in the fighting looking to reduce the number of deaths. Not so with dungeons."

"They are still similar enough," Salis grumbled. "You are staring, barbarian. Have you never seen a half-elf, half-dwarf before?"

"No," he admitted. "I lived with dwarves for many years and had the opportunity to meet a few High Elves in the past, although never drow. They tend to avoid barbarians. Bad blood."

"The High Elves return?" Grakoor asked and leaned forward. "It has been many centuries since they have graced our shores."

"Plagued our shores, more like," Salis muttered.

"I met a few of them," Skharr said, dunked his bread, meat, and cheese coalition into the dregs of the stew, and took another bite. "I saved the life of one of them. She ended up giving me a dagger in thanks."

"A dagger for her life?" Abirat asked. "It seems like she holds it cheaply. But anyway, we were told to find you by the high priest of Theros. The word has been spoken that you will attack a dungeon."

Skharr nodded. "I had a mind to attack the place, yes. Myself and another warrior."

"Of sound mind and body?" Salis asked as she took a bite from what looked like a pear.

"Of sound body," Skharr ceded. "Not many who are willing to attack a dungeon are of sound mind."

"From what we have been told, you are quite adept at dealing with dungeons," Grakoor told him. "I've heard you survived quite a few in your time."

Skharr narrowed his eyes at the man before he shrugged. "Aye, survived. Of late, I was the only survivor in my party, mostly because I was the only member of the party. Another found me and two others survived out of hundreds. The third... Well, I was not the one who faced the dangers in that one."

"You killed a dragon," Salis commented.

"I...fought a dragon," he corrected her.

"Whatever the case, that still means you've survived at least three more dungeons than all of us," Abirat interjected quickly. "But we can help as well. We know the way, although it is bound to be perilous at this time of year. Between us and the dungeon you have a mind to attack, there is a dark forest, a mysterious lake, an abandoned city, and a demon's asshole."

Skharr tilted his head and stared at the man as he processed what had been said. He had questions about what exactly made the forest dark, the lake mysterious, and the city abandoned, but one question pressed to the fore ahead of all others.

"There are few things in the world that I am not willing to do," Skharr growled. "Climbing into a demon's slime-greased asshole is one of them."

"It's only a name," Grakoor commented, took a map from his pack, and spread it over the open space in the center of the table. "I am told that it makes sense—in a metaphorical manner—once you go through it but aside from that, it's nothing more than a name."

"All right." Skharr paused to take another sip of the apple tisane as his headache began to pound again. "Why would we need to go through such dangers? We'll face enough of them once we enter the dungeon, no?"

"The abandoned city burrows beneath the mountain range here." The orc pointed it out on the map and sure enough, the city did tunnel directly under the mountains. "All other passes in this region have already closed with the advent of the winter snows. We could travel further south to find a pass that is still open or perhaps one that is open the year around, but it would take us at least a month or maybe two to find it and the same time again to travel north again. That is all time that might end with dangers as forbidding as those we might face with the other option."

Skharr nodded. He had been hoping to spend the winter hidden away preferably nowhere close to the kinds of elements that could freeze chunks off of him with no effort.

He could have done so at the new emperor's palace, of course, but it was only a matter of time until the folks there decided that he needed to continue serving the emperor. It seemed wiser to avoid a situation that might lead to the kind of commitment he never wanted to engage in with a member of royalty.

As was the case with most nobles, being involved with royalty tended to make him far more enemies and involve him in the type of fights that he wouldn't be able to beat his way out of.

Instead, he thought gloomily—and the irony wasn't entirely lost on him—in the end, he chose a dungeon he would likely not be able to beat his way out of.

With that in mind, he could always simply say no.

He ignored the small voice within, leaned closer, and moved his empty platter to the side so he could see the map a little better. "How recent is this map?"

"Not very," Abirat answered and shook his head. "Not many have traveled that way recently and of those, none were cartographers."

"So, there is no way for us to know what will wait for us in these places? Or why this city is abandoned?"

The three exchanged nervous glances between them.

"If it makes you feel better, we can likely assume that whatever made the inhabitants abandon their city is probably gone by now," Abirat said.

"Most likely," Salis agreed.

"Possibly," Grakoor added.

It was interesting that the orc descendant was the most reasonable of the three, but it didn't seem like they had much in the way of options.

"I'll consult with my partner," Skharr stated finally as he stood. "If she agrees to this, we will meet at the gate before noon. That should give us time to gather the provisions we need, yes?"

The group agreed, and he turned away and headed toward the door. There was barely enough time for him to gather what he needed if Cassandra was willing to go along with the insanity that was this dungeon attack.

He doubted that she would make any dissent. The fact that the three had come on word of the high priest meant that they were at least capable fighters, and he had seen that they were already well-armed.

He still thought it a fools' quest but as long as they had enough fools, there was more of a chance that some of them would come away from it alive.

"I didn't think you barbarians believed in magic."

Skharr looked up from his inspection of the variety of trinkets on display. The owner hadn't been present when he arrived, which left him with nothing to do other than inspect the items that were visible for sale.

It was clear that everything being displayed were the dregs, those runes and inscriptions that were made easily and sold for a pittance. It was most likely the kind of item the owner made the most coin on by selling to those mercenaries who had no idea what they were purchasing, although they were useful as charms and the like. They would have to be, especially if the mercs who bought what he was selling were to be encouraged to continue their purchases.

He replaced the charm that he had been inspecting a little impatiently. "We believe in magic. We merely don't like it in our part of the world. Given the kind of dangers mages can thrust the world into, can you honestly blame us?"

The mage tilted his head in thought and shrugged. "No, I suppose I cannot. I am Adept Fiarae. I have worked with and been blessed by the high priests to the gods of this city to provide enchantments, charms, and other magical paraphernalia to the various fighters and mercenaries associated with the guild. I am always happy for the work and the coin although, once again, I am surprised that one of your kind would search for magical accoutrements."

The mage clearly attempted to make some kind of a statement that would reassure him as to why he was trustworthy, but Skharr couldn't be bothered to engage with him in it. They simply didn't have the time.

"I find myself in need of what is called a 'memory stone,'" he explained as he moved toward the counter opposite the mage. "I was told you were the one to speak to about it."

"A...memory stone, yes." Fiarae nodded quickly. "And I am the only one in this region capable of performing the enchantments."

"Which I am sure is merely due to the difficulty involved?" Skharr asked.

The mage smirked and shrugged. "I would be lying if I said that the reason that I keep the ingredients and the like a secret isn't to maintain my clientele in this city. I am not proud, but certain dishonorable tactics are required to survive in our current economy."

"I cannot judge. All I ask is that this stone only pull memories of what I have killed or those that I think should die."

"Oh...that should be...interesting." The mage retrieved an old, dusty tome and began to sift through the contents. "And difficult, it should be noted. Always more difficult to... sift through the memories than to let them all through unabated."

"I'd argue that it'll be more difficult for me to deal with a husband should his wife choose to seduce me and succeed," Skharr explained.

The mage narrowed his eyes at him. "I take it this is a regular occurrence?"

"Regular enough to be of concern to me." He nodded firmly. "I am willing to pay the extra cost for this, of course. My ego is not worth any extra cost to my teammates."

"I see. Will there be anything else?"

"The regular assorted items needed to counteract the magic usually found in a dungeon. Something that works against poisons and other magical influences as well as something that would help to sustain my well-being in the event that I should be injured. I am also not above hearing what you might have to recommend for such a venture."

Skharr could see the avarice on clear display in the man's eyes, tempered only by what he assumed was his instinctual caution against trying to overcharge a man who not only knew what he was looking for but was also capable of tearing him in half.

"I do have what you might require," Fiarae answered. "And if you are interested in a particular recommendation, I have a potion that helps with keeping you awake. It has effects similar to the brown, burnt-bean concoction that they are beginning to import from the desert kingdoms."

"The bitter stuff?"

"Indeed, and while I cannot promise that it would taste better, I can say that it does not produce the same degree of addiction the bitter stuff causes."

The barbarian considered it and tapped the table. "I'll take it all. How much for everything?"

Another long moment of consideration made Skharr wonder if the man was thinking about cheating him. Instead, however, he quickly wrote the price on a piece of parchment and added the individual prices for all the different items the barbarian intended to purchase.

"I generally provide a discount to all our different guilds, mostly because you provide me with my most reliable source of coin." The mage paused and tilted his head with a small smile. "I provide it to most, not all. The absolute bastards get the full pricing for all my products."

Skharr nodded. "That...does make sense, I suppose. Which category do I fall under?"

"You have been reasonably polite. There are those who feel that simply because they can swing a sword with a hint of skill, it means they can treat the rest of the world like chattel."

"And you teach them their place in the world, yes?"

The mage shrugged. "Well, it is the petty revenge schemes that give one the most satisfaction."

A soft ping from the door immediately drew the attention of both men, who turned as a woman stepped inside. She wore a long, flowing gown in a deep-red velvet with patterns in gold and silver to denote flowers or stars. Skharr couldn't tell which, although they were pleasant to look at.

Still, he decided, it did seem like the type of thing Cassandra would wear, especially with the long flowing sleeves that boasted the same inscriptions, all marking the form of the woman beneath her dress in the patterns.

Her thick brown hair was tied back in a loose braid, and she grinned openly when she realized that Skharr was staring at her.

"Fancy finding you here," she said and played idly with her braid. The movement made something clink underneath her clothes and the barbarian's eyes narrowed.

"Yes, fancy that," he replied, took a step back and motioned her to have a word with the mage. He had already decided before he'd even arrived at the little store that he was willing to wait for her if she was able to meet him there.

She leaned across the counter to speak privately to the mage, and Skharr couldn't hear what she was saying. Fiarae nodded and whispered something in response before he motioned for her to follow him into the back of the shop, leaving the barbarian alone in the front.

Although immensely curious as to what she could be up to, he merely shook his head and counted out the required coins to pay for the items he'd ordered. It was best to get it out of the way while the two were off doing whatever a paladin needed to do before she embarked on a quest.

After a few minutes, they exited the back of the shop and Cassandra now wore garb that appeared more appropriate for a fighter. The leathers were bound to fit her form well without sacrificing mobility or defense, and he studied her movements in it as she tested the way that the armor felt.

He wasn't sure if there was anything to say about how she looked, aside from the fact that the armor did look somewhat like what he used to wear himself.

"You came to be fitted for the armor?" Skharr asked as she experimented carefully with arm movements and tried to avoid knocking anything over.

"Gods no." She laughed. "I needed a magical charm for the armor I'm wearing. It adds a little more protection, to parts of me not covered by the armor, see?"

Skharr examined her with a small frown. "Do you mean your head? I thought you knew that was what a helmet was supposed to be used for."

"Not the helm, no." She seemed a little impatient and pulled at the straps of her leathers to show him what she wore under them.

It looked like what he would expect from a woman's undergarments, especially in the warmer regions of the earth, and covered her breasts and between her thighs well enough. Surprisingly, it was all made from light mail.

"I…huh." Skharr grunted, at a loss for words.

"They'll be adequate for defending those bits," she explained. "But less so for the rest of me, so magic should do the trick. I'll need to get used to it, though. It feels like it might end up chafing after a while."

"I have no doubt. Why…why are you wearing that? And why do you intend to wear it for a while?"

"I decided I would dress the part of a barbarian if I was traveling to a quest with one." She grinned and patted him on the shoulder.

"Barbarians do not dress like that. Not even the women."

"Well, they should. They do in the stories, and that is what matters."

Skharr collected what he was owed and pointed the mage to the coins he'd left on the counter before he strode out of the store to catch up to Cassandra.

"And where are you off to, then?" he asked.

"You said we should meet with our new partners in arms at the gate before midday," she answered calmly. "It's a few hours away, but I thought you would not want anyone to be late. I've never had to wear a charm with my plate armor before. It is another thing that I will have to get used to."

"The charm will chafe less," Skharr noted. "Why aren't you wearing your plate armor? You are supposed to be off your sabbatical, yes?"

"Of course, but it would give me away as a paladin in a heartbeat." She looked at him, then at his hair before she adjusted the strap that held her hair in place. "This way, none will think of me as a paladin, and especially not like this."

She undid a few of the higher straps on her leathers and

opened a wide V over her chest that led interested gazes directly to the bared skin between.

"No. I suppose none would suspect you of being a paladin."

"See? And they will even less so if they see what's beneath."

"Do you expect there to be many that do?"

She shrugged. "Not many. But I wouldn't discount the possibility of a few."

Her wink made him pause before he looked around to where he'd secured Horse. The beast did not look perturbed by the sights, sounds, and smells of the market and barely reacted as he approached and undid his restraints. These had, of course, been for the benefit of the folk around rather than for the stallion. That done, he checked to make sure that none of the supplies were missing.

Horse was smart enough to ward off all but the most insistent of thieves and Skharr was not surprised to find everything where he had left it.

He clicked his tongue and the beast followed him, drawing a few looks and whispers from the people around them. Skharr paid them no attention and his long legs carried him purposefully across the square toward the western gate. The three mercenaries were already assembled and waiting for them from what he could tell.

The barbarian looked at the sky to judge the time from the sun's position. They still had more than an hour until midday, which told him the group were enthusiastic. That much was comforting, at least, although he wasn't sure why they were so anxious to get on the road.

Cassandra reached them first and paused to strap a few new items to her horse's saddle while the others discussed something as a group. It seemed likely that the woman that had just joined them might be the subject of their whispers.

They stopped when Skharr approached, and Abirat cleared his throat as a less-than-subtle warning.

"Skharr, it is a pleasure to see you again," the man said and took a step forward. His hands rested on a pair of sabers that he had strapped to the belt around his waist. "I take it this is the partner you made mention of at the inn?"

That explained the whispering. They had doubts about the newcomer, who was still focused on arranging her additional equipment on the packhorse.

"This is Cassandra, she is my partner in this venture," the barbarian said in response to the question that none of the three had asked him.

"It's a pleasure to meet you all," Cassandra said without looking up from her work.

"Likewise," Grakoor mumbled.

"Cassandra, this is…oy, look this way," Skharr called and gestured sharply for her to look up from fastening the saddle. "The flame-crotch is called Abirat. The half-elf, half-dwarf is named Salis."

"I wondered about her," the paladin admitted. "And the half-orc?"

"Quarter-orc," Grakoor corrected her. "My maternal grand-mother was an orc from the western desert tribes. Her marriage to my grandfather was…unique, but none would question the word of a chieftain."

"Is that similar to royalty?" she asked.

"Closer to gentry," he explained. "The tribes are highly indi-vidualistic with no centralized government. If any larger problem faces the tribes, they come together to find a joint solution. There is no king or emperor."

She nodded. "I see. Well, it's always good to have solid fighters in our ranks."

"Show her the map of where we'll be traveling," Skharr instructed, and the quarter-orc nodded and retrieved the maps that he carried to show her their planned destination.

They certainly looked experienced. Even the barbarian had to admit that much. They were all well-armed—Abirat carried his swords, Salis held a spear in her hand and a handful of javelins were secured in bags on her saddle, as well as a shield. A seax hung from her belt, although he had a feeling that she liked to keep her enemies at a distance.

The quarter-orc had a bow as well, although a smaller, more compact weapon than the barbarian used. A heavy war hammer hung from his belt, although Skharr couldn't see any sign that he carried a shield. Instead, what looked like a massive pauldron attached to his left shoulder and a gauntlet of similar steel-plate for his left arm could act like a shield in battle, although it appeared a little unorthodox.

Skharr decided that he would not make any assumptions about prowess until he'd seen the group fight. For the moment, all they could do was make sure they were off to a good start.

Cassandra didn't appear to have any objection to the path they would take. She mounted her horse quickly and without a word, guided it and the packhorse toward the gate, followed quickly by the rest of the group.

The barbarian strode behind them with Horse at his heels, and the small group moved steadfastly toward the gate as they started on the path out of the city.

Salis was the first one to notice that Skharr was the only one not mounted for their journey. They kept the horses at a walk, which made it easy for him to keep up with the others.

"Can't you ride?" she asked as she eased her smaller, stockier mount alongside him. "I imagine that riding a horse would be hell on your back, as tall as you are."

Skharr shrugged. "I could ride, I suppose. But I don't ride brothers."

"The horse is your brother?"

He simply nodded.

"Not by blood, I take it."

Skharr and Horse exchanged a glance and the beast tossed his mane gently.

"No," he answered. "Our bond is tighter than that."

"You don't mean to say—"

"I do not."

"Ah. Well, then." Salis patted her mount gently on the neck. "I adore my little Geordie, but she doesn't mind me riding her."

Skharr turned to look at the smaller horse and patted the shaggy, skewbald coat gently.

"Her name is Forra," he told her rider gently and focused on the half-elf. "And she would like to see how you would care to carry her for a few hours."

The half-elf paused, looked at her horse, and settled a somewhat confused gaze on the barbarian. "Truly?"

Horse's whinny sounded very much like laughter, and Skharr grinned.

"No. I jest."

CHAPTER NINE

I t was funny how each one of the four—including Cassandra —asked him why he wasn't riding Horse like they expected him to give a different answer.

Grakoor and Abirat both asked him what the stallion's name was, and both appeared to be confused by his response. The other two didn't bother to ask.

He assumed it was because they had realized by now that this particular barbarian was an odd one, at least when it came to horses, and merely dropped the matter entirely.

Their journey progressed without any major incident, and Skharr enjoyed the company on the trip, even if Horse was usually all the company that he needed.

The fact that they went for a full week without being attacked or even harassed by any of the bandit groups was not much of a surprise. All five were heavily armed and armored, with horses and ready to fight. They also showed no indication that they carried a large amount of treasure that would justify the losses any brigands would sustain if they tried to attack the group.

Skharr noticed that Salis and Cassandra pitched their tents

close together when night fell and it was time for them to set their camp up for the evening.

It had been interesting to see the paladin flow almost effortlessly through the group to initiate conversation. While she certainly contributed most to the various discussions, the group appeared to warm quickly to her.

The same could not be said for Skharr. The trio appeared to almost hold him in an interesting but somewhat distant regard. They always addressed him respectfully but hung back from him a little like they didn't think he would want to mingle with them.

He didn't mind, of course, and assumed their attitude would change the moment they entered into combat together. If they thought he was somehow a mythical creature, that idea would change when they saw him fight.

While he was a talented warrior and difficult to defeat overall, Skharr knew he was far from whatever legends they'd heard about him. He hated the fact that people saw someone big and strong swinging an ax and immediately decided that he was somehow more than he truly was.

There would be a reckoning and everything would settle into its proper place, but it would take him a little while to get there. For the moment, he would sit in his little corner of the camp and make his evening meal.

"What are you doing hidden out here?"

Skharr almost jumped. He hadn't heard Cassandra approach him, but there she was, perched on the rock that he leaned against. It was vaguely irritating that he had a feeling she'd intended to sneak up on him.

He shrugged and tended to the pot that had barely begun to simmer. "Making some dinner for myself. What are you doing in my little corner of the camp?"

"I smelled what you were cooking and I had to come over to try a taste. The last few days have been indulging in my love of the cold foods I usually enjoyed during my time on one campaign or another, but the smell coming from here was a little too enticing to resist. Who knew a barbarian was such a good cook?"

His gaze drifted upward to where the other three now sidled closer and looked similarly enticed.

"It's mostly the spices," he admitted. "And if you all want a taste, you'll have to add some of your rations to boost what's in the pot as well as some water."

He'd hoped that the price to pay would make them back off, but it did no such thing and they were eager to add their food to the pot if it meant having a warm meal.

"Barbarians of the Western Clans are famed for their spices," Grakoor noted as Skharr served him a portion of the stew he'd made from root vegetables, dried meat, and oats.

The warrior nodded as he served the rest of the group. "You sound well-studied. Where did you acquire such knowledge?"

"There are many universities in the human cities south of the deserts," the quarter-orc commented. "I had worked through most of them before Salis found me. Once we joined forces, my love for knowledge was expanded by our travels."

"I half-expected you to be the type who carries hundreds of books around with him, everywhere he goes," Skharr commented.

"Why carry the books in my saddle when I carry them up here?" Grakoor tapped his temple.

"Do you remember them all?" Cassandra asked.

"Every letter and every word. it's a blessing and a curse since that memory extends to more than book learning."

"Do all orcs have such a mind or is that from your human side?" Skharr asked.

"I have realized that it is from my orc heritage," he explained. "It is why the orc tribes have never taken to writing anything down. Their minds are like traps. They capture any knowledge they learn and pass it down for generations at a time. It is not a skill that is well-known about the tribes. I think that was intentional on their part. Acting the dull, witless orcs makes many underestimate them."

Skharr narrowed his eyes. The ploy sounded a little familiar.

"How long have the two of you traveled together?" Cassandra asked.

"About…a hundred years now, isn't it?" Salis asked and looked at Grakoor.

"A hundred and fifteen years," he replied quickly. "And from my calculations, you were traveling on your own for almost two hundred years before you met me."

"So you're about three hundred and fifty years old," the paladin commented and leaned forward. "The famous elven longevity that I've heard so much about."

"Indeed." Salis drained the bowl of stew she had in her hands and proceeded to nibble on some bread. "Although elves were here first, so it would be more accurate to say that most other species are short-lived. I will likely not live to the millennia that my father will, which is why he cast me out. Even drow can be bastards to their children sometimes."

"Did you never try living in the dwarven cities your mother hailed from?" Skharr asked and stirred his meal with a wooden spoon.

"I tried for a few decades. They were a little more welcoming, but I never felt truly at home among them. It was never in my blood to live under the ground, and I found happiness traveling the earth and killing things that needed it over the years to pay my way."

He nodded slowly. "I can see why a kinship was formed between you and Grakoor."

The quarter-orc nodded. "Aye. Our shared love for wandering the earth did make for ideal companionship, and when we found Abirat, it seemed almost like destiny that the three of us fight together so well."

The barbarian turned his gaze on the human with hair that

was a little brighter red than his own. "I did wonder. Few humans are fond of fighting with a weapon in both hands, especially one that requires such dexterity as a saber. It is a skill that the drow tend to favor."

The man laughed. "That is not the only drow skill I've learned since I was a child. They love to remain in the trees at all costs, even the trees their villages are not built into. I've discovered that I have that kind of dexterity."

"An acrobat?" the barbarian asked. "I can see how that would be a sound skill to learn."

"Indeed. Although I fear you'll see those skills in action before too long. We approach the woods that are said to be more than a little dangerous."

Skharr nodded. "I know the like. In fact, I built a small farm at the edge of one of these cursed woods."

Cassandra tilted her head and finished her stew in a single gulp before she turned to him. "You…built a farm at the edge of a cursed forest?"

"Why would you do that?" Salis asked.

"The land was cheap," he answered simply.

"I'll bet it was," Abirat commented dryly.

"DeathEaters." The paladin cackled and shook her head in exasperation before her voice took on a thicker tone to mimic Skharr's. "Oh yes, we'll build a farm at the edge of a cursed wood so I can occasionally go out and kill a few monsters if this whole farming business gets a little boring."

He smirked and the conversation wound down quickly. Traveling was tiring work, and it appeared as though they were about to enter the most difficult part of the journey. They wanted to be well-rested when they entered the cursed forest.

Working quickly and quietly, they collapsed their camp when the sun began to rise again. Skharr strung his bow before he headed into the foliage. They had no way to tell what might find them inside. While he had been cavalier about the concept before, choosing to walk straight into an environment like it without some type of preparation for what lay ahead would be unwise on his part.

This was possibly another point where reality fell well short of the legend. Being prepared for a possible fight was not something he would forego simply because something might be expected from him.

"What kind of monsters were in your forest?" Abirat asked after a short silence.

Skharr turned as the man had brought his horse beside him. "The creatures rarely left the woods, and those that did were usually weak and hungry, driven out by others deeper within."

"Truly? What types?"

"Direwolves were fairly prevalent, although they were thin and not interested in causing trouble once I caught a handful with traps and arrows. The packs remained inside the forest, so I only ever had to contend with a handful that had been driven out."

"What do they look like?"

"Mostly like regular wolves I suppose, although almost the size of a horse, and they have two fangs that extend well beyond their lips." The barbarian motioned with two fingers over his canine teeth and all the way down to his chin. "Useful, I guess, for bringing down the larger elk that live inside those forests. I think a few of the locals call them vampire wolves because of the fangs."

"And were there any actual vampires?"

"Do you mean men turned immortal and forced to feed on human blood for sustenance?"

'Yes.'

Skharr tilted his head in thought and shrugged. "I can't say I've ever met one myself, or not knowingly anyway. I cannot even say for certain that such creatures exist, although if I were to guess, I would say that they are the result of magic. Perhaps a human tried to make him or herself as long-lived as an elf and failed to recognize the consequences of such a decision."

"That…does make sense, I suppose. But why would there be a need for blood? And why would they be allergic to sunlight?"

That was a good question, and he shook his head. "Fucked if I know. I don't even think they exist."

"Would you kill one if they did?"

"If they tried to kill me, I would try to kill them," he replied firmly. "Under no circumstances should you not try to kill anything that tries to kill you."

Abirat laughed. "Well, I suppose that is an admirable ideal to have."

Skharr looked up at the sound of clopping hooves approaching them. Cassandra circled to them, although her usual calm and ready to laugh expression was notably absent.

"You mentioned that creatures and monsters in the cursed woods were generally bigger than those that mirror their likeness outside?" she asked as she pulled the horse around to continue on the path they were following.

"Yes," he answered. "Although there were a few other changes."

She nodded and looked out into the woods around them. "So…would it be safe to assume that the droning we hear in the air is something to be concerned about?"

He looked up, his head tilted in concentration, but he couldn't hear much of anything for a few seconds aside from the regular sounds of the forest. Once he was focused on listening for it, however, he could finally hear what she had drawn their attention to. A low drone sounded like they were approaching a hornet's nest, although considerably larger and louder than anything they might usually expect.

"Safe to assume, yes," Skharr replied as he took his bow from the saddle and a couple of arrows from the quiver. There was no way to know if they were hearing something that would attack them, but they couldn't be too careful about it in a place like this.

Cassandra nodded and circled again into a position where she could see the rest of the group. "Eyes up! We may have a fight on our hands!"

She certainly sounded like a paladin snapping orders to her troops before battle, and her voice was edged by a certain will that made people follow it without question. And in the end, it seemed like she was used to being in command, no matter what she presented herself as. She had already drawn the arming sword she carried at her hip, although a few throwing daggers positioned around her belt would likely be of more use against the flying creatures that now approached them.

The droning sound suggested they were flying creatures, at least. Skharr narrowed his eyes and tried to determine which direction it came from.

The barbarian first caught sight of movement above them and he pressed one of the arrows to his bowstring. He peered above the path they were following to where the wings were beating quickly enough that he could feel the wind they generated on his face. The creature was mostly obfuscated by the shadows cast by the trees around them, however.

Suddenly, seconds before he managed a better view of it, something launched from the surface and caught it in the abdomen, and the creature plummeted onto the road they were on.

He nodded as Salis took another javelin from her saddlebag and looked around for her next target.

"That was a fine throw," he said as he approached the felled creature. "I might have held off on killing it, however."

"Why?" she asked.

"I have learned that one shouldn't attack creatures unprovoked," he replied, dropped to his haunches beside it, and yanked the expertly thrown javelin from the abdomen to hand it to the woman. "If they didn't plan to attack before, they will now."

The woman nodded. "It is always better to strike first, though."

"Yes. Yes, it is."

The creature was a somewhat intriguing oddity and he took a moment to examine it quickly. It resembled the type of dragonfly that buzzed over the water in the marshlands he'd traveled through, but the long, translucent wings were almost six feet long and the creature itself was three feet long, which included a long tail that still twitched at its rear.

Skharr's featured darkened at the sight of a stinger at the end of the tail that made it far more dangerous than merely an extra-large dragonfly might be. More to the point, killing only the one hadn't stopped the sound of droning around them.

In fact, it grew more intense and sounded like a swarm was closing on them. Horse pranced and shook his head, and Skharr took that as the warning that a confrontation was meant to be.

The first creature that caught his eye darted in and out of the tree cover as it advanced, and he could see more than a few close behind it. They appeared to be trying to surround them, although they kept to the trees for the moment.

"Skharr!" Cassandra called.

He didn't reply but instead, drew the arrow back on the bowstring and kept his gaze locked firmly on the creature he could see instead of being distracted by the swarm that moved in behind.

The barbarian took a deep breath and released it slowly as he waited for the winged beast to hover out in the open a little longer than it had already before he loosed the arrow.

He knew it would hit and smiled as it cut toward its target fast enough to whistle. In an instant, the winged creature was pinned to the tree behind it.

"A fine shot," Salis noted as Skharr fell back to where the group was closing its ranks. Grakoor had already pulled on the pauldron and enlarged gauntlet that worked in tandem as a shield for him, as well as his powerful recurve bow. The monsters plunged from the trees as if they had decided to throw caution to the wind and swarm the mercenaries below them.

Skharr didn't need to time his shot. Instead, he selected a target out and nodded with satisfaction when it was punched back into the darkness of the woods and out of sight. Unfortunately, those directly behind it were quick enough to avoid being tagged by the same arrow.

Another dropped with an arrow from Grakoor's quiver, and yet another from one of the half-elf's javelins. One more appeared to fall. It crashed into a nearby tree and slid out of sight and the barbarian saw Cassandra reach for another one of her daggers.

It was good to see that her aim was as precise as his own and perhaps even better. He doubted that he could throw a dagger over that distance with that kind of precision.

Abirat was already off of his horse and when one of the beasts dove to attack them, he jumped clear and his sabers flicked out to reflect the sunlight as they moved in tandem. Skharr wouldn't have noticed that they were moving if it hadn't been for these bright reflections, and the dragonfly tumbled as the blades flashed. One of its wings had been severed and the wound had culminated in a deep slash through the creature's protective carapaces. Another slice, perfectly perpendicular to the first, had cut deeper and removed the tail cleanly.

The beast wasn't dead but flopped across the earth while dark-green blood flowed freely from its wounds.

The redhead swung into motion again as Skharr took another two arrows from his quiver. Another one of the dragonflies attempted to dive-attack Abirat, its tail pushed forward in a clear intent to kill.

He swayed out of the way like he was dancing over the road instead of fighting and again, the sabers swung in almost without being seen. They cut the beast in half effortlessly.

Another volley from the ranged attackers among them cut a group of the airborne assailants down, although Cassandra doubled up on the same target Grakoor had struck. From the looks of it, however, the beasts seemed to share a common consensus that they'd had enough.

Those the team could see began to pull away, still using the trees for cover, most likely to head off and find easier prey.

Skharr didn't want to see what kind of prey they were hunting or what the creatures could do to those creatures that they were able to overcome.

"Collect your projectiles quickly," Cassandra called. "We don't want to be here when they change their minds."

She made a solid point, and the barbarian moved quickly to collect his arrows. He yanked the paladin's dagger from one of the felled creatures and handed it to her.

"Much appreciated," she said with a small grin and cleaned the blade before she tucked it into her belt.

"Will you teach me to make a throw like that?" Skharr asked and inspected his arrows before he slipped them into their quiver.

"Can you not throw a dagger?"

"I can and have on occasion. I couldn't make a throw as accurately at that distance, however."

She tilted her head before she swung into her saddle. "I'll consider it. You never know when I might need you to save my life with a well-placed dagger."

Skharr smirked and clicked his tongue as he and Horse stepped onto the road again.

The group was considerably less relaxed after the attack. That much was obvious. Even while they set up their camp later that day, all five remained tense and alert to their surroundings.

It didn't help that they could hear screeches and growls from the forest around them, which appeared to have truly come alive once the sun went down. Even when he wasn't on guard for the evening, the barbarian realized that sleep wouldn't come. The best he could muster was a doze when things quieted considerably as dawn turned the sky gray.

From the looks of the other members of the party, he could tell they were in a similar condition. Abirat appeared to be cooking something over the campfire while his comrades prepared a morning meal.

Skharr recognized the dark powder that the man added to the water as well as the thick, bitter, and not unpleasant aroma that seeped through their little camp.

"What is that?" Cassandra asked and her nose wrinkled as she gathered her hair into the leather band.

"They call it koffie," Salis explained, although she also had her nose turned up in disgust. "It's an addictive liquid made from the burnt beans of a plant mostly grown in the south, where the forests turn into jungles. Horrible, horrible stuff."

"It is pronounced coffee," Abirat explained and it appeared that this was not the first time he was explaining it to her. "And while I admit it is a taste that must be acquired, it is far less addictive than other potions and chemical additives, all while giving a nice morning jolt of energy. Which we all need, I think, after the night we had. It's like being an acolyte to the Lord High God Janus without the horrifying side effect of being an utter bastard."

Skharr could not disagree with any of that, and he took a cup of the questionable brew. Cassandra did the same and shared what Abirat had to offer. The other two declined and the team dismantled the camp in preparation to head out on the path they were following.

Although he'd been a little skeptical, he couldn't deny a jolt of energy or that his heart beat a little faster. His fingers felt a little jittery in response to the bitter black liquid, and they moved with more purpose than they had before. The horses felt it as well and looked nervously around like they expected some kind of an attack due to the unsettled nature of their riders. The barbarian took a moment to calm Horse and make sure the beast knew they weren't in any trouble.

Or at least not anything of concern that demanded an immediate response. He strung his bow again, unhooked it from the saddle, and retrieved a couple of arrows. Sounds had built gradually around them now, but he couldn't shake the feeling that something was watching them, stalking and waiting to strike.

He drew a deep breath and winced as the bitter scent of the coffee dissipated and was replaced by something heavier and fouler. It smelled like rotting flesh gone rancid. He froze and took another deep breath. Despite the foulness of the stench, it had a source and he needed to try to determine what and where.

"What the fuck is that godsbedammed smell?" Salis shouted as she brought her mount to a halt.

The warrior raised his hand to his lips in a gesture for silence and studied their surroundings intently.

And suddenly, he discerned it within the deeper vegetation. The sound was a little more distinct now and sounded like a gutter that slowly emptied itself but too loudly and deeper.

The eyes betrayed the creature's location when they caught and reflected the light. Once he could see the basic shape, the shadows around it began to make more sense. The monster shifted as if it considered each member of the group and how best to attack.

Skharr focused on the massive form as he slipped the arrow into the bowstring, raised it quickly, and loosed before the creature realized it was under attack.

The arrow streaked directly into one of the massive eyes that were the most visible feature and the whole body of the beast slumped forward. It hadn't even realized it was being attacked before it was dead.

It fell heavily but a thunderous clamor rose from deeper within the forest, and the barbarian immediately nocked another arrow into the bowstring when he caught sight of another of the creatures moving in the dense foliage. It was about the size of a horse, although longer, and a thick, sinuous tail whipped furiously and sliced into the trees around it.

The arrow flew and he saw that it went true, but there was no sign that it slowed the monster. Thankfully, however, it appeared determined to run away from them and return to the safety of the deeper forest. He released a slow breath and looked around warily but could see nothing else moving in their vicinity. The death of the first creature was enough to scare the other one away, at least for the moment.

"What the hell was that?" Cassandra asked.

All Skharr could think about was how the monster had run off with his arrow stuck in its hide. There would be no opportunity to recover it.

"Let's see, shall we?" He growled and turned his attention to the beast that had been killed. The stench of it still hung heavily over the area and he needed to cover his nose to approach it.

"Is that a dragon?" Salis asked, her tone edged with disbelief.

"No," Cassandra answered quickly. "It has no wings. Maybe a wyrm."

"Wyrms have no legs and they burrow through the ground, spewing acid to melt the stone ahead as they move," Grakoor corrected her. "That appeared to be some kind of fireless drake, although larger than any I have ever seen. Most are the size of sheep or goats."

The barbarian dropped to his haunches next to it. The quarter-orc appeared to be right. The beast was long with a thick tail and bony spikes that protruded from the tip. A strike from the large appendage would kill almost about any creature it caught.

The body about the size of a horse with thick, stubby legs that could still move rapidly when it needed to, as evidenced by how quickly the other had run away. Its elongated jaws were weaponized with thin, dagger-like fangs in both the top and the bottom.

The skin was what Skharr found most interesting. The scales were tough and leathery—the kind that wouldn't let an arrow through, although a good shot could bury the arrowhead into the scales without letting it slip into the flesh beneath.

He was tempted to take a strip of the leather to see if he could tan it, but then he realized that the scales were the source of the foul smell, together with the thick, gooey drool that seeped from the reptile's mouth.

"Why does it smell so terrible?" Abirat asked and covered his nose and mouth with his hands.

"If I had to guess, I would say it brings its kills to its nest, likely in a nearby swamp, and leaves it there." There wasn't much that Grakoor didn't know, it seemed, and the quarter-orc seemed unfazed by the smell. "It roots in the kills and eats them as they decay, resulting in a smell powerful enough to keep most harmful parasites away. I would say those it attracts are likely eaten by the creature as well."

Abirat made a retching sound as he pulled his horse around to put a little distance between himself and the huge corpse.

"That means one good thing for us, I suppose," Skharr noted.

Grakoor nodded. "We are approaching a body of water. The lake, most likely."

"I could go for a swim," Cassandra commented.

CHAPTER TEN

The smell of a large body of water nearby was unmistakable and thankfully, far from whatever marshes the lizards had attacked them from. It was fresh and clean, the kind that came from the wind blustering across the surface to spread a fine spray across the whole area.

Certainly, if nothing else, it was the kind of thing to raise their spirits as they began to draw away from the wood's confines.

The land eased into a gradual decline and the trees there weren't as tall as their forest counterparts, although still fairly prolific, and allowed them a good view of the lake that extended ahead of them.

"Now that's a gorgeous sight," Cassandra said as they descended steadily toward the water. "I've ached for a massive body of water to dive into. And that smell—fresh water from the top to the bottom. We might even be able to drink that."

"Aye," Grakoor commented, his words a little more slurred than usual. "Although I would think twice about diving into those waters. From the looks of the map, we'll have to find our way through one of the two prongs and there is a warning that something will be waiting for us in the lake that could attack us at any time."

"So...no swimming then?" the paladin asked as they finally reached the place where the trees and plants gave way to the rough stone beach that surrounded the lake.

"It would likely be wise to not agitate the water, so no swimming."

"Damn." She scowled, slid from her saddle, and cast a longing gaze over the water. "If I cannot swim, I will be very displeased. And none of you would like me when I am displeased."

Grakoor laughed and scratched his chin pensively. "In fairness, most of the tales surrounding this lake say that the attacks happen when the traveler comes to the other half of it, on the other side. If you would care to risk it, this would most likely be the safest place to do so."

"That's better." Cassandra grinned. "I'll take a knife when I go in, just in case. Come on, Salis, I'll need you close by if there are any fish to be caught or if something attacks. And you three had better be close by as well. Should you hear screams, you'll come to save us. Should you come in hearing no screams, you'll be the ones to scream."

The warning was fair, and Skharr headed to a small section made flat by a heavy slab of naturally smoothed granite where it appeared they would be able to set up a small camp as they prepared to cross the lake.

"Do any of you feel the need to peek out and see what the ladies are doing?" Abirat asked as he removed the bags from his horse's saddle.

"I prefer to keep my cock and balls where they currently are," Skharr replied. "And not used as bait to catch the monsters in the lake."

The other two chuckled nervously, and he assumed that they felt the same way.

The water was cold. A little too cold for her taste, to be honest, which meant the lake was probably fed by glaciers at the top of the mountains or maybe from the snowfall.

Still, it was better than no water at all, and Cassandra had lived through similar situations more times than she was willing to admit.

She kept the undergarments made in mail on but pulled the rest of her clothes off before she stepped gingerly into the water.

"Fair warning," she called to Salis when she heard the woman approach the lake edge. "It is quite cold."

"Refreshing, you mean." The half-elf had all her clothes off and showed no sign of modesty as she stepped into the water. She also showed no sign that the cold was affecting her, and after a few steps into the lake, she dove forward with a fairly impressive splash and knifed smoothly and expertly through the gentle waves she had created.

"What type of clothes are those?" she asked when she came up for air and pulled her thick hair out of her face. "I never thought anyone would want to wear mail under their clothes like that."

"It does take some time to adjust to it," Cassandra admitted. "I have grown more used to other kinds of armor and I thought that I'd try something new."

"I see. Would that armor be similar to something that Skharr wears?"

The paladin moved deeper until the water reached her stomach and made her breathe in sharply. "I suppose that was a subtle attempt to question whether Skharr and I are romantically linked? Are you interested in the barbarian?"

Salis shrugged. "I make no insinuations, but are the two of you involved? He did refer to you as his partner."

"Partner in business only, so if you are interested in seeing if he is proportionate to his size, you are welcome to try."

The half-elf smirked and rolled onto her back, floated lazily on the surface, and spat a small fountain of water from her mouth. "I doubt I would have to try too hard. As for proportion, in my experience, very few men are—although the barbarians I've met were the exception. Grakoor said it had something to do with their women taking more than one lover, although I fail to see how that balances the equation."

Cassandra tilted her head as she considered the possibility that maybe the barbarian women were more likely to fuck men with larger cocks and thus produced male children with a similar tendency. Perhaps that had something to do with it, but she wouldn't spend too much time thinking about that. It seemed the half-elf was of the same mind.

"So, you have not been tempted to discover the power of his dragon, as it were?" Salis asked aloud.

"No, but you certainly seem interested. Would you ask him yourself?"

"Well, if he is a little too large, I wouldn't want to find out in person. I am smaller than you are and as such, if he is...shall we say, proportionate, I think I might scream."

"Only scream?" The paladin raised an eyebrow. "A woman should face her fears and overcome them."

"When facing one's fears and overcoming them results in walking bowlegged for a week afterward, it should be undertaken with caution," Salis replied. "Especially keeping in mind what one must do for the week. Running into battle while sore between the legs is not a pleasant experience."

"You say this from experience?"

"Yes."

Cassandra leaned back and sucked air into her lungs so she could float like the smaller half-elf. "I'd try to not walk bowlegged while around him. I wouldn't want his head to grow any larger than it already is."

"Wouldn't commenting on the size of his dragon already indicate a head that is large enough?"

"I mean his ego," she retorted. "And you never know. The dragon might merely have a long body."

"Hmm, maybe." Salis floated closer to her. "How did you meet the barbarian anyhow?"

"We traveled together from the capital. I was bringing my wares here and he did not mind traveling with company. He didn't talk much the whole way and I talked a great deal. We seemed to offset one another very comfortably. When we were attacked by bandits, he was surprised when I stabbed one of them through the throat."

"Why would he be surprised that a warrior joined in the fight?"

"I wasn't dressed like a warrior. Instead, I wore a long, flowing dress covered in flower and leaf patterns in red and green. I made it myself."

"Ah. And your wares were…"

"The material with which I made it myself."

"You like making clothes? It's not the kind of skill that comes naturally to a warrior."

Cassandra breathed out and sank slightly into the cold water before she sucked air in to keep herself afloat. "I learned to darn my clothes while out in the field and I found I had a talent for it. I took to fixing and correcting the clothes of others for added income, and it was a relaxing way to keep my hands busy during the quiet times between battles."

Salis turned onto her stomach. Dwarves were famous for their avoidance of being in the water, which suggested that this was something she had inherited from her elf side—or perhaps something she had picked up for herself.

"I suppose that makes sense. And you decided to take that passion up to support yourself in the fight?"

The paladin nodded.

"Then why did you choose to join us on this venture? Was it because you had a mind to follow the dragon and the man it was attached to?"

Cassandra turned her head to look at Salis, who was watching her carefully. As old as the half-elf was, she didn't want to try to lie to her. It seemed like it would end poorly.

"I was curious about Skharr, yes," she admitted. "But there was also something of an honor element involved. Unfortunately, that is all I can say about the matter for the moment."

Salis looked curious but didn't seem eager to pry, and she floated lazily in silence for a short while. Cassandra found the silence almost comforting given that it was matched by the sound of the water lapping all around them.

"I could make a few dresses for you if you like," she said finally.

"I've found that dresses don't particularly suit me. My shoulders have always been a little too broad and make me look a little mannish when I wear them."

"It's only that you've never found the right person to make the dresses—the kind that don't tighten around the waist but flare out. It is also important to emphasize what is nestled between those shoulders, which you have an…well, an abundance of."

The half-elf chuckled. "Well, I did notice you staring but did not want to comment."

"It is true, and a way to distract from shoulders is to draw the eyes toward the center, which you are perfectly built for. Of course, like with all clothes, they take some time to grow accustomed to, so I would not want to force dresses on you. Still, if you are interested…"

She let her voice trail off and her companion laughed. It was an oddly melodic sound that she hadn't heard from her before.

"I might have to try it. Well, once we are finished with our impossible task, that is."

Skharr narrowed his eyes. "You're lying."

Abirat shook his head. "I shit you not. I was bare-assed naked, and her husband was coming in through the door. She was a handmaiden to one of the ladies in waiting so was living in the tower with the lady she was waiting on."

"So you climbed down the tower with your ass hanging out in the breeze?" the barbarian asked.

"I always wondered why we found you all but roasting yourself over our campfire," Grakoor muttered. "I rather regret learning the real reason."

"It was in the middle of winter, yes?" Skharr asked.

"Yes. My ass was numb for weeks afterward. I talked to a mage about it, and he said that if it did not heal on its own, he would have to lop chunks of it off to keep the gangrene from killing me."

Skharr tilted his head to inspect the affected region. "That explains it, then."

"It healed on its own!"

"Well, you say, that, but—"

Grakoor laughed and shook his head.

"I do have you beat on that front," Skharr commented. "When I was in my teens, my trainer told me that my rite of passage would be for me to strip to my bare skin in the middle of winter, in the mountains, with a bright blue eagle painted on my back. I had to climb the rocks to where a caravan was camped for the night, steal the wheels from their wagons, and throw them down into the ravine."

"Did you do it?"

"I managed to climb half the way up the ravine before I encountered a small patch of ice and was stuck. No matter what I tried, I could not climb up and could not climb down, and I was stuck there for the whole night until they found me again, shivering and chattering on the side of the mountain. My group thought I was dead and attacked the camp in the night."

"How did you survive?" Grakoor asked.

"I was deathly ill for most of the winter. Thankfully, it was determined that it was the fault of my instructor and I was not struck with the eternal shame of it, while she was sent on her pilgrimage at an early age."

Abirat shook his head. "I will admit, that is the dumbest thing I have ever heard, mostly because you chose to do it with forethought. My action was less the result of careful consideration and more not wanting to have to fight a city guard with my cock hanging out."

Skharr nodded. "It was a careful, calculated risk. Unfortunately, I am terrible when it comes to such calculations."

"I could tutor you in some mathematical equations if you like," the quarter-orc offered. "As a beginner lesson, I can tell you that climbing up the side of a freezing mountain without your clothes was plain fucking godsbedammed idiotic."

"Interesting," the barbarian mumbled and rubbed his chin thoughtfully. "I'll need to take that into consideration."

"It would be best."

The sound of footsteps returning from the lake caught the attention of all three, although Abirat was clearly disappointed that both women were fully clothed when they returned to their camp. The campfire had already been lit, although the preparation of the evening meal had not yet begun.

Skharr was somehow relegated to the role of cook for the whole of the party, which he truly didn't mind. It was a far more favorable role than the others that went into preparing the campsite for their evening stay. Besides, it was less of a thankless job as the other four were always enthusiastic and grateful for a tasty if simple meal of stew and the waybread they'd brought for the journey.

He would need to find a way to continue as the cook once his spices ran out. It would take a few weeks, at least, which gave him more than enough time to find out what he could do to make the meals equally as tasty without the additives.

It was the second evening that passed without incident, and Skharr couldn't help but feel that something was on the way to interrupt that.

Still, it was easier to sleep near the lake rather than in the forests, and he was considerably better-rested when he felt the warmth of the sun make it a little too warm to sleep comfortably.

The bitter smell of Abirat's coffee was there to welcome him again and this time, he was less interested in the bitter liquid now that he'd had a full night of sleep.

"It's an addictive, foul drink," Salis snapped and rubbed her eyes as she sat cross-legged on her blanket and chewed on something dried for her morning meal.

"It'll keep you awake and alert for the full day," Abirat argued. "Honestly, do we need to have this discussion every time?"

"Until you break your addiction to it, yes."

Skharr smirked and shook his head as the man looked at him.

"Would you care for a sip, Skharr? To prove my half-elf friend wrong?"

The barbarian shook his head. "I did not care for the taste."

"And yet you guzzled a full cup of it?"

"I was tired. Something to drink that would help with that was welcome. It is not necessary now and as such, I would say that Salis is correct. You are addicted."

"I…what?"

Cassandra moved to where he was preparing the brew in a small steel pot and poured some of it into a cup.

"I like the bitter taste of it," she stated and took a few sips. "It brings the whole body to life. It's probably the kind of taste that would require some time, but once you get used to it, I could see myself having a hot cup of this every day. Especially on the colder days where waking up is a chore."

Skharr couldn't remember when waking up wasn't a chore for him, but he had nothing to add, especially as she poured herself more from the pot and she drank it quickly.

"That...that was my cup!" Abirat shouted. "You know I'll have to make more, yes?"

Cassandra shrugged. "You do want me to enjoy this drink of yours, yes? So I can join in the defense of it?"

"Well...yes."

"That means that I'll need to acquire a taste for it by drinking as much as possible."

The man scowled as he began to make another cup for himself. "Well played."

"Thank you." She offered him a mock curtsey before she returned to where she needed to gather her portion of the camp, still sipping the bitter, black drink slowly.

"We'll need to decide on our path," Grakoor mentioned once they were all packed and ready to leave. "We won't need to move across the lake as such."

"We couldn't anyway," Salis pointed out. "As we have no means of moving over the water except for swimming."

"Indeed. There are two paths that lead around the lake, although we'll need to remain close to it as the mountains drop off rather quickly as we progress if I read this map correctly."

"If?" Skharr asked.

"It's an old map in an ancient dialect. I am doing my best to translate it, but there are...holes. It does say that one of the paths is fraught with dangers and the other is peaceful, but there is no mention of which is which."

"If there is only one monster in the lake, I suppose that would make sense," Skharr pointed out. "It would only be able to sit on one side or other to catch its food outside of the lake, and it could mean that either side could be the one fraught with danger."

"I suppose we'll have to test our luck, then," Salis interjected. "I say we move to the right. It's always a good choice to try the right side first, eh?"

The group exchanged a look but none of them could come up with any idea as to why they shouldn't follow her suggestion. After a moment of silence, they moved as if by general consensus to the right.

The barbarian grew more and more uncomfortable as the day went on. As Grakoor had told them, the landscape began to sheer off to their left to give them a massive view of what amounted to a clifftop dropping into another cliff. A handful of small breaches in the rock allowed the water to fall from the clifftop into the forests below to form slow-moving rivers that were mostly obscured by the underbrush, but the waterfalls were truly a sight to behold.

"You don't think this was formed by nature, right?" Skharr asked as the quarter-orc moved close to him. Together, they peeked over the edge of the cliff that inched closer and closer to the lake with every step they took.

"What else would it be formed by?" his companion asked and shaded his eyes, although more from habit than necessity. "I suppose one raised in the mountains would find himself quickly accustomed to heights, but I am not fond of them."

They moved hastily away from the edge.

"In one of the dungeons I attacked, there were walls that appeared to be carved out of the mountains it was built up against, but I could not see any sign that any instrument had been used on it. It was as if the mountain had been formed with a wall jutting out from it."

"Magic?"

"Of course. I cannot help but wonder if a similar kind of magic was used to create this place."

Grakoor scrutinized the area more closely and narrowed his eyes as they continued to walk. "That would require some powerful magic—some I doubt could be replicated without serious consequences. And it would be old. You can see where the water has eaten into the rock."

Skharr nodded. "The sort of magic that might have been used to put an elder god to sleep, do you think?"

It was a hefty consideration and one he wasn't sure he could believe, but it certainly seemed possible. He peered over the edge again to reinforce the idea that there was something unnatural about what he saw before returning to the rest of the group, where Horse was waiting for him.

"You're not fond of the heights either, are you?" he asked and patted the stallion on the side of the neck. His four-legged friend had no answer for him, although he refused to so much as budge within ten yards of the edge of the cliff.

The beast's response came as no surprise. The fact that the barbarian had spent his younger years turning his fingers bloody by climbing the sharpest of inclines in the mountains of his home didn't mean he could apply the same recklessness to others.

"Do you think there are fish in the water?" Abirat shouted as he stepped closer to the edge. The water was mostly clear and there was no sign of movement under the surface. "Grakoor has a trick where he ties a piece of rope to an arrow and uses it to shoot a fish and drag it out of the water. I've never complained about tasting fresh fish cooked over a campfire."

"Hunting for fish with a bow," Skharr muttered and shook his head. "I can't say I've ever acquired the skill. I did learn one where I slip into a pond or a river and catch a fish with my bare hands but never with a bow."

"Those arrows you have are likely too large anyway," Grakoor noted as he picked a pebble up from the edge of the water. "If you were hitting anything other than a salmon or trout, you would skewer the fish beyond any man's skill to cook and eat it. You need smaller fish, the likes that are commonly found in lakes like this. A good way to scare them into activity when the water is cooler is to toss a rock in and see what moves."

He hurled the pebble a long way—at least fifteen paces—before it arced into the water with a splash that thrust a large ripple outwards.

A second later, another ripple rose from deeper within the lake and culminated in a wave that splashed against the beach. It wasn't a large wave and not enough to do much more than send the water in higher than a few feet up the beach line.

Still, it was enough to catch the attention of the entire group. Everyone froze and stared at the slowly radiating wavelets, and they tried to make out what exactly had caused the reaction.

"I have to insist that you not do that again," Salis whispered and reached her hand out to calm her horse. The beast now pranced nervously from the ripples that had begun to spread out from deep inside the lake.

"I'll agree with that," Skharr whispered and turned to check on Horse, who looked a little nervous as well. His hands reached instinctively for his bow but he realized he was already too late when the ground below them began to shudder and shake and the water grew choppy from the movement beneath it.

He snatched the sword instead and dragged it clear of its scabbard as the water swirled and spun. Whatever came toward them was certainly not a small beast by any means.

The others had the same idea and grasped their weapons as a foul smell permeated the air, although Skharr had no idea what it was.

Something long and sinuous erupted from the water and writhed and twirled as it reached for something to latch onto.

The barbarian slapped Horse on the rump, and the message was immediately clear. The stallion broke into a gallop and the other horses followed as he sprinted away.

Another long, powerful strip of flesh lashed out and sprayed them all in liquid. Skharr skidded to a halt as the tentacle flailed nimbly like it had no bones inside it.

He did not want the monster to reach him. Large suckers

under the limb grasped chunks of rock with enough force to rip them out of the ground and drag them into the water.

The water roiled—almost like it was boiling, and something seemed to advance from the impossibly deep center of the lake.

"Move!" Cassandra shouted. Salis had already been on her horse when it galloped away. She wasn't able to regain control and instead, jumped from the saddle, landed heavily on the hard, rock-covered earth, and rolled over her shoulder a few times before she finally regained her feet. She had a couple of javelins in hand. Without so much as a moment of hesitation, she hefted one in her right hand and hurled it toward Skharr.

He knew he shouldn't have thought that she would hit him but it was a purely instinctive thought. Instead, it began its descent before it reached him and buried its head into the thick, meaty tentacle that continued to search for the prey it knew was there but couldn't seem to catch hold of.

In that moment, the earth shook, accompanied by a loud rumble that left them feeling that they'd heard monster roar in pain. The injured tentacle quickly lashed out, caught him across the chest, and catapulted him away. The single blow was powerful enough to thrust the breath out of him with a painful heave. Thankfully, none of the suckers caught onto him, and the fleshy limb retracted hastily into the water.

After a moment of tense silence, dozens of the tentacles suddenly thrust from the surface and a large wave surged onto the rocks and spilled over the edge of the cliff. The barbarian sucked in a deep breath and grimaced at a twinge of pain around his midsection. He ignored it for the moment and pushed to his feet.

"Skharr!"

He twisted and his gaze alighted on Cassandra, who was caught by one of the tentacles. It looked smaller—like a tendril—and extended from something closer to the center of the creature, whatever it was.

"Shit! Fucking godsbedammed crotch-licking suck-face." He growled annoyance and forced himself forward. She hacked at the flesh of the tentacle, but it showed no inclination to release her and instead, began to drag her into the water.

With little time on hand, he pushed into a run and drove his body as fast as it would go, his sword still clasped firmly in his hand. He moved in smoothly and swung the blade into the tendril. Whatever the metal was made of suddenly made the creature's flesh burn and acrid smoke rose from the severed piece as well as the bleeding stump. The latter slid hastily below the surface like it had been stung—or burned, he corrected with grim satisfaction.

Skharr looked into the water, which suddenly seethed with hundreds of the smaller tendrils that writhed endlessly like angry snakes. A few had found purchase on the rocks and it appeared that the creature was slowly dragging itself up to the surface.

There were no eyes that he could see and no sign that this creature had any place on the surface world. It appeared to be nothing more than a wriggling mass that smelled of death and darkness. Merely looking at it made his stomach roil with nausea.

Larger tentacles reappeared and anchored themselves on the other side of the cliff face as they worked with the smaller appendages to heave the monster out of the water.

And in that moment, while dozens of the smaller, wriggling, snake-like tendrils reached hungrily for him, Skharr realized that he now had the full focus of the creature. He had a few ideas as to why but there was no time to consider that in any detail.

He spun to avoid one of the grasping limbs that almost caught him, but before he could retaliate, it dropped, rolled, and withdrew to safety.

Abirat flicked black blood from his sabers.

"Let's go!" he shouted over the sound of rushing water and the ground shaking around them.

The barbarian couldn't agree more and rushed to where Salis and Grakoor were already helping Cassandra, who limped heavily as a result of the injury the tentacle had inflicted while wound around her leg.

One of the larger appendages lunged abruptly from the water and waved hungrily as if searching for them. The barbarian bellowed an impromptu war cry and attacked without thought. "Slime-sucking godsbedammed spawn of fucking Janus."

He drove his sword into the sickening protrusion and the same dark smoke rose from the wound. It was like the creature's flesh pulled away as quickly as it could from the silver blade, and it was almost effortless to cut through it.

Abirat looked confused but withheld his questions as they vaulted over the severed limb and raced toward their companions.

The earth shook violently again and for the first time, the thick body of the monster cleared the water. Air blew away from it like it had suddenly exhaled and the air filled with the scent of acid and rotting fish.

The tendrils moved with more purpose now, this time toward Abirat although they still appeared to be focused on Skharr. No eyes were readily visible on the body, but whatever the creature was, it could now sense them more clearly.

Tentacles ripped viciously at the rocks and snatched angrily at him as if they could somehow sense where he was. The redheaded bladesman beside him cut one in two, but the rest were carved smoothly by Skharr's sword until he finally faced the last of the larger tentacles.

There was nothing on his mind in that moment but escape, but as Abirat vaulted over it, the warrior acted without thinking. He roared and drove his blade into the tentacle to push it aside as he moved through.

In that moment, the whole earth shuddered violently and the upheaval propelled him toward the lake. The sheer weight of the creature was dragging a part of the cliff into the water but his last assault had shaken the balance somehow. Now, the entire precipice had somehow sheered away.

"Oh...fuck me," he whispered and whipped his head around. It wouldn't be long until the weight of the monster heaved everything into the lake behind it. Already, the platform he was standing on had begun to slide toward the fathomless drop to his left.

The only advantage was that no tentacles were reaching for him anymore, and Skharr pushed his body as fast as it would go toward the crack that had appeared on the rock face ahead of him. It moved slowly, yet he couldn't help but feel that he would be too late.

In the last second before the whole cliff caved in under the weight of the lake, he jumped out and flailed for handholds in the rocks ahead of him.

His powerful fingers dug into any purchase they could find. He grimaced and cursed as bones broke and sharp rocks lacerated his skin, but he held on and didn't dare to look at what was happening below him.

Hands caught hold of him. Not the tentacles he feared but solid hands with fingers and everything. They closed around his flesh and began to pull him up.

"Put your backs into it!" Cassandra shouted as he was dragged over the edge and into his four teammates who had worked together to snatch him from the jaws of certain death.

The barbarian scrambled to his feet almost immediately and shuddered as he peered over the edge he had barely escaped. The monster still lurked in the water that had become an instant waterfall to plunge into the forest below.

The creature fought the powerful drag of the current but its efforts were as futile as the force of the raging waterfall it had created that dragged it inexorably to its hopefully final landing.

He couldn't even fathom how impossibly large it was. Droves

and droves of tentacles, from the smaller ones to the impossibly large, simply overwhelmed the mind. A few looked to be as thick as tree trunks, while others were about the size of snakes. Irrespective of their size, all flailed desperately for anything to stave off the inevitable fall.

Nothing worked and eventually, with an odd sound that might have been a wail, the beast tumbled over the edge and plunged hundreds of feet into the forest that had suddenly been inundated with the contents of the lake. The area that had once been filled with water now looked considerably emptier as the water flow slowed and finally stopped.

There were still hundreds of feet of water beneath, but some third of it had disappeared into the forest.

"What the fuck was that?" Cassandra asked and sat to inspect the damage done to her leg.

"Was that the Old God?" Abirat asked, and Skharr appreciated the man's optimism. If the Old God was dead, that meant their mission was finished. Of course, the man wasn't to know that as he and Cassandra hadn't shared any of those details.

But the warrior knew their eventual target wasn't dead, although how he knew it remained elusive.

"I...I don't think so," Grakoor answered, still gasping for breath.

"I hope it wasn't," Skharr said suddenly and looked into the forest, where he could see swathes of trees being knocked over in what he hoped were the monster's death throes. "Otherwise, we just released the old one from its watery prison and I doubt I would ever outlive that shame."

He pulled his shirt up to examine the place where he'd felt the twinge of pain. It looked like a rib had been broken by the strike and although painful, it wasn't as bad as what had happened to Cassandra's leg. Her ankle had been twisted violently and two large red welts marred her skin. From the suckers, Skharr assumed, and shuddered at the thought.

"I hate to curse us, but I think we are past the dangers of the lake," Grakoor noted. "And I would not tempt fate by remaining in this place for long. There is no telling what else might fall now that the structure is weakened around us."

The man made a good point. Skharr and Salis helped the paladin onto her horse and they moved hastily from the scene of the bizarre battle. By the time the area between the lake and the cliff grew larger and larger, the sun had begun to set and they had started their approach toward the mountains on the other side.

It surprised no one to see a massive gate carved into the mountainside that evidently led into the caves within.

The quarter-orc's presumption had not cursed them and thankfully, it seemed as though all five had the same idea at the same time. None wanted to head into the cave for the moment. They'd had enough adventuring for the day.

Without so much as a word, they paused in their advance and set up a small camp.

Skharr could only think that they were beyond lucky that they hadn't lost any of the horses or supplies. No one wanted to take water from the lake, and he doubted that it had anything to do with the fact that it was now farther away than it had been the day before.

He therefore didn't need to cook this time, and they all had something cold to eat, set the night watches, and settled in to sleep.

Cassandra's watch was first but the barbarian had difficulty falling asleep. He held his sword over his lap and inspected the blade. There was something about it that caused a reaction with the monster—something that, in his limited experience, could only be attributed to magic.

What kind precisely was beyond his realm of expertise.

"Thank you."

He looked up from his weapon over to where Cassandra pressed her fingers tentatively into her injury.

"Hmm?"

"Thank you," she repeated. "For saving my life. When I was being dragged into the water by that...that thing."

He nodded. "You did save my life a little while later when I was falling off the cliff. I suppose you could think of us as even, in case you were considering swearing your life to me or something."

She laughed and nodded slowly. "Were you injured? I thought I saw you holding yourself a little stiffer around the midsection."

"I think it broke a few of my ribs when it caught me with one of its tentacles," he answered. "I took a potion to heal it, but it's uncomfortable while the potion works its magic. How about your leg?"

Cassandra scowled at it. "It twisted my ankle and the suckers caused a few contusions. I cast a couple of healing spells for the bones and for the arteries to keep them from bursting and causing a blood clot that could kill me or leave me without the use of my leg."

He nodded as though he understood what she was talking about. Paladins were learned in the arts of healing and knew more about the bodies of those they would treat on the battle-field than he ever would. There would be no point in asking her to explain.

She noticed his confusion easily. "When there is this...suction on the skin, it causes blood vessels under the skin to burst. Damage to the blood vessels triggers clots to form to stop the bleeding, but in a few cases I have seen, the clots can be driven up through the veins and can stop blood flow to whichever part of the body they end up in and possibly even cause death."

He narrowed his eyes. That did seem a little clearer but he would assume that she was right anyway.

"I remember that there was this one battle where one of the men that I was treating had taken a rock to his thigh that caused a contusion and a similar blood clot. I managed to keep it from causing him any undue harm, but it triggered a raging erection for three days."

His eyebrows raised and he looked at Cassandra, who grinned broadly. "You're joking."

"This is absolutely the truth. I thought he was lying at first. I was pressing my hands on him and using magic and suddenly, up he went. He said he had no idea what was causing it and once it lasted for longer than four hours, I had no choice but to believe him. He was in a great deal of pain before he finally...uh, deflated."

Skharr nodded. "I don't doubt it. Did he survive?"

"Aye, but I think I heard that he had some trouble bringing himself to full mast, as it were, for a while after. He consulted me about it, and I directed him to a couple of the mages. I had a feeling they had a mind for that kind of thing."

He chuckled deeply, shook his head, and winced when his ribs twinged again.

"How about you? Do you have any interesting moments in your long career as a mercenary for Theros?"

"A few, yes," he replied. "Although I must say the most amusing has been a thief I encountered for the first time before I was a Theros mercenary. He tried to rob me and I took everything back, as well as the gems he had hidden in the lining of his clothes. Amazingly, I found him again in Verenvan, boasting that he beat me senseless. I punched my fist through a wooden wall, dragged him through it, and proceeded to teach him and his friends another lesson. A while later, though, I found him disparaging me and citing how merciful he had been to leave me alive after our last encounter."

"Pride does make fools of men," she commented and chuckled softly. "Do you think he ever learned his lesson? Is he still alive?"

"He was alive when I left him last," he told her. "Although I cannot speak for him later. A fool like him is bound to anger folk who lack my restraint. He was on some kind of pilgrimage when

I first found him, armed and armored, with a group of his friends. I forget the precise name."

"A religious man, then?"

"In name only. Any who believe in the gods would find it above themselves to lie so brazenly. Unless maybe they were followers of the Lord High God Janus, troll-fucking dickwad asshole that he happens to be."

The paladin laughed, finally finished with her leg, and lay back on her sleeping bag to stare at the stars. "It's an odd thing but there are so many odd things in this world. None that I would have even dreamed of in my youth when all I could think of was rushing through the world in search of worthy causes to champion."

"Not many causes are wholly just," Skharr said softly and looked at the stars as well. "Unless you make them so yourself, of course. Is that why you withdrew from your order?"

She shook her head. "I haven't withdrawn, only taken a sabbatical. In the end, I realized that paladins were merely mercenaries, gathering gold and favors for those like the high priest. They'll always say our work is the will of the gods but I realized—a little too late—that the will of the gods aligned so closely to theirs that it could be no coincidence."

Skharr chuckled, pleased that his ribs felt a little more comfortable now. "As long as you choose what you fight or not fight for, you'll find a cause worthy enough, even if it has nothing to do with your vows. Now, you should get some sleep. I'll keep watch."

She sighed and nodded gently. "Remember to wake Grakoor before the moon reaches its peak."

Her eyes were already drifting shut and he looked at Horse, whose head was tucked down and his eyes shut as well.

No, this was not the kind of fight that he ever thought he would find himself in, but neither were so many of the others. He'd stopped the endless questioning and reminded himself only of what he was fighting for. If it felt as though it was not worth it —that his life was not worth it—he would leave.

Or so he told himself. He knew he would always find a way to drag himself into some fight or another for the oddest of reasons.

All he could hope for was that the last would be a good one.

CHAPTER ELEVEN

The air was getting colder, a sure sign that winter was just around the corner. There was no doubt that most of the passes would already be closed thanks to the snow that would have fallen early in the higher altitudes. This left them no choice other than to continue around or through the mountains unless they wanted to wait until spring.

He assumed there was no time to be wasted wandering the wildernesses or waiting for spring, as those who were summoning the Old God would not be so hindered.

There was something bracing about the icy wind that whipped across their camp. The barbarian was up before his teammates and settled beside the fire with a blanket wrapped around his shoulders. Grakoor was supposed to be on watch for the early mornings, yet he could hear the quarter-orc snoring softly in his corner of the camp. He'd tried to prop his head on his hands but it had done little to stave off the need for sleep.

Skharr felt no judgment for the man. The early morning hours were the hardest to stay awake for, and as long as they hadn't been attacked or robbed while he slept, there was nothing to complain about. After a moment's consideration and warming himself by the fire, he returned to his saddlebags. Careful to not wake Horse, he removed a selection of dried ingredients from the packs and ventured warily to the greatly reduced lake to claim a little water.

Seeing the monster had made him squeamish the night before but having slept, he decided that the water would have been kept fairly clean. That aside, it was probably the only water they had access to anyway since they had needed to refill their skins from the lake the day before. They were damned either way.

Once he'd collected everything he wanted, he settled next to the fire, placed a pot on the burning embers at the edge, and started to add his ingredients to it.

Despite his attempts to not wake any of the other members of his party, Cassandra groaned and drew herself slowly from her blankets. She seemed to immediately regret it, as she yanked them close and draped them around her shoulders.

"Holy hell," she whispered as she inched closer to the fire. "It was not this cold yesterday."

Skharr shook his head as he cut a few pieces of dried meat and tossed them into the sauce he had on a rolling boil. "We were out in the sun yesterday, with most of the wind coming from the comparatively warm forest behind us. Here, we are in the shadow of the mountains and out in the open with the wind whipping across the cold water of the lake before it sweeps into us."

Cassandra scowled at him as she came closer to the fire. She opened the blanket to let the heat inside while protecting herself from the wind.

"What are you making?" she asked once she appeared to be a little more awake.

"A traditional meal I always cooked whenever we were in the colder regions of the world," Skharr explained. "Dried beef, potatoes, carrots, and wheat middling made into a thick stew with a handful of spices. I can guarantee that you'll feel warmer after having a bowl of it, although you might want to have a few pieces of waybread at the ready, just in case."

"In case what?"

Skharr looked at her and shrugged. "You'll see."

The other members of their party had slowly begun to wake as well. Grakoor straightened himself hastily and pretended he had been up the entire time.

"What are you cooking?" Salis asked and rubbed her eyes as she shambled forward to sit near the fire. Even half-asleep, she made sure to place herself in the path of the rising sun.

"It's a food that Skharr guarantees will cure us of the cold," Cassandra explained.

"It's called Guadid," he said and stirred the pot a little more vigorously as the contents grew thicker and the danger of them burning became more than a possibility. "It means fire in an older tongue that has mostly been forgotten by the clans, except when it came to naming food."

"How will food make us feel warmer?" Abirat asked as he poured some of the water into his small steel pot to begin preparing the morning's coffee. "Well, I mean any more than a warm meal would, I suppose."

Skharr didn't want to explain the effects of the powerful spices that were generally used to preserve food and keep pests and other animals from consuming them. With some things, it was better to make sure it was a surprise.

He used a ladle to pour some of the concoction for himself. The heat from the spices was the kind he'd grown used to, especially in the instances when he traveled through the mountain passes and away from any source of fresh foods and had to go to extremes to keep from anything spoiling or being eaten by pests that were similarly desperate for sustenance.

The heat radiated from his mouth, across his face, and down to his chest. He even felt like he was about to break out into a sweat under his clothes. It wouldn't last but it certainly helped to wake him fully and raise him to a warmer temperature that would be easier to maintain once they started the day's journey down the path.

A quick pause to bite into a piece of waybread felt necessary to soothe the tongue before he continued with his meal.

"I am intrigued," the half-elf commented as she found a clean wooden bowl and filled it with some of the thick stew. She took a quick mouthful, then another before she shrugged and frowned in confusion.

"There is a heat, but nothing...oh." Salis' eyes widened as she swallowed the food. "Oh...fuck. That is...warm. Too warm."

She coughed hoarsely and sucked in a deep breath, which only appeared to make it worse as her face began to turn red. Skharr snaked a hand out to stop her from attacking her water skin next.

"Not water," he advised. "Waybread is best."

She ignored him and stumbled instead to where Abirat was breathing over a steaming cup of his thick coffee.

"What?" The man looked aghast. "Hey!"

She paid him no mind, downed most of the liquid, and breathed out slowly, shaking her head.

"That was..." She seemed at a loss for words to describe the meal. "Well, I do feel warmer."

"And I need to make more," Abirat complained. "I thought you didn't like the stuff."

"In fairness, I can't taste much of anything right now," Salis answered, picked her bowl up and tentatively tried another mouthful. "But after the first reaction...I suppose it's not so bad once you are accustomed to the heat."

Skharr shared the stew with the rest of the group and all turned a bright red. Abirat broke into a sweat as he finished his bowl.

"They said it would put hairs on your chest," the barbarian quipped as he sopped the last traces from the pot with a piece of waybread. "I don't think that is the case, but I certainly believed it at the time. I used to think there was some magic that made the food so hot."

Cassandra, still breathing a little heavier and fanning her ruddy cheeks, laughed. "Well, I'm sure I could believe that. Or I would if I didn't know a few things about magic. Still, I do feel warmer and more alert now than I did before."

The barbarian narrowed his eyes when he realized that she still looked a little tired and had bags under her eyes. Perhaps it had something to do with the spell she had used to heal her leg. There was a difference, he supposed, between the effects of someone else's magic in the form of a potion and using her power to heal herself. It must surely take a toll. All magic did.

"Are you sure it is not because of my coffee?" Abirat asked from where he cleaned his pot and the used cups with water from the lake. "And for the record, I do expect all of you to contribute toward replenishing my stock as you all contributed to emptying it much quicker than I expected you would."

They all exchanged a look and nodded in agreement. It was only fair, after all, since they appeared to be delving into the man's personal stock.

"I might have underestimated the effects of that liquid," Salis said as they trudged on toward the gate carved into the mountain. "I do feel more…uh, energetic and powerful now than I remember having felt in years."

"I told you," the man retorted smugly as he brought his mount level with hers.

"It might also be why it is so easy to develop a dependence on it," Cassandra interjected. "If it is like other types of similar stimulants, you would need more and more of it to achieve a similar effect as the first time."

Abirat had no answer to that, but the barbarian was more curious about Grakoor's distraction. The quarter-orc hadn't participated in the conversation at all and instead, inspected the gate that they were approaching with careful scrutiny. He added a few notes to a scroll he carried in his saddlebags.

The gate itself was enormous, easily larger than almost anything he had ever seen. Carvings of large, bearded and armored men with their spears pointed toward the gate adorned the mountainside, although the elements had worn the carvings to the point that the individual features were mostly gone.

As they approached the opening, it became clear that the gates were meant to be closed, possibly when they were being attacked, but the doors had since crumbled. They lay scattered in large, boulder-sized pieces on the ground outside the cavern.

"It looks like the doors were burst open from the inside," Skharr said as he inspected one of the crumbled pieces that, like the rest of the location, appeared to have been exposed to the effects of rain, snow, and sleet for a few decades.

"I was thinking the same thing," Grakoor said. He dismounted from his horse, used a small knife to break a few pieces of rock from the larger boulders, and slipped them into a pouch. "These did not fall to pieces after the ravages of the weather weakened them but rather... My guess is they were flung from their place on the mountain face."

"An explosion?" Cassandra asked. She was not so curious as to dismount herself, but she watched them closely.

"Possibly, although I cannot think of what might have caused such an explosion."

Skharr tilted his head and studied the gate that was large enough to allow a few of the large houses he'd seen in his lifetime to pass through without issue.

Salis brought her smaller horse to a halt beside him and also inspected the carvings on the rock face.

"Is it odd that I am considering how a general might be able to lay siege?" she asked aloud once Grakoor moved to another pile of rocks that had once been the doors and Cassandra followed, still on her horse.

"It is likely, yes," Skharr muttered. "With that said, I thought the same. There would be no way in through this route, not when the gates were sealed, but there would also be no way for the defenders to retaliate. A well-supplied mage would be able to tunnel in from the side and there would be no way for the defenders to stop them."

The half-elf focused on him as she brushed a few rebellious strands of her thick hair out of her face and forced them into the band that was supposed to hold them all back. "You have been in a handful of sieges before, haven't you?"

He simply nodded.

"Odd. I think I've heard most of the tales on the Barbarian of Theros and none involved protracted sieges."

"I was not the Barbarian of Theros during those sieges," he answered, his expression bland when he looked at her. "I was merely another soldier profiting from the dozens of wars that needed mercenaries to bolster the ranks of the armies involved."

There was little to add to that and they both moved back to join the rest of their party, who now began to tentatively approach the gate ahead of them.

It seemed almost impossible, but Skharr was sure he could discern a light inside despite the long tunnel that the gate led into. He moved through first with Horse close behind him. Of course, he took that to be a good sign. The stallion's instincts were generally trustworthy, and if he had refused to enter, he would take it as a sure sign that danger waited for them inside.

Not that it would change his mind about continuing, of course, but there would be second thoughts.

Even so, he rested his hand on his sword as they moved into the cavernous entry. Once they were inside, it looked more like a hallway they might find in a castle that led deeper and deeper into the mountains.

Not a word was said between the group as they were on high

alert. Each scanned the shadows cast on the walls for any sign that trouble might be awaiting them.

The barbarian's gaze was drawn to the end of the tunnel, where the light from inside had grown even more intense. It wasn't enough to rival the sunlight outside but cut easily through the shadows as the group crept closer.

He was still at the front of the group when they exited the hallway and stepped into an inconceivably large chamber that spread ahead of them. The map had not been incorrect in stating that a city awaited them, as it was precisely that. Carved into the heart of the mountains, hundreds of buildings sprawled over a larger space than he remembered Verenvan taking up but less than the capital city.

Waterfalls graced the east and west points of the chamber and fed into two rivers that flowed in an impossibly straight line down the middle of the city before it disappeared into the same pool in what appeared to be the perfect center.

They could see it all clearly from above as the path that they were on steadied into a gentle decline that brought them into the city. The entire sweeping tableau was illuminated by what appeared to be vines of pure light wound around dagger-like stalactites that extended hundreds of feet from the ceiling, while still held well above the tops of the tallest buildings.

His gaze was drawn to the opposite side of the city, where a similar entrance had been carved into the stone. The road itself bisected the city like the river did and diverted only to circle the central pool before it continued in the other direction. The symmetry of it was oddly pleasing to the eye.

There were no words to adequately describe the incredible vista.

No. Skharr changed his mind about that almost instantly as he studied it a little closer. Despite the beauty and symmetry of the city, the single factor that seemed to define the scene was the fact that there was not a single living soul in sight.

"What is that making the light at the top?" Abirat asked.

"Is that a Birafun Root?" Cassandra asked.

Grakoor nodded. "I think so."

"A…what root?" the barbarian asked.

"There is a type of tree at the top of the mountain that absorbs the sunlight," Saris explained. "The myth is that they form the roots the mountains grow from, pushing the tree up farther into the sky for the purest form of light. They bring the light down into their roots to bring light to the darkest places."

"That is the myth," Grakoor said. "It's more likely that it is some kind of monolith erected at the top of the mountain, created specifically to bring light down into tunnels and larger underground cities. The dwarves have writings about such structures, but most of the complex spellwork has been lost to time."

"I suppose the question should be asked," Skharr said and gestured for them to continue down the path that led into the city below. "What happened to all the people here?"

"It has been a few centuries since the city was abandoned, and most of the depictions of what happened were changed with retelling," Grakoor explained and fell into step beside him as the rest of the group quickly followed suit behind them. "There isn't much consensus between the stories we have on written record, but most scholars appear to agree—those who have studied the history of this region of the world, at least—that something poisoned or polluted the water in the cavern, which resulted in thousands of deaths. They had no other source of water and were forced to leave and find another home."

"Do you think that it was the monster we found outside that did the poisoning and polluting?" Abirat asked.

"It could have been," the quarter-orc conceded. "What worries me more is the condition of the gate we entered through. It has been centuries, of course, but it does appear that something blew the doors out from the inside."

"I might say that those who left the city closed the gates

behind them," Skharr suggested as they reached the bottom of the decline. "Either to keep themselves from being tempted to return or maybe to seal something in."

His words echoed through the empty city and none of the party had any response for him on the topic. They scanned the empty buildings around them as if to find anything in there that would explain everything. None of them thought they would find the answers they sought but the fear was there.

"I wish you hadn't said that," Cassandra whispered and her gaze flicked from shadow to shadow as she tried to make sure that nothing was about to jump out at them.

"I'll have to ask Grakoor to not try fishing with rocks anywhere in here," Salis commented, and the quarter-orc couldn't help but agree as they continued their slow but steady journey.

The horses were still relatively calm when they reached the center of the city, where they all approached the pool of water. None were tempted to refill their skins, however, and when Skharr leaned forward, he realized that the water was swirling. It moved slowly but spun in a slow circle and a small dimple in the middle revealed that it disappeared slowly through a drain.

The question of where it ended up remained unasked. All they wanted to do was move through the city as quickly as possible—which proved fairly quickly indeed, given that the streets were empty.

It wasn't until they reached the second stretch of road that they saw any signs that the abandoned city had been previously inhabited. Skharr paused and studied a heavy chariot that had been abandoned in the middle of the street. Any signs of the beasts that had pulled it were gone except for the leather straps that had held the horses to the harness.

He moved in closer and ran his fingers over the leather until the end, which had been thoroughly shredded.

"Look out!"

The barbarian turned to Cassandra, who raced toward him.

He followed her gaze and noticed something grasping for him from beneath the ruined chariot.

A hand, thin and wispy-white with threadbare rags hanging from it, moved slowly across the ground toward his leg.

The paladin was already in action. She drove her sword through the hand, broke the bones in a smooth strike, and kicked the conveyance away. It was ancient and collapsed with the impact, but something moved under it and rose faster than the hand had done.

A pair of eyes, glowing a deep and nebulous purple, stared out through the cloud of dust that had been kicked up and a piercing scream echoed through the unnatural silence.

She showed no sign of hesitation but with a smooth thrust. drove her arming blade directly between the two eyes that were visible.

A skeleton suddenly stilled where it stood in the dust. The scream stopped, and Cassandra drew her sword back and slashed across its neck to sever the head. She nodded as it tumbled down the road away from them.

"Are you all right?" she asked and turned to Skharr once the remains of the skeleton fell and showed no sign of coming to its feet.

"Yes," he said, feeling and resisting a tremble in his voice. "I'll be fine."

His statement was quickly contradicted as the call that the undead creature had sounded was picked up farther away in the city. It was soon followed by another, then another. The clamor sounded almost like wolves howling but was more of a low, hungry, angry groan that grew louder and louder as more cries were added.

"Necromancy," she whispered. Her face went pale and slack and an odd fury burned in her eyes—the kind Skharr had never seen in her before.

"There's a whole city of them, from the sound of it," Salis commented. "We should be running."

"We woke them, and unless you want to see them run amok in the countryside, we'll have to deal with them now." The paladin rummaged through a few of her pouches and retrieved an ancient-looking silver star with seven points. "Protect me. I'll need…five minutes, I think."

"And then what?" the warrior asked.

"And then I'll deal with them!"

Cassandra dropped down to her knees, closed her eyes, and held the star with both hands while she whispered hurriedly. It was clear to her teammates that they wouldn't be able to drag her out, and they also wouldn't be able to help her in whatever magic she was summoning.

"Shit." Skharr looked around. They were in the road with openings of possible attack from all sides. There was also no better place for them to set up a defensive position, however.

He drew his sword and the others gathered hastily around Cassandra. It was interesting that they immediately believed her when she said she had a way to handle their situation, and he realized that he did too. All they needed to do was keep her alive until she could save their lives.

The first surge of movement came from the pond in the center of the city, and he positioned himself to face the advancing group.

At least a dozen of the same monsters that had been hidden under the chariot. Unlike the skeletons he had seen and fought before, these appeared to move at the same speed that a human could, although they sagged somewhat like they weren't quite used to walking yet.

Their speed increased dramatically when their dark-purple eyes found the team and they now raced forward in a full sprint.

The warrior dragged in a deep breath and took a step forward as more shrieks joined the unholy cacophony.

The closest of the creatures had no weapons in its hands, but its fingers looked like they had enough force behind them to drive easily through his armor. He swung decisively and severed the hand away with a sharp, downward stroke, and a rapid reversal targeted the head and knocked it from its neck in another clean strike.

Before he could confront the next, Grakoor launched into the fray as well. He uttered a powerful roar as he charged into the group of skeletons, powered his plated gauntlet through the skull of the first to shatter bone without pause, and brought his hammer smoothly into the fray next to kill two of the monsters with a single stroke.

Skharr had heard the calm, collected, learned side of the quarter-orc for so long that he almost forgot there was a beast of a fighter hidden inside as well.

With a smile at his foolishness, he swung his blade to decapitate another of the creatures that carried what appeared to be a blacksmith's hammer in hand. Like the others, removing the head —or crushing it, in Grakoor's case—was all that was necessary to stop the monsters.

But more of them appeared as if out of nowhere—too many— and hundreds of roars were added every second until the cacophony filled the subterranean city. It was deafening and even a conservative estimation must put them at thousands by now. This was a small army, ready to attack any intruders who tried to pass through.

The question of who raised the army and why paled when compared to the question that the presence of the undead answered. This was what happened to the people of this city. It was what had driven the survivors away and this was what they had attempted to seal in.

Worse, it gave rise to another, more chilling question. Who or what blew the doors open?

That was a question for later, of course. Skharr drew back a step as twenty or so of the creatures surged out from inside the buildings around them and his blade cut a path for Grakoor to retreat to their ranks. They were drawing most of the attention of the attack, leaving the stragglers to Salis and Abirat, who deftly kept the last line of defense over Cassandra. She continued to whisper, the star still clutched in both her hands, and sweat dripped from her face and drenched her clothes and armor.

Her eyes were clenched shut and she seemed to struggle to remain upright, although she didn't relinquish the star and her whispered words seemed more fervent. It felt as though the light was being drawn from the space around them and sucked into the star that had begun to glow in her hands.

Skharr ducked a blunt ax that was swung at his head by a creature on his left, and he finally positioned himself to fight shoulder-to-shoulder with Abirat and Salis. They were soon joined by Grakoor. The quarter-orc had a handful of shallow wounds on his face and arms but none that would slow him, fortunately. Skharr had lost count of how many of the monsters his teammate had pulverized with strikes from his plated gauntlet and hammer, and he looked like he was genuinely enjoying himself.

Cassandra's whispers turned to shouts, and she raised the star above her head. Her eyes were open now and glowed with the same light that streamed from the star in her hands, and she looked directly into it. The words were lost in a sudden ringing that rocked through the barbarian. It was odd to think that he could feel sounds, but the vibrations shook him physically. Not a painful feeling, but it was certainly uncomfortable.

It appeared to have the same effect on the monsters, which were being pushed back by the pulses of the vibrations emanating from the star. He looked down when he noticed the silver on his sword had begun to glow as well. It spilled a cold brilliance, although there was no vibration from the weapon in his hands.

Cassandra yelled one final word and screamed like it was her last breath as the light suddenly turned too bright to look at, and he closed his eyes. Even then, he could see the brilliance through his eyelids, and he raised his arm quickly to block it all out. He feared that it would sear his eyes in their sockets, leaving him blind.

No such thing happened, however. The light vanished almost as quickly as it appeared and he lowered his arm and tentatively opened his eyes.

He felt like he had been blinded for a second and needed a moment to let his eyes adjust to the comparatively dim light in the cavern. When he could finally see again, he looked around. All the skeletons were sprawled on the ground. The light was gone from their eyes, and their limbs were scattered like the magic had been all that held the corpses together. Once that was gone, they were left simply as bones.

"Fucking troll-snot-scoured godsbedammed bone bags." Skharr growled and glanced at his sword. He wondered if he'd imagined it or if its glow had flared briefly again for a moment.

"All right. then," Cassandra sounded a little hoarse where she remained on all fours. "I think I need a little help here."

CHAPTER TWELVE

Skharr hurried forward to help Cassandra up. She looked drained and immediately sagged against him, although she tried to move her legs in time with him as he guided her to her horse.

"Unless you lay me across it, I don't think I'll be able to ride," she whispered, her voice still rough with strain.

"I could carry you on my shoulders," Skharr ventured, and she laughed weakly. It had been a genuine offer, but if she preferred to take it as a joke, maybe it was that too.

"That would be an interesting ride and not quite how I imagined my first time riding you," she said and patted the arm that held her upright.

"That was holy magic you cast," he said quietly while the rest of the group began to gather themselves to continue their journey.

"Yes, all paladins carry old relics that are used to remove the effect of necromancy," she replied. "It is our duty to remove the stain of that whenever we find it."

"You're no longer a paladin."

"As I keep reminding you, that's probably only temporary.

Besides, that was one of the few parts of my oaths I never wanted to set aside. Necromancy is dangerous magic, the kind that always rips free of the control of the necromancer. It is best to do away with it whenever I find it."

He wondered if he should mention the effect her spell had on his sword, but it felt like a topic for another day.

"It is the first time I cast that spell on my own," she admitted as he clicked his tongue to call Horse and her mount to follow them as they moved toward the other side of the city. "I've always had three or four other paladins with me. We were sent in groups, and I feel like it might have killed me if I had tried to cover a larger area with the spell."

"You engulfed the whole city, then?"

She nodded. "Aye. And as many tunnels as I could reach. There were quite a few, so I might have missed some of the monsters. Still, their power was fading. A fresh skeletal rising has bright eyes and these were almost faded. I am curious how the necromancer turned so many in the city."

"It might be that the necromancer had nothing to do with the poisonings," Skharr pointed out and felt in his pouches with his free hand until he found the vial he was looking for. "He might have heard of thousands dead from a poisoning in a city that had since been abandoned and thought it a perfect opportunity to test his abilities, and…well, as you say, it all got out of his control."

She nodded. "It's an interesting theory. The answer may never be found among the living and the dead… As you know, they aren't the talkative kind. What do you have there?"

"A potion the mage sold to me while you were fitting your chain mail undergarments. He said it helped to give a person energy like the coffee Abirat carries, but without the side effects. I think a sip would do you no harm."

He placed the vial in her hands, and she nodded and tried to pull the wax seal off. After a few failed attempts, he broke the seal for her and helped her to raise it to her lips.

Cassandra smiled but looked a little embarrassed as she took a sip from the contents before she sealed it again and handed it to him.

"You might find a need for it later," she said, and he could already feel her walking with a little more force behind her step. They continued up the incline that headed toward the exit and with every step, she slowly regained her strength until she was able to walk on her own.

The darkness in the tunnel grew deeper and deeper. This was not an exact mirror of the other side, Skharr realized. They now climbed slowly into the mountain and the winding path led them farther and farther.

Despite this, he felt confident in his sense of direction, even underground. They were en route to the other side of the mountain, although they now followed a more circuitous path and had to light torches to be able to see where they were going.

"Oh...fuck!" Salis shouted and took a step back.

The whole group froze, and Skharr already had his hand on his sword hilt when he looked back to where the woman stood, her expression one of utter disgust.

Thankfully, no monsters were in evidence. The half-elf had taken a step back and hauled her horse with her. She wiped her feet to try to remove something thick and foul-smelling that she had stepped in.

"What is that?" Abirat asked.

Grakoor approached and sniffed the pile before he shook his head and sneezed loudly.

"It is guano in certain civilizations," the quarter-orc explained. "Bat shit. There is likely a colony of the creatures nearby, preparing to hibernate for winter."

"Bats would need to find a way in somehow," Cassandra pointed out.

Skharr nodded and studied the tunnels. For the first time, he realized that the ceiling was much taller than it had been before and a hint of a chill had crept in. His gaze ventured upward and he lowered his torch until it was dark enough to see.

Small lights twinkled in the distance. The ceiling above them was open to reveal cold starlight.

The rest of the group followed his gaze and stared at the clear sky above them.

"Now if that isn't a welcome sight," Grakoor whispered.

"I think we found our demon's fucking slime-greased anus," the barbarian muttered, a little irritated that he'd missed this. "Or at least the demon's godsbedammed crack, which might have been mistranslated. And it has more than enough shit to fit the name."

Salis was the first to laugh. "We'd best watch our step, then, lest we turn batshit crazy."

It was odd to hear laughter in hallways that had likely been silent for so many years.

As they continued, the piles of guano became more and more frequent. In some cases, they narrowed the hallway to where the group could move through in single file only and the team had to guide the horses as they picked a careful path through without sullying or dirtying themselves in the muck.

There was a natural need to not be covered in the stuff, of course, but Skharr knew pests and insects likely wallowed in the waste that could prove as deadly as any necromancer army.

He paused when he heard a small gasp behind him and whirled to catch Cassandra before she planted, face-first, into one of the larger piles.

"Thank you," she whispered. "I guess I'm still not quite steady on my feet. I might suggest that we find a place to set up camp."

"That might take a while," he informed her, and she nodded slowly as she hoisted herself slowly up his arm until her balance was regained. That left her pressed against his side, which meant he was unable to move until she did.

Instead of moving back, she took a light step forward, placed one foot between his, and spun carefully—still using the massive barbarian for balance—before she stepped out in front.

"I think you've wanted to do that for a while," Skharr said and chuckled as he took a moment to make sure she wouldn't fall back. "If you think there are precious few opportunities for you to press yourself against me, you are mistaken. You need only ask."

She grinned but looked away quickly and made sure the torchlight didn't touch her face as she moved forward.

"At least there is a pleasant view ahead of me this time," he added. "It was getting tiresome having to stare at Grakoor's ass."

"You don't need to stare at all, you know."

"There isn't much else to look at."

"You know," the quarter-orc shouted from the front of their narrow line, likely in the interests of changing the subject, "in places where bats are most numerous, you'll find that farmers use their shit to fertilize fields and grow fantastically-sized fruits from it. There are many who make their living collecting the shit from caves and selling it to farmers."

"They would make a fortune if they found this location," Abirat quipped. "And it would have the additional benefit of clearing the way for us, although I suppose they'd have to find another name for it."

It wasn't long until another gate opened for them, although much smaller than the first. It was of a similar design. A long crack that had appeared and continued down most of the hallway they had followed started at the gate itself, where there was evidence that the doors had been brought down in a similar fashion as those at the front entrance.

He had to assume that this was somehow the rear, if only from the name.

"We've traveled far enough for today," Grakoor stated once they were clear of the shit-filled hallways. "I suppose it is about time for us to set up camp, get some rest, and be prepared for what comes tomorrow."

The group agreed without any argument and were relieved to find a small creek running near the gate to provide access to fresh water and enough firewood for the camp.

"I'll need a hit of the coffee come the morning," Cassandra said softly as she slid into her sleeping bag and drew the covers over herself. "But for now…"

Her voice trailed off, and Skharr realized that she had fallen asleep right then and there.

"Of course," Abirat grumbled as he settled into his blankets. "She drops off before we can arrange a watch schedule."

"Give her some slack," the barbarian retorted. "She saved our lives in those caves and managed to keep walking regardless. She earned a good night's rest."

"That was holy magic she used in there," Grakoor said calmly and took a bite from a strip of dried meat. "Only one type of warrior I know uses magic like that—paladins."

"It doesn't matter," Skharr cut in quickly. "All of us need to get some sleep. I'll take the first watch."

"I can take the second," Abirat said with a dramatic yawn. "I'll use the opportunity to brew some of my koffe."

"Koffe?"

"It's the proper name. I found it inscribed in the last pack I have of the stuff."

The barbarian shrugged and left the man to fall asleep undisturbed.

It had been a long day, and he impatiently watched the quarter moon move across the sky and counted the hours carefully until it was time to wake the redheaded human.

It felt like he had barely closed his eyes when someone nudged his shoulder.

He was awake almost instantly, his hand already on his sword, and he looked around while his mind and senses readied for an attack.

None was forthcoming, thank goodness. They had slept a little longer than they usually did, and the glowing sky indicated that it was a few hours past sunrise.

"We slept long?" he asked, straightened, and waited for Horse to stand carefully as well.

"We might have needed it," Cassandra answered and scratched her arm idly.

Something was wrong. It looked like the whole group was in a foul mood, and Skharr narrowed his eyes to study the other four. All seemed to avoid looking at Abirat, who was in a much better mood as he loaded his horse's saddlebags.

"What happened?" the barbarian asked and rolled his neck.

"Abirat made his koffe and refused to share any," Salis explained and shook her head in disgust.

"I thought you didn't like it."

"Sure. And I don't like making sure that my teeth aren't rotting out of my skull by having a specialist mage blunder about with my mouth as wide as it will go, but it's still necessary."

"Drinking my koffe is not necessary, and it may prove to be beyond us, given how quickly we are going through my supply. Until we find civilization where I can buy enough for us all, we'll have to be sparing."

Skharr nodded. "That does seem to be a reasonable approach to me."

"Well, yes." Grakoor shook his head and his voice slurred a little more than usual. "But we don't much care for it all the same."

The warrior had a feeling that this was the case for Cassandra as well, although she did less to voice her complaints than Salis, who was determined not to let the topic rest.

"If you intended to insist on sharing it with us," she resumed once they were on the move again, "you might have brought enough to share for the entire journey."

"There was no way that I could judge how long the journey would take," Abirat protested. "And besides, I didn't expect all of you to want it every day, plus drink the portions I made for myself." He directed a glare at the paladin before he returned his gaze to Salis. "And I certainly didn't expect you to demand it every morning!"

"We don't demand it every morning!" the half-elf shouted as her temper got the best of her. "Only this morning!"

"Hush!" Skharr said and raised a hand.

"No," Salis snapped. "I want to know why you have waved it in our faces during the trip, only to remove it when we need it!"

"Quiet!" the barbarian shouted, yanked his bow from the saddle, and strung it quickly. "You idiots drew company to us!"

An odd meowling pierced the sudden silence and increased rapidly in volume. The group turned hastily to their weapons. A pride of larger cats climbed down from the rocks they likely used as a home. Their fur was thick and gray, and their long, tufted ears flicked to listen in all directions.

He had seen the like before, but those had been a great deal smaller and only reached to his knees. These were larger—the size of lions and stockier around the shoulders—with elongated, tusk-like fangs extending from the top half of their jaws.

His gaze fixed on the predators, he took three arrows from his quiver but paused when Salis yanked her javelins from their pouch and began to advance on the animals. She had a murderous glare on her face and was joined by Cassandra, Grakoor, and Abirat, all in the mood to take their frustrations out on something. It seemed the felines had volunteered, the whole dozen of them.

After a moment of thought, he returned his arrows to the quiver and unstrung his bow.

"This should be interesting," he said, placed it on the saddle, and turned to watch the fight.

Cassandra made good use of her sword to keep two of the cats at bay. Salis had already used all three of her javelins and now hefted her spear to corner a fourth.

Abirat and Grakoor both caught it before she could. They sliced into the creature and crushed its skull with a hammer before they turned their attention to the rest.

It was not a fair fight. There were a few benefits to fighting when angry. They usually only came in instances where tactical thought was not necessary since cool heads would not be found, and dealing with the large mountain cats did appear to be the time for that.

Horse snorted and turned to nudge him in the shoulder.

"No," Skharr replied and shook his head. "If they need my help, they'll ask. For the moment, it seems as though they all need to…unleash on something. I would only get in the way."

The beast did not appear to be convinced, but he smiled as Salis and Grakoor surged toward the two that Cassandra had been toying with and drove both to their deaths on the paladin's weapon.

"Weren't you going to join us, Skharr?" Cassandra asked once their weapons were recovered and Abirat inspected the bodies. The fur would have likely fetched a high price in a few markets, but they did not have the time or the patience to treat it properly.

"You had everything under control," he replied and patted Horse's neck. "Besides, I took the first watch last night. I've done my part for the collective safety of our group already."

She grinned at him and cleaned her sword before she tucked it into its sheath. "Where do you think we should go now?"

"I think we should ask our guide." He raised a finger to point at Grakoor. "He is the one with a map, after all."

"The map is a little vague about what happens now," the quarter-orc admitted as he took it from his saddlebag. "I suppose the assumption is that if we got through all the other trials and tribulations alive, we would be able to find our way to the dungeon without issue."

"I hate it when map writers make those assumptions," Skharr muttered. "We should search for clues, I suppose—any sign of magic that the dungeons tend to be steeped in. It shouldn't take too long."

The fight had done wonders for the mood of the group. All the aggression had been expended and while Salis still looked like she needed a little more of the koffe—or whatever it was called— if she was to make it through the day without berating Abirat a little more.

Skharr frowned in concentration as they continued on their way. It seemed impossible, but he could hear footsteps on the same path they were following—heavy footsteps and heavy breathing too, now that he focused on it. He raised his hand to catch the attention of the group and pointed in the direction from which he could hear the movement.

There was no argument this time, and it wasn't long until two heavily armed and armored mercenaries moved out from the underbrush. They didn't notice Skharr or his group until they had taken a few more steps out, then they froze in place and reached for their weapons.

"You fight, you die," Skharr warned them roughly, his hand on his sword. "Talk. And maybe live."

The two were covered in sweat and grime like they had been running in their heavy armor and didn't look like they believed they would survive if they tried to fight anything larger than a duck. It seemed like the group they encountered was a little reasonable. They would talk.

"Who are you?"

"Pilgrims on our way to the nearest worship site, ready to sacrifice lambs and fuck under the full moon," Salis snapped. "Who the hell do you think we are?"

"Mercenaries?" the other asked.

"Aye," Skharr answered. "You ran from the dungeon?"

The two exchanged a quick look before they nodded in unison.

After a moment, the one on the left—smaller and with a thick beard—took a step forward. "There...there were eight of us. But there was a...a..."

When his words failed him utterly, his companion stepped in to finish for him. He was clean-shaven with long, greasy hair and a crooked nose.

"A...fear filled the air. Something attacked and we...we ran. We were in the dungeon already, so I grabbed this." He fumbled in his pocket and pulled out a ruby the size of Skharr's fist. "I thought we had enough to set us up for a few years."

"Don't show it to them!" the first man snapped, took the ruby, and shoved it into his pocket.

"We do not intend to rob you," Cassandra assured them.

"How can we believe you?" the bearded man asked.

"Because if we did, you would already be dead," Abirat pointed out.

It was a good point, and they agreed after a brief moment of deliberation.

"Where is the dungeon?" Skharr asked. "We have business there."

"Business?" the one with the crooked nose asked. "What business would you have in a dungeon?"

"Blood and the spilling of it," he answered quickly. "Where?"

"Back the way we came." The one with the beard pointed over his shoulder, although he seemed too afraid to even look in that direction. "You'll be able to follow our tracks easily enough if you've a mind to do so."

He nodded. "Get back to your running and don't look back. And you would be wise to hide that treasure from those you find in this place. Others will be greedier than us."

Both nodded but made no effort to even thank the group before they continued at a slightly slower pace.

"Why didn't we take the ruby from them?" Abirat asked as they moved down the path. "It would have been easy enough to pick them off with bows."

"Because if there was a ruby like that so close to the entrance that they were able to escape, the chances are there will be more treasures than we can carry in there," Skharr answered. "There is no need to spill blood pointlessly. I'm sure there will be treasure enough for all of us."

That seemed to convince the redhead, who made no further protest. Sure enough, the two mercenaries' tracks were easy to follow.

Cassandra paused and an odd look crept over her face.

"There is...magic here," she whispered. "A wrongness I cannot explain."

"Nothing like a paladin to admit a place is cursed to get the blood flowing," Grakoor commented from behind them.

"Well yes, but this one has my blood flowing simply by walking in front of me," Abirat answered.

Cassandra looked at Skharr and a flush touched her cheeks as she pulled a few strands of her hair back.

"Don't look at me," he protested. "I did not say a word. They reached the right conclusion on their own from your display in the abandoned city."

"Not that," she whispered.

"Oh." He looked at the three who brought up the rear of the group. "Well, do you not deal in truth? In this case, the truth is that you are quite attractive."

She grinned. "Not when I wore plate armor."

"Of course. That would hide the assets they were commenting on. Or, at least, the ass."

She punched him in the arm to silence him. Hard.

"Barbarians," she huffed. "You can't leave them behind when

you are done with them and can't stab them in the ass when they are making asses of themselves."

He shook his head and glanced at Horse. "See, this is why human men do not understand women. I don't suppose it is any easier between you and mares?"

The stallion tossed his mane and nickered softly.

"Well, at least males of all species can fraternize in their shared misery." He sighed and consoled Horse with a pat on the shoulder. "What?" he asked when he realized that Cassandra was watching him closely.

"These conversations with Horse," she said, "are not as one-sided as they appear, are they?"

The beast tossed his head up and down in a nod.

Her eyes widened. "I'll be…"

"Don't say it," Skharr cautioned her. "I don't want the big man dropping into my dreams to talk to me about you. With my luck, he will blame me for your actions."

"So, you truly did speak to Theros," she mumbled and regarded him with open interest. "How have we not discussed it?"

"There isn't much to discuss. He appeared to me as the old man who bought my farm. I did realize there was something odd about him, of course, but never thought it would be more than a strange old man before he appeared to me in a dream—one that saved my life, as it turned out."

"You mentioned that before. How did he save your life?"

"He warned me of creatures that killed us in our dreams and woke me in time to save the lives of a few others."

She nodded. "Interesting."

"I've always taken his dreams as portents of something dangerous. I thought he would show himself to me soon, but perhaps he now only appears when I am inside the dungeons."

Skharr stopped and narrowed his eyes as they approached a line of trees where a group of eight horses had been secured.

"There are eight of them, so at least the men weren't lying," Salis pointed out. "Why would they run without their horses?"

"I doubt they did much thinking as they shat themselves in fear," Grakoor commented. "You all did smell that on them, yes?"

Skharr hadn't but he would take the quarter-orc's word for it.

"Release the horses," he instructed. "And we would do better to not tie ours up. Should we leave, we will find them again. If we do not, it would be cruel to leave them bound and at the mercy of the predators in this region."

"I assume someone will come along and steal them anyway if we were to tie them," Abirat added.

"What will happen to the horses if we don't come out?" Grakoor asked as he did as Skharr instructed.

"They'll find their way to civilization," the barbarian answered. "Horses are crafty animals and know where they'll find food and shelter."

"There are no doubt many who could find them and take them anyway," the man commented. "With considerable movement in the region, it wouldn't take long. No offense."

He directed the last comment at Horse, who ignored him and lowered his head lazily to graze on a patch of grass.

Skharr grinned and patted the beast comfortingly on the neck.

"You remember our deal, yes?" he whispered so only the stallion could hear him. "If I don't come out in a few days, you're to find Sera Ferat's farm and live out your days spawning little Horses and eating apples until you're sick of both, you hear me?"

Horse bobbed his head gently as the barbarian gathered his armor, weapons, and supplies from the saddlebags and arranged them carefully over his shoulders to make them easier to carry. After a moment of thought, he lifted the small pouch carrying the healing medallion Horse had worn. The beast looked healthy enough already and Skharr had a thought that he would need some of the effects for himself.

"Who is Sera Ferat?" Cassandra asked. She had already hoisted her supplies and left her horse untied.

"That was a private conversation," he answered.

"And I was dropping eaves."

He nodded. "A blademaster. She taught me how to use the sword."

"She must not have been a great instructor," the paladin commented. "You have some skill but lack all finesse."

"She was a fine instructor. I was merely a poor student," he countered. "Come on. Chewing the fat all day won't kill an old god. We move!"

CHAPTER THIRTEEN

As they continued to prepare for the dungeon, Skharr began to feel what Cassandra had been talking about. She was better attuned to the magic of places like these but it was powerful enough that even one as thick as a barbarian could feel it.

An animosity permeated the air as if something didn't want them in the region. Skharr felt at least one part of himself desire to go and discover the cause of it, but two parts seemed angry that they were there in the first place.

He moved to where Cassandra held what looked like a charm hanging around her neck and whispered a few different prayers.

Out of respect, he waited for her to finish before he spoke.

"What is it?" she asked as she tucked the charm into her shirt.

"You know something about Theros, yes?" he asked, his gaze fixed in the direction they were headed in.

"You met him so you should know more than I do."

"But in your training as a paladin…they taught you something about him, yes?" he persisted. For some reason, he had trailed his hand to the dagger he had tucked into his belt and he tried to remember what the elf had said about how to use it.

"Oh. Yes, I suppose so."

"And about the Old Gods?"

Cassandra nodded.

"I don't suppose there is any teaching about how to kill an Old God?"

She narrowed her eyes. "There...wasn't much about the Old Gods, aside from how they are gone and still leave their mark on this world in dreams. From what I heard, even those who battled the Old Gods in the past had no way to kill them, only to...well, put them to sleep."

Skharr scowled and glanced at the other three. They were talking about what they would do with the treasure they would find inside. There would always be priorities to face when they entered a dungeon. They had to keep their mind on what they intended to do on the other side.

As odd as it was, dreams and desires were what drove folk to survive when it felt impossible and to succeed when failure was on their mind. He knew that failure would be difficult to shake with the magic hanging over the location like a thick blanket.

"Why do you ask?" Cassandra whispered.

"There aren't many things you can't kill in the world," the barbarian muttered finally. "I merely wish we had known more about what we were facing before we...well, faced it."

She nodded and he realized the thought had plagued her as well.

"What do you mean you cannot die?" Abirat said loudly enough to bring Skharr out of the dark reverie his mind was slipping into.

Grakoor laughed. "I mean it. There will be treasure inside, and there is nothing that can stop me from taking that coin for myself and spending it on all the many, many vices I've acquired over the years."

"It's an odd thing to curse yourself like that before we enter a dungeon," Cassandra commented and patted the quarter-orc on the shoulder. "But if you die, I'll spend your share on all your vices for myself."

Grakoor laughed. "Well, as long as you spill a few drops in my name, I won't haunt you from the afterlife. Come, then. It's past time we got to making ourselves rich."

Richer, in Skharr's case. He was there for the purpose of killing a god, but he would not refuse the possibility to fill his coffers in Verenvan more than they were already. The project he'd commissioned the dwarves to forge had proven to be a fairly greedy consumer of coin.

"Well, we've both left instructions for how our shares are to be spent should we die," Salis noted, speaking for herself and Abirat by the sound of it. "The guild will make sure survivors pay to those causes."

Skharr chuckled and shook his head as he adjusted the pack on his shoulder and stepped forward to lead the group. The horses, including those that had belonged to the other mercenary group, moved away with Horse at their head. The barbarian trusted that they would all return once they exited the dungeon, but it would take the team time to find their way out—if they did.

A mist seeped and swirled into the valley they were entering, and he felt more comfortable with his bow already in hand, an arrow pressed to the bowstring in case they found something that was not friendly upon their arrival.

Something had likely killed the members of the party whose horses had been left behind, and it was always best to be prepared for it.

"Ahead," Abirat called and Skharr frowned at what looked like a cave emerging from the mist. The rocks were covered in moss and there was no other way for them to go.

The entrance was clearly marked and the barbarian pressed forward first, still ready with his bow.

He recognized the feeling. Recollection from his time in another dungeon reminded him that there were magical charms out there that could make people feel uncomfortable simply by being close to a location as long as they were all placed in the right positions.

Irritated by both the sensation and the memory, he shook his head and tried to physically shake the feeling as he slipped through the entrance.

It was immediately apparent that he wouldn't have much space to use the war bow so he lowered it, slung the weapon over his arm, and settled his hand on his sword instead.

The first chamber looked like a cave. It was covered in moss and might as well have been one of any of the hundreds that were spread across the whole region. But as he moved through a narrow crack in the back wall, he realized that was likely the intent of the builders—to mask the presence of what had been built within.

He rolled his shoulders as his gaze traced the curious design of the next chamber they entered. It was clearly man-made and contained a few statues that had begun to fall apart. Skharr wondered what they had looked like when they had originally been created. Perhaps they weren't quite so chilling back then.

Or maybe they were more so. In places like these, it was difficult to tell since they were not built for the benefit of bringing guests in. He studied the empty eye sockets and tried to determine what the original had been before time and the elements that filtered in through the crack in the wall and wreaked their slow destruction. It must have been left untouched for centuries for it to be in the condition it was in now.

"Look here," Abirat said. He settled onto his haunches and rummaged through the piles of dust and other things that Skharr didn't want to think about before he drew his hand back out with a triumphant grin on his face.

The redhead's eyes were sharp and he held two sapphires about the size of his knuckles. With a grin of triumph, he held them aloft for the rest of the group to see.

"I guess I have the eyes of…whatever the hell this used to be," he said and patted the statue with a chuckle before he turned his attention to the group. "How much do you think these might be worth?"

Grakoor leaned closer to inspect the gems. "I would say close to a hundred gold pieces depending on where you sell them. Each."

"I would say that is a fortunate beginning to our little venture." The man tucked the gems quickly into his belt and out of sight. Skharr had a feeling that it would be the last time they saw any sign of those gemstones but made no comment on it. There would be more than enough treasure to go around for the rest of them, and the treasure wasn't what he was there for anyway.

The next chamber looked similar to the last, although a handful of torches on the wall sconces had been recently lit and still carried a few hours of flame on them. The barbarian took one off the wall and swept it slowly over the room, which extended into a long hallway ahead of them. He stopped short, his gaze fixed on the floor.

Something had disturbed the heavy coating of dust there, but he wasn't able to determine that the remains were human and stooped for a closer look. The corpse had been all but ripped apart. Four ribs were missing, along with the right arm and part of the skull, leaving only the bottom half of the jawbone.

Most of the meat was missing from the dismembered, almost unrecognizable corpse.

Skharr moved the torch closer to where he could see teeth marks on the ribs and spine and after a moment, reached in with his free hand.

"Ugh," Cassandra whispered. "Can he not rest in peace?"

"Wherever that mercenary rests, it is not in peace," Salis whispered and shook her head in disgust.

"In pieces maybe," Abirat noted, and Skharr heard Grakoor chuckle at the turn of phrase.

He moved his hand between the ribs and felt a few chunks of organs that remained, but he was looking for the spine. Something had chewed on the corpse and taken its time before it suddenly left. He had a feeling that something had driven it away.

His somewhat messy exploration was rewarded when he shifted and felt something a little harder. Carefully, he tugged it out of where it had been caught in the spine.

A long, curved fang had broken off while the creature had been feeding.

"What is that?" Cassandra asked as he cleaned the blood from it.

"Remnants of whatever we might be facing," he answered and studied it intently. "Something large and powerful enough to force the smaller creatures that killed him to run away, taking what chunks they could get their teeth on before they left."

"You determined that from only one tooth?" Abirat asked.

"No, from the bite marks on the limbs compared to those along the stomach, which are smaller nibbles and rips. Not only that, something large peeled the shit armor off and immediately went for the liver, then the heart. While it was chewing on the lungs, its tooth got caught in the spine and broke off. It was painful enough to drive the creature away."

"Do you think it will return for its meal?" Grakoor asked, although he already knew the answer.

"We'll have to be ready for it when it does," Skharr answered, tossed the tooth aside, and straightened. He used a piece of cloth to wipe the blood and viscera from his hands. Whatever was waiting for them inside was very likely still hungry.

They moved through the hallway that opened up in front of them, which made it difficult to put a finger on what was wrong about the place. He raised his torch as they moved in front of what had once been a painting etched across the wall, although the artwork had been severely damaged.

The damage was not the result of time and the elements but rather direct action. Claw marks over the paint dug into the wall behind and ripped into the work of art until little of it remained. A tiny area had gone untouched by the rampant damage, and Skharr noticed this and leaned closer. He ran his fingers over what appeared to be a small group of people standing on a boat with no land anywhere near them.

"What do you suppose it means?" he asked and looked at Grakoor.

The quarter-orc shrugged. "Art never held much interest for me, aside from its depiction of history. Without the context of the rest of the work, it would be difficult to pin down what this means precisely."

None of the group had anything to add, although Skharr couldn't shake the image from his mind as they continued down the hallway. Finally, they reached what had once been a door. The hinges were still in place, although thoroughly rusted, but the door itself had either rotted away or been torn down.

It was difficult to place which was the more likely scenario, and he moved past it quickly to illuminate the next room.

"Oh, gods," Salis whispered behind him.

The warrior scowled and took another step forward to sweep the torch higher so they could see a fuller picture. Of course, the half-drow saw better in the darkness than the rest of them, but it was still difficult to look at. Piles upon piles of bones had been left in a single space. A few looked like they had been bitten or gnawed on, but not all.

"This must be all the adventurers who entered here," he mumbled. "Killed and...brought here for what?"

"Raw material?" Cassandra answered quickly. "Burn them all and smash the bones. There's no point in...uh, in..."

Skharr frowned when the pile heaved gently as something moved beneath it.

"What did you intend to say?" he asked as he drew his sword.

"Oh...leaving it here to attack us from behind later," she answered and readied her blade.

"No paladin magic to finish them off here and now?" Salis queried with a small smirk.

"There's no point. There aren't many of them and I am sure my magic would be best kept for later use."

Skharr wanted to counter that statement, but there was no time. A skeleton rose from the pile and it shuddered and struggled to remain upright as it stretched mindlessly toward where he stood. A simple strike from his sword was all that was needed to fell it completely.

"This is my kind of fight," Grakoor crowed, immediately stepped forward to crush the skull of another, and quickly reversed his strike to apply the same power to a second that emerged from the pile.

Another one rose, with legs and a jawbone that came from some other indefinable species. Others appeared to have bones of various creatures drawn into them, which made them seem more terrifying than they were. Skharr noted that these creatures were slow-moving, carried no weapons, and were easy to crush into dust.

It wasn't long before most of the bones in the piles had been splintered and powdered to leave nothing moving in them.

"They're called boneyards," Cassandra explained and cleared a small space on the floor of the dust and bones to reveal a variety of runes that had been inscribed on the rock, although they were all inert. "It works to create a large number of creatures to fight but requires little magic to raise or maintain them. Writings told of old battlefields where necromancers gathered hundreds of thousands of dead of all kinds of species—humans, elves, dwarves, orcs, goblins, horses, cows, sheep, and the like—and raised them into a force that would pose little danger in smaller groups but were useful in larger numbers."

Skharr kicked a piece of skull away from his boot. He would never understand the appeal or the greed that went into using magic to raise the dead.

"Are the bones any danger as they are now?" he questioned.

"Not much, but they could be used to make more bones gathered in the future stronger, as they do now," she confirmed. "Which is why I suggest we burn them as they are. Fire has a… cleansing effect on runes like these."

They worked to quickly gather the shattered remains into a pile. Skharr poured pitch over the stack that came almost to his waist and set it alight with the torch.

Despite her calmness, he could see that the sight of so many corpses was bothering the paladin. She had a vibrant hatred for necromancy and all things like it, but this appeared to be more deeply ingrained—certainly beyond what he felt comfortable asking about.

They waited to see the fire die down. It didn't take long and the bones wouldn't be turned to ash, but all were left scorched black by the flames before Cassandra finally looked satisfied and indicated that it was time for them to go.

"Down this way!" Abirat called and gestured them to another crack in the wall that had been hidden by the skeletons they'd burned. It looked accidental like the bones were supposed to be sealed away from the rest of the place, but a crack had developed across the wall in the back and gave them a view of another chamber on the other side.

"You look uncomfortable," the paladin whispered to Skharr as they went through the crack one at a time.

"Aren't you?"

She nodded. "Yes, but I might have a reason to be. You…well, you've been in situations like this before, yes?"

"And I survived by never feeling comfortable in any moment

of it. If nothing is attacking us now, it only means that something larger will be waiting for us later. As long as we stay uncomfortable, we might stay alive."

Cassandra nodded. "I suppose that makes sense."

"I am also unsure if I'll be able to fit through that opening."

That brought a grin to her features as she studied the crack in the wall that Grakoor now moved through.

"You'll have to move through it sideways," she suggested. "It will be a squeeze but I think you'll make it. If all else fails, you could simply remove your clothes and try that way."

"I worry that was always what you wanted to see."

She tilted her head and smirked unashamedly. "I will never admit to it."

Skharr motioned for her to go ahead of him. "I believe you are next to move through. And it is for the best, truly, as it would give me something to push toward."

Cassandra laughed and made sure to shimmy as she glided through the opening without difficulty. "It would be best to get moving then, barbarian."

He shook his head but the amused expression faded rapidly from his face when he looked at the pile of corpses they were leaving behind. It was probably not a sound idea to think about it too much but he couldn't help it. How many had been warriors who, like them, had entered the dungeon with all the confidence in the world?

CHAPTER FOURTEEN

"What do you suppose that is?' Abirat asked.

"It looks like instruments of torture," Salis responded.

"It is likely that these instruments were used for the infliction of pain," Grakoor explained, "but their true use is the presentation of the victim as a sacrifice. You can see how they all force the victim to look in the direction of the statue against the wall. The pain is meant to be some kind of offering to the god involved, although whether it is a willing offering or not... Well, that is the question."

"Why would anyone willingly offer themselves up to be subjected to this kind of pain?" the half-elf asked.

"There are a few cultures where it is a way to escape a dishonorable death."

"Fuck that." Abirat growled his disgust. "An honorable way to die is with a sword in hand, preferably in someone else's gut while I die. That is how I plan to leave this world."

"It's good for you to plan," Cassandra muttered. "I'm sure the gods will take your plans into consideration."

Skharr scowled as he pushed himself a little harder through

the crack in the wall and felt it scrape across his chest. There had been no need for him to step out of his armor to pass through but it was still an uncomfortable squeeze to get through an aperture that the rest of them hadn't had too much trouble climbing through.

Still, it wasn't long until he was on the other side and could finally see what they were talking about.

Three torture devices were easily recognized as that, and a handful of others that he couldn't identify were in pieces.

One of those assembled was clearly a stretcher, the kind where a person's hands and feet were roped behind them over two hard beams so the ropes could be drawn back by a crank a few feet behind it. It was fairly common among torturers in the world, as was the breaking wheel on the far side. He had seen them in action and his stomach still churned at the thought.

The one in the center was the most recognizable and one he remembered seeing as a boy. It stirred the memories of dull fears at seeing what traitors, murderers, and rapists were condemned to. The clans could not tolerate crime, nor could they see to the death of their people lightly, which left them no choice but to make any deaths sanctioned by the clans to be levied in a painful manner.

There were two pedestals in the front, where the penitent was meant to kneel. Barbarians were meant to hold the poles on their own and never release them, but straps and chains were fixed in place for this particular iteration. The second piece was a small cage that would be wrapped around the penitent's ribs, with a hook blade that was driven into them. This would latch onto the ribs and with the use of a crank, would open the ribs out to expose the lungs, which would then be left out to freeze. Most penitents would be dead before the ribs were fully opened, but Skharr remembered seeing one man who survived in the freezing cold for almost three hours.

A penitent would regain all honor after his crimes if he

suffered through the torture in silence. All honor would be lost and it would become about punishment if he cried out in pain as his ribs were slowly forced apart.

He didn't think he would see any of the devices so far from his home. It was one of the practices he'd found to be truly barbaric among DeathEaters. He could understand it but he'd never enjoyed seeing it.

"What is that one?" Salis was asking.

"Maybe something to remove the internal organs?" Grakoor asked.

"It's to give him wings," the barbarian explained. "The skin on the back is sliced into near the spine and hooks are inserted to catch the ribs and opened out again."

"Oh." The quarter-orc narrowed his eyes like he was trying to picture the precise effects of the device. "Yes, I think that would work. The victim would die fairly quickly, yes?"

"Only if you break the ribs quickly." Skharr approached the post on the right and shook his head at the straps. "If done slowly and carefully, it could last for hours."

"You've seen something like this in use before?" Abirat asked.

"It is how DeathEaters put their foulest criminals to death." His scowl deepened when he realized that Grakoor was taking notes of what he was saying, and a quick check revealed that he was making a rough sketch of what the wing-giver looked like for what the warrior hoped was for academic purposes. His type didn't pick or choose which parts of history they transcribed.

Still, the barbarian didn't want anyone else to take ideas from Grakoor's writings and making the torture device a mainstay.

"We should continue," he said brusquely and adjusted his pack from where he'd let it hang lower for his move through the narrow crack in the wall.

Abirat approached the statue the torture devices were meant to honor, checked the floor, and sifting through the dust and chunks of something Skharr did not want to speculate on.

Odd how his stomach had suddenly turned squeamish. He didn't like it. Something about this dungeon unsettled him more than he would have been otherwise. At any other time, he would make a crude joke or three about how the world was a darker place than folk tended to think, but none came to mind.

They would later. He sucked in a deep breath as the man moved away from the statue.

"There were no eyes in that one either," the redhead explained. "I thought they would be gems too."

"Judging by the size, I would say that the eyes might have been the rubies our friends who escaped were carrying out," Cassandra pointed out. "The jewels were likely grabbed by something small that likes to play with shiny things and brought it out to where the men escaped from."

They pressed forward into another long hallway, where more defaced paintings hung on the wall. Again, the only parts that were left untouched each time were the people on the boat. Some of the depictions had waves and others had icebergs in the background. The paintings were depicting a journey being taken by these people, but the story was incomplete.

"What is this place?" Abirat asked.

"It looks like a temple," the paladin said. "Although what exactly the temple is honoring is difficult to determine. All depictions of it have been destroyed."

"Hidden," Skharr agreed. "Intentionally obfuscated."

"Do you think this is a temple to the Old God?" Salis asked. "But why would it want all images of itself struck away?"

"Perhaps they were struck away by the folks who put them to sleep," Grakoor muttered. "If this is where the Old God was put to sleep, perhaps all that we see is conjured from its mind. A sleeping god can still dream, after all."

"What does that mean?" the warrior asked.

"I don't know but I don't like it." The quarter-orc tapped his extended teeth and shook his head. "We should leave this place and never come back."

"I never took you for coward, Grak." Abirat smirked.

"It is not cowardice to know when you have no chance of success and choose life over pointless death."

"Surviving by running away is not survival," the man retorted.

"Enough!" Skharr snapped and raised his voice loudly enough that it echoed through the hopefully empty hallway. "Whatever we choose to do, we do together. Bury any animosity and remember that you'll die on your own here."

Abirat and Grakoor both stopped their squabbling as if they could agree on that, at least. As the group proceeded warily, the barbarian dropped back, concerned that something might like to attack them from behind.

Cassandra followed him and tucked a few strands of hair into the band. "Do you think that there is something here that causes strife?"

"It could be. Or it could merely be nerves. My advice is that we should not make assumptions about anything here."

She nodded and peered cautiously over her shoulder to make sure nothing was moving beyond the line of their torchlight.

"Have you had any godly visitations?" she asked after a moment. "Does Theros have anything to say about our presence here?"

Skharr shook his head slowly. "Nothing so far. But I'll be sure to inform you the moment he pops into my consciousness."

The paladin smiled and looked back again like she expected something to follow them. It was beginning to wear on his last nerve.

"Over here!"

The welcome distraction drew their attention and they turned immediately to where Grakoor squatted over breaks in the dust that coated the ground.

"I've made some rough measurements," the quarter-orc whispered and ran his fingers over the traces. "We are moving in a circle and from what I can tell, if we continue along this path, we'll end up in the torture chamber again."

"What are you looking at there?" Cassandra asked.

"A door." He straightened and narrowed his eyes at the wall, which revealed no interesting markings or any sign that markings had been ripped and torn from it.

"And you simply happened to find it?" Abirat asked. "How?"

"Because I was looking for it," the quarter-orc snapped, annoyed.

Skharr moved closer and frowned as he lowered his torch over a few marks farther away from the door than it would swing.

"What do you see there?" Salis asked.

"Boot marks—old ones," he explained. "And...they appear to be dragging a body. Or...something."

He had to remember his own advice. Making assumptions about a dungeon was a dangerous business and one that he had no intention of indulging in.

"Well, there is no way to open the door," Cassandra said and pointed out the obvious. "While we try to find our way forward, we should get some rest and food and gather our bearings."

Skharr didn't like the idea, but the rest seemed to be weary and ready for rest. He would certainly be outnumbered if they voted on the subject. He settled next to them as Cassandra started a small fire.

There was no talk about setting a watch. The fact remained that they most likely didn't want to risk falling asleep for fear of never waking up again.

"Do you know what we could use right now?" Salis asked and glanced at Abirat.

"Son of a whore," he hissed. "I already told you. Until I can restock my supply, I will be the only one who partakes of my koffe—me and me alone. You can buy your own if you feel the need for it."

"We could do that now," Skharr suggested.

"What?" Abirat asked.

"You already claimed some treasure for yourself that you'll share with all of us once we are clear of this," he continued. "If you were allowed to keep your hands on those sapphires you found, you'll share your supply of the coffee—"

"Koffe," the man corrected him.

"Whatever. Consider it your way to earn the full cost of those gems you intended to keep anyway, yes?"

Abirat stared across the fire at him for a few moments and finally shook his head, confirming his suspicions about his intentions. They all poured water from their skins into his small pot, and he added the thick black powder and stirred the contents until the whole hallway was filled with the rich, bitter smell of the brew.

Skharr still wasn't partial to the taste but he appreciated the way it staved off the exhaustion he'd felt creeping over him.

"You don't strike me as the type of person who is often deep in thought," Grakoor commented, seated next to Skharr as Cassandra moved closer from the other side. "And I fear that might be your way of letting folk underestimate you."

"It might be possible that you know something about using the prejudices of others against them." Skharr raised an eyebrow at the quarter-orc, who laughed.

"Aye. I might. Which means that when there is something on your mind so consuming as to allow you to drop your façade, it is likely important."

He nodded slowly. "I…I have a feeling. It concerns how most of the dungeons have some type of connection to the gods. I am merely wondering if there was some kind of connection between this dungeon and the Lord High God Janus. Perhaps he created it, which might be why it is causing us so many troubles."

"It's an interesting thought," Cassandra whispered and leaned her back against the wall. "But I am not sure how that would help us."

"It might give us an idea of what we are up against, if nothing else," he said quietly. "But it is a feeling only and nothing more. We should get some real rest but must have someone awake at all times to make sure that nothing attacks."

Skharr looked at Grakoor, and the quarter-orc nodded.

"I can take the first watch," Cassandra whispered. "I don't feel comfortable sleeping here anyway."

"That is understandable," he agreed, but he felt the need to close his eyes. Only for a moment and no longer, he promised. He didn't want to be killed in his sleep.

CHAPTER FIFTEEN

Sleep came and went. Skharr didn't know what he had expected, if anything, but when his eyes opened—almost of their own volition—he could remember none of his dreams.

Annoyingly, he didn't feel any better rested than he had before his eyes closed, but once he was up, he knew he'd not fall asleep again.

Cassandra had curled against the wall, and it was Salis' turn to watch over the group.

"Did you get some rest?" she asked as he pushed up and stretched with a low groan.

"Aye." He scowled and shook his head. "I'm not sure I feel it, though."

She nodded and looked like she felt the same way but didn't want to say it aloud.

There would be no cooking from him today, and all he could spare for himself was a few strips of dried meat and waybread, which he shared with some water with Salis once he sat next to her.

"Has anything struck you on how we might be able to open that door?" he mumbled around a mouthful of the dried foods.

"Nothing," she whispered and pressed her back against the opposite wall. "I tried to search for any handles hidden in the stonework. Cassandra tried to cast a handful of revealing and opening spells. Nothing worked. Has this ever happened in your other trips through your dungeons?"

Skharr nodded. "There were doors in the Tower. They always required that folk died for them to open, but I hope it will not be the case this time."

"What is the alternative?" she asked as she took a sip of water.

"Waiting outside for the door to open from the inside. There is someone in there, that much we know."

"How did you know that folk needed to die outside the doors in the Tower?"

Skharr shook his head. "There was writing on the doors in dozens of different languages. It was what told us to start killing each other until the necessary numbers were reached."

The half-elf lowered her gaze and toyed with her javelins. "Grakoor and I have traveled together for years. Abirat as well. I wouldn't kill them to get in here, not for all the coin in the world."

"In that case, Grakoor might have had the right of it," Skharr whispered and shook his head. "Turn, leave this place behind, and never look back."

She nodded. "I know Abirat and I quarrel, but it's more along the lines of siblings bantering. Nothing that I would ever consider worthy of death."

"I wouldn't kill folk for treasure, not unless they were trying to kill me," Skharr noted. "No, that's not quite true. I've killed more than my fair share for coin. But I wouldn't turn on those that I've been fighting alongside for coin."

Salis laughed. "Well, I appreciate hearing that. If there were a stipulation that only one could pass through, I would place coin on you surviving."

"Me too. But you would have to attack me first."

The half-elf opened her mouth to reply when she was cut off by the sound of stone grinding on stone.

Skharr was on his feet almost immediately, his sword already cleared from its sheath as the door across from them began to open. It was larger than they had expected and knocked their fire over with enough of a crackle to gather the attention of the rest of the group and drag them from their sleep.

On the other side of the door, three men stood and looked almost as surprised as Skharr and Salis were. Their eyes widened and their hands reached for the clubs they carried on hooks hanging from their belts.

The barbarian was already in motion. He jumped forward and leveled his sword across the neck of the man closest to him. The blow severed the head from his shoulders in a slash clean enough that it tumbled into the wall beside him.

Another had already drawn his weapon and tried to swing it at Skharr but he fell back with a javelin protruding from his chest before he could so much as blink.

The third and last of the group reacted the fastest and was already racing out of sight.

"Come on!" the warrior roared. The door had begun to swing closed, which left them almost no time to snatch their possessions and race through again.

Lit torches illuminated a winding, stone staircase that descended to where they could hear footsteps pattering. Skharr was at the front and took the steps two and three at a time to catch up. He didn't pause to listen for the rest of his group behind him.

All he could hope for was that either the man running for his life was alone, or that Cassandra and the others would be close behind him in case he ran into a trap.

The steps came to an end and led into another hallway, although Skharr didn't spare the time to look for the same ruined paintings on the walls, which were illuminated by torches on sconces.

At least the light made it easier to keep running after the man who tried to escape.

The man was flagging visibly as he tried to reach a door at the end. A heavy steel lever on the door itself was likely what had been used to open it to the staircase above, but there was no time to think about that.

Skharr closed quickly and a roar ripped from his throat almost before he realized it as he drove his blade forward and through the man's back with a thrust powerful enough to punch out the other side. Blood sprayed across the stone door.

The handle had already been turned and the same sound of stone grinding on stone rumbled as it swung open slowly. The fact that these mechanisms were still oiled and functional showed that there were more people in the dungeon than the three who had been killed.

A glance over his shoulder confirmed that the rest of the group were close behind him. Salis had retrieved her javelin from the man she'd killed and now tried to clean the blood from the head.

"Couldn't you have kept him alive?" Cassandra asked, her sword already out. "We could have questioned him."

"Put the torture chamber above to good use," Abirat added.

"And now we have no one alive who can tell us what is happening down here," the paladin continued as the door began to open.

It moved slowly but there was no sound aside from the noise that the stone door made as it scraped the floor when it pushed out into another, larger chamber.

This one was well-lit with torches and a chandelier hanging above and it opened into what looked like a small amphitheater. A massive statue stood at the front. The head had been removed and the arms had been placed on top of the stump of the neck to make it look like a creature with horns—or perhaps tentacles, as the hands were splayed with the fingers spread.

Approximately sixty people were gathered inside—men and women and mostly human, although Skharr noticed a few elves and five dwarves. They all wore the same drab robes as the three dead men and the acolytes now turned as one to look at the five mercenaries who had appeared at their doorstep.

On the stage of the amphitheater, a dozen or so beds each held another robe-wearing individual, and a single man stood among them. He looked like he was performing some kind of ceremony and waved a fresh oak sprig over those on the beds while he sprayed what the barbarian hoped to all the gods was water.

The man was massive and was dressed in a long, pristine white robe with a gold rope wrapped around his waist. He was taller than Skharr was, with broad shoulders and thick arms that bulged through the sleeves of his robe. A thick, bushy brown beard complemented his long auburn locks with thick streaks of gray through them.

"He looks a little like a barbarian," Abirat commented as they made their way down the steps that led to the stage. "Are the two of you related?"

Skharr snapped the man a sharp glare and shook his head. "His features are too fine. No scars. In short, a little too beautiful to be from The Clan."

His teammate seemed content with the explanation, and they stopped short of the seats that were filled with the robe wearers,

"Welcome to the Temple of BaroonPatel, travelers!" The bearded man's voice boomed through the room in an almost unnatural volume. "I am High Priest K'Shallot, and I hope that the road that led you to us was lush and peaceful."

Skharr looked back at the way that they came and raised an eyebrow. "You can see the body we left at the door of this... temple. One of your kin?"

"Followers," Cassandra corrected him.

"Followers." He nodded firmly.

"True, but the misunderstanding serves a higher purpose. I can only hope that peace fills your soul from this point forward in your journey."

"I have one question," he retorted and took another step down, still gripping his blood-soaked blade as he narrowed his eyes at the group that stood closest to him. They shuffled away quickly. "Who the fuck is BaroonPatel? Not any god that I've ever heard of, and I doubt that you were ordained as high priest by any of the Elevated Temples that I've ever seen. They tend to choose an aesthetic who is lean, frail, old, and scholarly. In short, very unlike you."

"BaroonPatel is one of the Old Gods," Cassandra explained, her voice a whisper although it carried well beyond what she intended. "Or at least one of the names they chose for themselves."

"BaroonPatel is a benevolent god, granting prosperity to all who ask it with humility and a pure heart," the giant said with a brilliant smile.

"And a little sacrifice, I suppose?" Cassandra completed helpfully as she stopped beside Skharr.

"Nothing in this world is for free," the man replied, still smiling. "All that one must consider is if the price one is willing to pay is worth that which is granted in return. It's simple exchange, the kind that all economies in this world are based on."

"As I recall, the kinds of economies that are based on exchanges involving those torture implements we saw above have been shunned by civilized societies," the barbarian stated, his tone accusatory. There was no need to comment on how his people were shunned for the barbaric practices.

The man nodded and looked at the people in the beds around him as he placed the oak sprig carefully on a nearby table and slipped his hands into his sleeves.

"Your lack of faith is your undoing, travelers," K'Shallot said. His smile remained but his voice suddenly dripped with menace. "But you can be taught the error of your ways, you may yet prove beneficial to others if not yourselves."

"Now that sounded like a threat," Skharr replied and glanced at his sword. "What do you think?"

"Most certainly a threat," Cassandra agreed.

"Did we begin to take threats on our lives lightly?" Abirat wondered aloud. "I wasn't aware of this sudden change of our group perspective."

"Not as far as I am aware," Salis agreed.

K'Shallot shook his head, and Skharr noticed that most of those who had been in the seats had begun to file out quietly.

Some remained and joined the high priest on the stage.

He removed his hands from his sleeves once most of the followers had vacated the amphitheater and now held a dagger in his hands.

"Observe," he instructed them. "And believe."

The dagger slashed across the throat of the young woman who lay closest to him. She didn't even raise her hands to defend herself.

The others— eight of them—who remained also held daggers in their hands. Deftly, they cut eight more throats.

Something white-hot touched the bottom of Skharr's gut and he took another step forward down the steps toward the stage.

"You're right," he said. "I do believe that you and yours need to be put down."

The high priest suddenly flung his dagger at the barbarian. His speed was impressive for a man that size, and he was barely able to raise his sword to deflect the blade to his left, where it buried itself almost to the hilt in one of the seats.

"Dispose of them, my warriors," K'Shallot ordered. "Show them your faith!"

He wasn't surprised that the high priest himself walked away from the fight in the same direction as the rest of his flock. Skharr grasped his weapon tighter and narrowed his eyes at the group as they began to move off the stage toward him.

"We'll see what your faith can do for you." He growled a challenge, twirled his sword, and felt the need to loosen his wrist a little as the first of them approached and brandished a dagger identical to the high priest's.

His eyes widened suddenly and he looked at his chest from which a black-hafted arrow now protruded. As if of its own volition, his hand groped to reach it before he sagged and fell, dead before he landed.

The second showed no sign that he even saw his comrade fall. Instead, he screamed defiance as he charged with his dagger raised.

He moved faster than Skharr thought a man like that could move. It felt safe to assume that he would be stronger too. He had felt the impact of the thrown knife and seen it embed itself in the stone.

Had killing those people made them stronger or was that some sick form of proving their faith to the high priest? He watched the man approach, readied himself for a fight, and studied his opponent's movements.

Even with increased speed, the man's movements were those of an amateur—one who had no idea how to fight. The barbarian took a step to the side to avoid the fierce thrust aimed at his chest. He drew the sword across the acolyte's chest, sliced easily through the gray robes, and hacked through flesh and bone.

The slash almost cut the man in half and his body spasmed as he dropped to stain the cold stone floor red with his blood.

The warrior turned to the next one, but one of Cassandra's daggers protruded from his neck. It was a lethal wound although the man appeared to ignore it. He continued his attempted assault on Skharr until a javelin caught him on the side of the head and thrust him back to the stage.

Seeing three of their comrades fall in rapid succession was enough to convince the five who remained that their faith was no substitute for proper armor. They turned quickly and ran in the direction in which the high priest had gone. Skharr shook his head.

"They're youths," Cassandra whispered. "Tossed at us like animals."

He scowled at her, yanked her dagger and the javelin from the last man to be killed, and handed her the blade. "Is that so unlike what they did to you as paladins?"

She opened her mouth but shook her head quickly. "In essence, no, but we were always sent off well-armed, armored, and ready for battle. These were not. He threw them at us like he did not mind their deaths but wanted to slow us."

Salis took the javelin from him. "We'll show him how his own medicine tastes when we catch up to him."

The paladin nodded and climbed to the stage and the three who were still alive on their cots. They appeared to be asleep and she opened one of their eyes with her fingers and inspected it closely.

"They've been sedated," she whispered, leaned closer, and sniffed close to the young woman's lips. "Henbane seeds."

"From the smell?" Skharr asked.

"Aye. It has a very unique foul odor."

"Will they live?"

She nodded.

"Then we should continue after the others. Come on."

She nodded and straightened quickly as they moved ahead through the same door the others had used. More hallways and tunnels led deeper into the earth, and Skharr could still hear footsteps from the last of the acolytes as they raced away.

They weren't too far ahead, and he had a mind to make sure that no others were pointlessly murdered for their faith. A few more doors were still open, and he slipped through one of them when he saw shadows cast. He was close enough to smell them now, growling and anxious for a fight.

Suddenly, something moved beneath his feet. One of the flagstones had elevated but was now depressed under his weight and in that moment, he could hear the mechanism moving inside the walls.

The sound issued from behind them, and a slab of heavy rock came down a few feet away. It was a trap, likely meant to protect someone playing acolyte from those who might be in pursuit although those who had fled hadn't thought to activate it to seal Skharr off.

But the slab was still coming down, directly over where Salis stood.

"Look out!"

The warning came too late, and the half-elf could only look up as the stone dropped over her. In the moment before she was crushed, something shoved her beyond the slab and fell onto the heavy stones that comprised the floor around them.

"Abirat!"

Skharr remained where he was and stared in horror as a dead weight dropped through his chest and into his stomach when he saw the young redheaded swordsman on the ground. The man lay still under the stone that had fallen on top of him.

CHAPTER SIXTEEN

"Abirat!"

Skharr didn't need to check the man physically to know that he was dead. The slab was made of granite and its impact had crushed the young swordsman's entire torso beneath it. Blood seeped out through the cracks in the stones as if to emphasize it.

That didn't stop Salis from trying to reach under it to lift it off the man. Tears streamed down her cheeks.

"Help me!" she cried and looked frantically at her teammates. "We can lift it off him!"

Skharr couldn't help. His feet felt like they were rooted to the spot and he simply stared at Abirat's head and shoulders that jutted out from beneath the slab.

He had caused this. His blood lust had been so consuming that he hadn't bothered to think there would be traps in place.

Salis would have died had Abirat not intervened, and his reward was being crushed. At least it was a quick death, which was likely more than what many of the folk who died in this dungeon were allowed.

Cassandra looked around and knelt beside the half-elf.

"We need to keep moving," she said, her voice soft and comforting. "We are not safe in here."

"Please...help me lift—"

"He's gone, Salis."

She turned on the paladin and her watery eyes flashed with anger. "You don't know that. He could..."

Whatever reasonings she had in her mind evaporated quickly before she could speak them, and she shook her head and ran her fingers gently through the dead man's hair.

"We...can't leave him here," she whispered.

"Never let our considerations for the dead endanger the living," the paladin said, and took Salis' hands in her own. "Honor his sacrifice by surviving. Please. We need you."

The half-elf shook her head, but finally pushed to her feet and cleaned her blood-soaked hands carelessly on her clothes.

"We should go," she whispered as her eyes transformed suddenly into cold orbs full of rage. "And kill the bastards responsible."

Skharr was the one responsible. He half-expected her to drive one of her javelins through his chest as she passed but she walked to where Grakoor was waiting instead.

Cassandra moved close to the barbarian, who continued to stare at the body.

"Are you with me, Skharr?"

He didn't know what to say. There was no answer that she would be able to understand.

His face stung unexpectedly, and he blinked when he realized that the paladin had slapped him across the cheek. Hard. He was sure there was a bright red handprint on his left cheek.

"I can't lead them alone!" she insisted and her voice cracked as she grasped his chin savagely to force him to look into her eyes. "So, I ask again. Are you with me, Skharr?"

He clenched his jaw and nodded slowly.

"I am with you."

"You can deal with whatever guilt you feel later. For now, we need to find a way to survive this. Come on."

She made an excellent point. He was responsible, of course, but for the rest of them to make it out alive, he needed to gather his wits. There would be time for Salis to use him for target practice with her javelins later.

"I'll kill all the fuckers!" Grakoor roared and hefted his hammer as they continued down the hallway.

"We should remain together!" Cassandra shouted and Skharr ran to catch up as quickly as he could. "That way we can avoid any further—"

Her voice was cut off as another click was heard and another flagstone slipping into the floor. This time, the half-elf had stepped on it.

Skharr's eyes widened as he looked for a slab of rock that fear told him would crush Cassandra this time.

The slab did come but thankfully, it was a few paces ahead of where the paladin stood.

The ground shuddered as it settled heavily and sealed them off from where Salis and Grakoor now stood.

"Shit!" Cassandra advanced on it and tried to pull it up but it proved as immovable as the one that had crushed Abirat. "Shit! Fuck! This…this is what happens when we lose focus!"

Skharr nodded. "I'm…I didn't mean to—"

She shook her head. "No…I didn't mean… That isn't what I meant and you know it. It's only…now, we are separated into tunnels infested with a…a murder cult!"

He could see that she had begun to lose the edge that had helped her calm Salis, and realized that it was his turn to ground her for the moment.

With a single quick step, he was able to close the distance between them and placed his hand on her shoulder, effectively clamping her in place.

"We need to stay focused!" Skharr added a clipped and almost cold tone to the words and made sure she was looking at him when he spoke. "We are still in danger and there is no time for wallowing."

She stared at him and her mouth opened and closed a few times before she shook her head. "Right... yes. We'll need to—oh, they need to stop doing that!"

Skharr stiffened at the sounds of doors swinging open behind them. His sword was already in hand and he spun toward the approaching footsteps.

He was thankful that it was an acolyte like the others and not an innocent, as the blow severed the woman's head cleanly from her body. It brought a quick surge of pleasure to have a weapon that was capable of that. At least three more pressed forward, holding daggers and ready to attack.

One fell back and clutched a knife that suddenly appeared in his neck. Skharr advanced on a second, who tried to back away as he sliced his sword across the acolyte's stomach. The blade penetrated deeply enough that he could see the contents of the man's bowels slide out of the wound.

The last one retreated hastily in the direction from which she'd come. Before the teammates could stop her, she took hold of another lever on the wall, but it wasn't to close the door.

The barbarian cursed when something shifted under his feet. Instinctively, he looked down but the flagstones that had felt so secure a moment before suddenly fell away as the support beneath them disappeared.

"Skharr!"

Cassandra flailed and clutched his arm, not realizing that his footing wasn't any more secure than hers, and they fell together. The darkness engulfed them and the warrior could focus on nothing more than the sensation of her tight grasp before everything went cold.

The temperature seemed to have plummeted in an instant.

The room was quiet, especially when the door shut behind them. Salis turned and tried to decide where they were. Her sense of direction was completely lost underground, which was why she hated being in tunnels for too long.

It was an unsettling feeling, and she loathed it. Still, there would be time for her to make that complaint later.

"They took all my weapons," Grakoor muttered belligerently and peered around the room. "Even my hidden dagger."

"Where did you keep it hidden?"

"Under my arm. Why?"

Salis shook her head. "Never mind."

She felt naked and missed her armor, weapons, and everything else that generally allowed her to feel safer. Of course, she could fight with her fists better than most, but it still felt unnerving, even if she wore the thin gray robes that the acolytes wore.

"I'm sorry I wasn't more help," Grakoor said as he shook his head and tapped his half-tusks. "I think I crushed a couple of skulls before they swarmed me."

"You did better than I did," she admitted. "I wasn't even able to bring my spear to bear before the bastards grabbed me. There must have been at least...I don't know, twenty of them?"

He nodded and looked around the room. "We need to find a way out of here. There has to be more of those...tunnels or traps hidden around here someplace, right?"

Salis sighed and rubbed her eyes. "Yes...I suppose so."

"Use your elf eyes to find something, then?"

"My elf eyes?"

"Your...you know what I mean." He growled a protest.

"Yes, I do. And you're lucky that I do."

There was something oily about the water. It smelled foul too, and Skharr found that his clothes drying after they were soaked in it only made it worse. As a solution, he removed them entirely.

Cassandra was the worse off of the two of them. She had been wearing her leathers and they reeked even worse. To try to ease the stench, she had stripped down to the mail undergarments she'd worn before and shivered gently when he pulled a few clothes that had escaped the water from his packs.

"You know," he said and offered her one of his shirts, "I don't think I've ever seen a warrior wearing anything...like that. It is oddly appealing."

She didn't put the shirt on immediately but paused, tilted her head, and regarded him calmly. The garment was too large for her anyway, and she smirked.

"No warriors?" she asked, glanced at the mail, and patted it where it covered her breasts. "Not even...say, a barbarian princess or two?"

"I don't think any of the clans have any semblance of royalty," Skharr muttered. "Why would a princess wear anything like that anyway? Royalty would want to be well-protected and not... exposed, I guess."

"Suppose the princess wanted to be exposed?"

It felt odd that they were commenting on clothes when they had fallen into the murky, foul water and were now separated from the rest of their group. But then again, he wasn't sure if there was anything else for them to think about.

And in the end, there was something appealing about her appearance in the mail undergarments. Distractingly so, and he tried hard to not stare too obviously.

"Well, they should," she insisted his shirt still scrunched in her hands. "A woman should wear what makes her feel powerful and I do feel that way. I have a mind to wear this and only this in the future. It would certainly make paladins look better than we do now."

"I cannot disagree."

"Besides, if I read your intentions correctly, the outfit does have a few tactical advantages."

"It might distract a few...more than a few," Skharr admitted. "But is it worth the potential risks?"

"You do remember that the armor is based on the magical amulet that comes with the outfit?"

His gaze drifted to her collarbone where the amulet resided and he attempted to make sure that was all his eyes were looking at.

He failed but it was a valiant effort, nonetheless.

"It's quite effective as a tactical diversion." She beamed and put her hands on her hips.

The barbarian nodded and drew a deep breath as he looked at where his clothes were drying. "I...yes, quite."

She walked over to where he stood and made sure to slip out in front of him. A smile touched her face as she moved closer to him than she had been before.

"I know what you're thinking, you know," she whispered and allowed her gaze to wander over his bare chest.

"Your abilities as a paladin extend to telepathy?"

"No, but you do make it a little obvious. And I enjoy seeing it play across your face while you pretend it is not there. You can be subtle about it but in some ways, you are as easy to read as the simplest man."

"Are you calling me simple?"

She placed a hand on his chest to ensure that his attention was on her and not their supplies.

"Never." Her voice was soft but intense. There was an underlying intention to it, and not merely a flirtatious quirk. "But your intentions are. I think you deliberately make them so. You are an odd creature in that you want to be the dull, dimwitted barbarian you pretend to be."

Skharr couldn't find it in himself to disagree. His gaze and his mind were focused fully on the way her hand glided lightly down his chest.

"What was I thinking, then?" he asked.

"Hmm?"

"You said you knew what I was thinking. What do you think I was thinking?"

She smiled, tilted her head, and inched forward, close enough that he could feel the heat radiating from her skin.

"You were thinking about whether the amulet would be able to protect me even if I am not wearing the chain mail."

That was amazing as it was exactly what he had been thinking although he didn't want to admit it outright.

"Was I right or not?" she asked as she moved her hand to his stomach.

"Absolutely correct," he answered. His voice was thick with something that had begun to build within him. It expanded rapidly as her hands caught the top of the trousers he wore.

"I am quite the psychic." She grinned.

"Are you?"

She pushed his trousers down as she slid her hand lower and a small smile touched her lips. Finally, she dragged her gaze away from his to look at what now pressed against her fingertips.

"I suppose you'll have to find out, won't you?" she murmured and licked her lips. "We won't be able to find a way out of here until all of our equipment is dry and functional again anyway."

Skharr tried to focus. "What?"

"I saw what you were thinking again. You were wondering about whether we had time for you to test the effectiveness of my amulet without the chain mail—which you'll have to remove if you have a mind to reach what's under it."

He knew he wasn't the type to be timid about anything and so pushed any momentary confusion aside as he moved his hands to the straps that held her undergarments in place.

It was simple enough to send them tumbling to the floor and

they clattered a little louder than most undergarments would have as she pressed herself against him a little tighter.

The barbarian caught the back of her head and tilted it up as he lowered himself to press his lips to her neck and breathe her heady scent.

"As much as I trust the amulet," she whispered and shivered against him, "I had better be able to walk after this."

He smirked and drifted a hand down her back, grasped her rear, and dragged her in closer to press her body tightly against his.

"Don't be afraid," he assured her. "I should be able to carry you if you have trouble remaining on your feet."

She bit her bottom lip and stretched up to grab his neck so she could pull herself up to wrap her thighs around his waist.

"I think I'm woman enough for the job," she retorted as she threaded a hand through his hair and twisted a handful in her fingers. "Now get to testing, barbarian."

CHAPTER SEVENTEEN

His clothes were dry, although the smell would need a deeper wash or ten to be removed in full. Still, Skharr felt as though they were pushing in the right direction once they were dressed again. As Cassandra had assumed, the place that they had fallen into was meant to be used as an escape instead of an actual trap. The water had been there to break their fall where a drop onto the hard floor would have killed or maimed them.

Once they were dressed and armored again and once they started looking in earnest, it was easy to find a small series of steel ladders that had been set into the walls and led them up to the level from which they had fallen.

It had been an easy decision to let Cassandra climb ahead of him. If something waited for them at the top of the ladders and one of them fell, Skharr would have a better chance of catching her than the other way around. In the end, if he was at the top, he would knock her down with him if he were to fall.

He wouldn't tell her the real reason why he hadn't protested her taking the lead. There would be a place and a time for them to talk about what happened while they waited for their clothes and equipment to dry, but it wasn't here or now.

"What do you think this place was?" she asked and broke his focus.

"I...what?"

"Well, we know it was a temple, but what kind of temple is built like this? Why would there be doors that close behind people? Traps that hurl people into foul-smelling water to keep them alive?"

She made a good point. It did seem to be built with an odd system that was intended to protect someone who was running through the hallways instead of endangering them.

"Skharr? Are you staring at my ass again?"

He jerked his head up, a little startled when he realized it was there for him to stare at.

"Would you be annoyed if I said yes?"

She paused to look at him. "Well, you did considerably more than stare at it earlier so I cannot see why I would be. But did you hear what I said?"

"I can stare and listen at the same time," he replied. "What do you have in mind?"

"Well, the fact that you cannot tear your attention from my posterior."

"In my defense, it is directly in front of me." He grinned, determined to enjoy the view while it lasted. "I could always take your place at the top, but you would have to make sure to catch me should I fall."

She considered this as they continued their climb and finally, she sighed. "Fine, stare all you please. Is it odd that I now wish for some godsbedammed plate armor?"

"Do you?" Skharr asked. "I assumed that you chose the...uh, attire you did for the sheer physical attractiveness that it imbued you with."

"I assumed I would be able to keep it covered until it was best to reveal it," she explained as they reached the top, where a small hatch opened in the rock for them to climb through. "I never thought the leathers that covered it would be ruined by a simple dive in the water."

"Leather is a fine, light armor, but it does have its disadvantages," Skharr growled as she reached down to help him up the last few rungs of the ladder. "Your armor is still functional, I suppose, although I think we proved that you do have to keep the mail on for it to be effective."

"Either that or the magic was not designed to take the full attention of a barbarian," she agreed hauled him as hard as she could while he pushed through the hatch. Neither took a step back once he was through it.

"Not much defensive magic in the world can withstand a focused attack from a DeathEater," he agreed and smiled when she steadfastly refused to back away from him. "Do you honestly think you should have brought plate armor?"

She shrugged. "I don't know but I do know that I'm not inclined to attract all the barbarians who are hiding dragons in their loincloth."

"A dragon like mine would be difficult to hide anyway," he countered.

She laughed. "You have a point there. Come on, we need to find Salis and Grakoor. Assuming—"

Her features sobered and her gaze lost some of the pleasant humor that had been in them since they had started their slow climb.

Skharr placed a hand on her shoulder. "They are alive and waiting for us, somewhere. We merely need to find them. Once we do, we'll locate this Old God of yours, kill it, and continue on our merry way."

She nodded firmly. Empty platitudes did have their place, he decided. In this case, they had to focus on the best possible scenario if they were not to descend into madness.

"Come on, we'll find our way back." He growled and hefted his weapon as they followed the hallway. The space was lit by torches, which he assumed probably burned magically since there were too many to replace on a regular basis.

It wasn't long before they reached the place where they had fallen through. Heavy slabs of rock had returned to the spots where they had been retracted, and Skharr was careful when he stepped close to them. Part of the floor had fallen out from under them and it left an indent on the ground from where the stone floor had fallen once the slabs beneath had retracted.

"How is this all still functional?" Skharr asked as he negotiated the open section to reach the area that appeared normal.

"There are spells that would keep the mechanisms in this place functional," Cassandra answered. "If those began to fail, the dungeon would begin to fall apart. And if the spells were repaired, it would become functional again."

"And how would they repair the spells?"

"An easy and simple way is the sacrifice of living creatures," she whispered as they continued down the hallway and were about to come to the end of it. "The sacrifice of sentient creatures always has more power, although it's more corrosive to the mind of the person doing the sacrificing."

"How corroded do you think the mind of the high priest is?" he wondered aloud.

"We should find out." She drew her sword as they approached the end of the hallway. "Preferably by removing his head from his shoulders and inspecting it that way."

Her anger was something to behold and Skharr wondered what it would look like when she was truly and completely a paladin in good standing. The rage of a paladin was said to be impressive.

He stopped short of the doorway and noticed that the temple construction stopped at that point and opened out into a large, uncluttered cavern that was illuminated by the same root-like tendrils that had hung over the city. He had never seen the trees these roots were reputed to grow from or the monoliths other tales mentioned. Perhaps they hadn't found their way to the mountains where he'd grown up.

The chamber was large enough to accommodate a small lake, although he couldn't see where it was fed from. Maybe a few underground rivers, he reasoned, but there was no real sign of those.

As they approached the water cautiously, Skharr realized that there was a small island at the center with a handful of statues present on it. Although he couldn't quite make out what they were supposed to be, he couldn't shake the feeling that he'd seen something like them before although his instinct showed a marked reluctance to explore the mystery of where.

"It's like in the paintings," Cassandra said and echoed the thought he hadn't been brave enough to give voice to. "A group out in the water. I always thought they were in a boat of some kind, but I guess it could have been an island."

The barbarian shook his head and stared across the beach against which the lake lapped gently.

"Oh, shit," he snapped. A small skiff had been tied to a pier that extended into the lake some five paces or so. A handful of people huddled in the tiny craft—real people, not statues like those on the island.

He rushed to the pier but paused at the sight of the fragile wood, unsure if it would take his weight. It seemed foolish to risk touching the water unless he couldn't help it. While it had no old, foul smell to it like the cistern that they had fallen into, there was still something about it that made the murky depths feel dangerous.

Truly, caution assured him, it would be best if he just kept his distance.

"I'll go," Cassandra said when she noted his hesitation. She moved lightly over the rickety planks, untied the rope that kept the skiff in place next to the pier, and tossed it to the shore where Skharr waited for it.

Quick, firm strokes hand-over-hand brought the skiff to shore and he counted five people naked and bound to the mast at the center, all of whom appeared to be unconscious.

One of them had a stocky build and thick hair and he recognized her without needing to even see her face. The quarter-orc beside her was fairly easy to identify as well, although he had no idea who the other three in the skiff were.

"Salis?" he said and drew a knife to cut the ropes that bound them. "Grakoor? Wake the fuck up, you godsbedammed addlepated sleep wallowers or by the gods, I will hunt you in whatever afterlife you think you can retreat to and beat some sense into both of you!"

He patted Salis in the cheek once the prisoners were unbound and after a long moment she gasped, looked up, and scowled as she tried to inspect her surroundings.

"What…what happened?"

"You tell me." The barbarian patted Grakoor on the cheek a little more firmly to wake him as well. "The last we saw, you two were sealed off from us by a slab of rock."

"Oh…" Grakoor grunted and stood slowly. He looked down hastily and covered himself with his hand as they clambered out of the skiff. "We…we were captured and put in a small room. And then a…a cloud that smelled of roses filled the room and—"

"And you slapped me in the face," Salis snapped on her teammate's heels. She stepped onto the rock and didn't bother to try to cover herself. "Did you have to, or did you merely want to?"

"I was…frustrated," Skharr admitted. "And truly, it was only a little tap. But I'm damn glad to see you alive."

"Who are the others?" Cassandra asked when she rejoined them on the shore. The two men and a woman—all human—who were similarly naked began to climb out of the boat as well.

"We were part of a mercenary group," the woman explained, her expression wary as her gaze swept the area. "When we were barely a couple of chambers in, the monsters attacked—dozens of them. We...we tried to run, and I think a few managed to escape through the door, but something hit me on the back of the head, and...well, I woke here."

"Does your head still hurt?" Skharr asked.

"I...no."

"Do you feel unsettled in the stomach?"

"Not that either."

He shook his head. "You weren't hit in the back of the head."

"A spell must have caught you," Cassandra whispered.

"Oh, all right, then." She didn't seem particularly interested in how she had been rendered unconscious, although she covered herself with her hands. "We had armor on. What happened to it?"

"They stripped us of our armor and weapons," Salis commented and scowled at herself like this was the first time she realized that she had no clothes on. "And they dressed us in those gray robes the rest of the acolytes are wearing, but...I guess that would have been too much to sacrifice us in."

"Sacrifice?" one of the other mercenaries asked and studied the large chamber they were in. "If they intended to kill us, why leave us on a skiff on an underground lake?"

Skharr paused. That was a good question. These people had been roped and readied for a sacrifice, but there were none of the instruments of torture that had been present in the other section where the sacrifices were made.

"I think we should move away from the water," he whispered. As if something could read his mind, he could see the placid surface begin to move. It shuddered and shivered faintly like something moved beneath it. Their past experiences with deep water and the creatures that lurked within made him extremely cautious about being close to the water itself.

It wasn't fear, he reassured himself. Merely healthy caution, which was good.

"We have more of them!"

Skharr turned at Salis' warning. Another hallway had opened

and almost a dozen acolytes poured through. These wore not only the robes of their order but also chain mail and leather armor. They carried hammers and swords, although none of them bore any shields. Whether it was because they didn't have a mind for defensive warfare or perhaps because they relied on the weapons they had taken from the fallen warriors who visited the dungeon, he didn't know. In all honesty, he didn't much care either.

It would make the battle a little less challenging and acolytes a little easier to deal with.

He rushed ahead of the group, well aware that Cassandra was the only one who had a weapon in hand. With his sword held firmly in front of him, he rushed toward the front line and scowled at a ball and chain flail that swung toward his shoulder.

The barbarian leaned back to allow the weapon to swing past him. The man struggled to bring the weapon back to bear, which gave Skharr the opening he needed to step forward and slice his blade across the man's throat in a single motion that made the man stumble back.

A spear followed, thrust at his stomach, and he lowered his left arm to brush the head aside before he grasped the haft and dragged the man who held it stumbling forward to drive his fist into his jaw. He wasn't wearing a helmet either, which made him think that these people were not used to being in combat. It begged the question of why they now threw themselves into a fight so willingly.

The barbarian snatched the unconscious man's spear and tossed it to where Salis stood. She caught the weapon deftly and grinned at the prospect of being able to fight back. Still smiling, she lunged forward to where another of the acolytes advanced with an ax in hand. He almost didn't see her before she drove the spear into his chest. The wide, leaf-shaped head cut through his lungs and likely straight into his heart. His body instantly went limp before she drove him to the floor.

Skharr narrowed his eyes when a few droplets of blood splashed into the water. The result was almost immediate and ripples bubbled from deep within the lake. Despite the buoyancy that the water surely provided, the ground shook where he stood.

It was an unsettling feeling but one that had to be put aside as he took a step back to try to evade an arming sword that swung toward his gambeson.

It was a weak strike that failed to catch him flush and the blade bounced away, leaving only a little superficial damage to his armor. The woman with the weapon fell back and looked at it like she almost didn't believe that it hadn't achieved anything.

One of the mercenaries surged forward, thinking that he saw an opening as he dove toward the first man Skharr had killed. The barbarian waved for him to fall back and wait, but he was too late. Another one of the acolytes saw him as an easier target than the massive barbarian and powered a seax into his gut.

He screamed and fell, trying to contain the wound where his innards had already begun to slither out.

Another of the mercenaries raced to where Salis had impaled one of the acolytes and tried to snatch the ax he had been carrying when something jerked out from the water. The movement was quick and sudden enough to spray water over the group that was still fairly close to the shore.

They all scrambled away as what looked like a massive leg stretched sharply to stab through the chest of the woman who had tried to arm herself. It crushed most of her chest with frightening ease. The limb was long and segmented and resembled that of a crab with a few bristles protruding from it. It might possibly even be delicious if it hadn't been almost ten feet long.

The leg helped to drag whatever was beneath the surface up, and more appendages were revealed as the creature thrust itself to the surface. It moved slowly and Skharr could see why once it was out of the water.

Of its ten limbs, only eight were used to support it. Compared to the thick, heavyset body, the legs that flared out seemed spindly and a pair of heavy claws swung out ahead. They sagged and scraped against the rock as the creature propelled itself forward and used the claws to drag the two bodies—the acolyte Salis killed and the mercenary who had tried to arm herself—toward the water. The monster lifted the arm of the acolyte to its mouth where a few chunks of the exoskeleton extended and dragged the limb inside after it was torn from the dead body.

"He approaches!" one of the acolytes shouted, laughed, and pointed his sword at the monster that dragged itself slowly even farther out of the water. "He approaches! Our faith is rewarded!"

Skharr scowled at the man's shouts. It seemed like the monster was more a scavenger drawn to the taste of blood and the sight of the corpses that it would feed on. The way it moved showed that it was uncomfortable outside its natural liquid habitat and it likely preferred to attack while still in the water—which explained the skiff, he supposed. Once it was pushed out, the monster would have little difficulty in submerging the small craft with its offerings.

"He approaches! He app—"

The yells cut off as the barbarian slashed his blade across the man's throat. The fool had seriously begun to annoy him.

He realized that Cassandra had peppered the other acolytes with her throwing daggers. This, combined with the efforts by Salis and the single remaining mercenary, made five of the acolytes realize that they were in as much danger of being sacrificed as their intended sacrifices, and they began a hasty retreat to the door they had entered from, closing it behind them.

For his part, Skharr had no intention to run from the beast and studied it intently from the relative safety of his position a short distance from the shore. Instead of attacking, it dragged another of the corpses of the acolytes toward it and began to ease into the water. Small waves were displaced as it descended into the depths with no interest in those who were still alive.

"What the hell was that?" the barbarian asked finally. "Is that the Old God that they are worshiping?"

Cassandra shook her head. "It's merely an instrument, a means to sacrifice the victims. I would think they would watch the skiff head out into the water. It would be enough to bring the monster out and they would only see the creature dragging it down."

"I think we should leave," the remaining mercenary said and glanced around nervously. "We are alive and that is enough treasure for me."

Salis was quick to shake her head. "This place is designed to draw folk in. Leaving will not be an option. We will have to go through the dungeon to survive it."

"Through?" the man asked and stared at the island.

Skharr drew a deep breath and shook his head. "We move to the island. If you prefer to not join us, I understand. For the moment, I would suggest that we take any weapons and armor we can scavenge from the dead and use their skiff. Of course, we need to be quick and hope that the monster is no longer hungry."

CHAPTER EIGHTEEN

It was a gamble, but Skharr felt it was a sound idea. The monster did not seem to be interested in killing anyone after it had feasted on the dead. It even left a few of the corpses behind once it had enough.

This last fact was beneficial. Salis, Grakoor, and the single mercenary left of those who had been captured all needed armor and weapons if they had a mind to be involved in the fighting. Skharr offered his bow to the quarter-orc, but his teammate found that the draw was too heavy for him to fire it accurately and decided it was best to simply let him keep it.

The dead had been well-armed and armored, which confirmed that their equipment had been taken from those that they captured over the years. None of it was specifically designed for any of them, but Grakoor was happy with the ball and chain flail, and Salis enjoyed the weight and balance of the spear the barbarian had tossed to her. That left a short arming sword and a dagger for the man who had chosen to join them. He looked less than convinced that going through the dungeon would help them, but he knew his chances of survival were better with the group than on his own.

Skharr stepped cautiously onto the boat and inspected it to make sure the structure was sound and would carry them safely across.

He grinned as Cassandra yanked and tugged to adjust the armor that she had taken from the dead acolytes. The most offending piece, it appeared, was a gambeson of thick padding and a light cover of mail that had been designed with someone possessing a much smaller bust in mind.

"You fought in plate mail," he said as they all boarded the small skiff and he pushed it out onto the water. "Do you find this lighter armor less comfortable?"

"The plate was designed for me specifically," she grumbled and shifted the piece around a little more. "It was comfortable and easy to use. This one gives me easy movement around the shoulders but less around the waist and chest. I can fight but it is…uncomfortable. It would suit me better if it offered a little more ventilation, even at the expense of less protection."

Skharr chose not to speak of the fact that she wore a charm that would protect her as armor would. Perhaps she merely didn't feel protected enough or had little faith in the device working as required. Either way, if she wanted to be better armored, it was her prerogative.

Their small boat had a mast and even a sail, but there was no wind to speak of once they were out on the water. It was best, they decided after a brief discussion, to use the oars that had also been provided with no apparent purpose. They were pointless if the intended sacrifices were bound and unconscious. Skharr took one and Grakoor took the other and between them, thrust them toward the center of the lake and the island.

None of them felt comfortable as they moved out over deeper waters, and Cassandra was the first to peer out over the edge into the depths while careful to not tip the skiff.

"I guess the creature is content with the meal he has," she

whispered as their rowers worked in unison to drive the vessel out toward the island.

It seemed like she was right, of course, but none were willing to test their luck as they continued to move across the eerily still surface. All of them waited warily and almost expected something to lurch up from the watery depths.

Skharr was facing away from the island, with Cassandra seated at the stern to guide them as they continued toward the island. It was an unsettling feeling to not see where they were going, but when she finally tapped his shoulder, he pulled the oar into the boat and turned to look at their destination.

For a moment, he wondered if they had somehow discovered a different one. It had seemed smaller from a distance, but when Salis bounded out to pull the craft onto the shore, he realized that they had reached something a great deal larger. The statues were taller than they appeared from a distance as well and rose almost fifteen feet from the rocks at the edge.

Skharr debarked carefully and paused to make sure none of the others needed any help before he advanced up the isle.

It was an unsettling sight. So much of it had somehow been hidden from sight from their previous vantage point, and it now seemed like they had reached a rocky beach that looked like it could stretch for miles.

He adjusted his sword for a better hold and looked at the rest of the group to confirm that they were following him before he veered deeper into the island.

"Don't you think we should reconsider this?" the mercenary asked as they climbed over the rocks to reach where Skharr was leading them. "There is more to this place than what meets the eye, and if we simply head on in, something will eat us. I'm sure of it."

The barbarian looked at the others. The man had something of a point, and if they all decided to leave this enchanted island and try their luck in the labyrinth of the temple, he wouldn't try to stop them. Even so, his battle lay directly ahead and he would not back down, not even if he had to continue on his own.

He had been brought in to kill this Old God before it could emerge from the depths.

"Do you truly want to row yourself back?" Cassandra asked and studied the man carefully.

"No, but..." His gaze darted toward the temple with a hint of longing in his expression, but he knew he wouldn't return on his own.

"We move forward," Salis asserted firmly and patted him on the shoulder. "Turning around now will only see us stabbed in the back—or with a slab dropped on our heads when we aren't paying attention."

"We're here to kill a fucker," Grakoor agreed. "We'll find it, kill it, and leave this place alive and with enough stories to dine for free for the next decade."

Skharr shrugged. "I suppose you have your verdict. Once more, if you think you would fare better going the other path, none of us will stop you."

There was no sign that he would leave the small group, but the barbarian didn't like having a man like that in his party. The chances were that once things became violent—as they inevitably would—they would not be able to count on him to stand his ground.

They continued inland and Skharr kept his sword in hand. The landscape was covered with rocks which made it difficult to see how the island had been formed. There were no plants and no signs of life, merely acre after acre of craggy rocks that seemed untouched by sunlight since the formation of the earth.

Skharr scrambled down a small decline and into the rocks. The light from above cast an almost reddish-blueish hue across the scenery which made it seem almost ethereal like he was looking at something from another world.

Which, he supposed, was what the lone, woeful howls he

heard from the distance sounded like too—otherworldly and ethereal.

"Oh, gods," the mercenary whispered. "They've released the monsters again."

"What?" Skharr asked.

"They keep the creatures in cages and released them to attack my party. Somehow, they can control how the monsters attack—and when too."

Skharr didn't like the sound of that. He took his bow from where it was slung over his shoulder, selected three arrows from the quiver, and tucked two into his bow hand.

The last was pressed up against the bowstring as he moved over the rocks and watched for any sign that the monsters were approaching them.

The first one seemed a little different than what he'd expected. One of the monsters crested the rocks and heaved itself up for a better view of the group. It was a lean creature and painfully thin and its rib cage was visible through its thin, gray skin. It had a long jaw with small, brittle teeth and large eyes with massive black pupils suddenly turned on the barbarian.

It had started on all fours and about the height of Skharr's knees, but it straightened its long and sinewy body. The head looked a little too large for the rest of it as it raised its snout and uttered another of the mournful howls that they'd heard before.

The warrior raised his bow and immediately let the arrow fly once he had the beast in his sights. The arrow flew true, drilled directly into the creature's chest, and turned the howl into a sharp yelp as it was punched from its perch on the rocks.

"That was one of the monsters!" the mercenary warned and clutched his weapons a little tighter. "There will be a whole pack of them coming, just you wait."

Skharr hoped that cutting the howl off would keep the rest of the pack from finding them, but his hopes were dashed when he heard a dozen or more similar howls from behind him. More of the monsters were coming.

"We need to move," he instructed. "Get up on the rocks and find us a path!"

He was speaking to Salis, who responded with alacrity. Despite her stouter appearance, she was light on her feet and climbed the rocks smoothly while the others struggled to follow her.

Their pursuers came within range and Skharr tried to pick one of them off as it stood on its hind legs to try to locate them.

The head ducked a little too quickly and the arrow flew over to splinter uselessly against a boulder behind his target. He scowled and retrieved another couple of arrows from his quiver to have them ready when more of the monsters began a concerted approach.

Most appeared to be of the same size as the first—smaller, painfully thin, and ravenous—but others were noticeably larger. They seemed to lurk deliberately at the back of the pack, while they were similar enough for him to see that they were at least the same species, there was a clear difference in hierarchy between them and the smaller ones, who seemed to try to avoid the larger creatures out of fear.

Those of the larger version were more powerful and sat on their hind legs with their forepaws in the air like they were watching and waiting to see what was happening with the rest of their pack.

It seemed likely that they waited for the smaller creatures to kill their quarry before they moved in to steal the food and feast first while the hunters were forced to wait.

Skharr paused and raised his bow to find one of the larger creatures. It saw him almost as soon as he had set himself for the shot. There was no sign of fear in the beast's massive eyes as it stared at him from almost a hundred paces away.

It was a difficult shot, to be sure, but the sheer size of it—

larger than most large cats he had encountered—made it a little easier. As did the fact that the beast didn't appear to move at all.

He loosed the arrow and traced its path to its final soft but powerful thunk into the beast's chest.

The monster responded with a pained howl as it fell back and blood dripped from the wound.

He placed another arrow quickly to the bowstring and let it fly to catch a smaller creature on the side of the head as it tried to approach him.

Another arrow was brought to the bowstring and he turned to see where the rest of his group were.

A deep scowl formed on his face. Salis had been leading them away from the monsters, but it seemed almost impossible that they had disappeared. The formation of the rocks and boulders made it easy to hide, but they had been in front of him a moment before.

"Stinking slime-spawned son of Janus' poxy whore." He growled with real annoyance.

CHAPTER NINETEEN

The low howls followed his every step and Skharr couldn't shake the feeling that something else watched him as well while he navigated the rocky landscape.

The monsters were better adapted to moving across the rough terrain than he was, but for some reason, they held themselves back from attacking him outright. Whether it was because they were afraid to attack or if they were merely trying to circle and launch an assault from all sides, he didn't know.

Pack animals tended to follow the latter option.

The fact that he had their full attention was at least one benefit of what was happening. At least he was keeping the monsters away from the rest of the group, wherever they might be.

There was the matter of how he would survive, but he would get to that later.

Skharr worked his bow and caught another of the monsters that stood on its hind legs and tried to find his location. The others had begun to learn quickly and now kept themselves low or ducked quickly when they saw him.

Although not entirely surprising, it would make thinning

their numbers a little more challenging. The barbarian had a few moments' reprieve now and then but it wouldn't be long until he finally found himself in a place where he could no longer run.

That was how wolves hunted. They simply waited for whatever they were hunting to find itself stuck or unable to keep moving, then made the final kill. He had never imagined that he would end up much like one of those elk or buffalo.

Finally, he reached an area of flat land where the rock formations rose in front of him almost thirty feet. It was possible to climb, of course, but it would not be quick work and especially not with monsters nipping at his heels.

He turned to look at a handful of the monsters that had already stopped at the entrance to what he now suddenly recognized as a dead-end.

"I guess you were guiding me here, then?" Skharr asked and touched his quiver to determine that he only had six arrows left, aside from the two he had in hand. It wasn't nearly enough to defeat the group of monsters that followed him. Still, the pack would be much smaller once he had put the few arrows he had to good use.

The creatures began to filter in and he raised his bow. A few scrambled back when one was caught and pinned by the arrow, its death instantaneous.

"Who'll be the first?" Skharr roared. The creatures probably couldn't understand him, but it certainly filled him with a stirring of fire as he took a step forward and fitted another arrow to the string. The beasts backed away hastily.

He grinned, his gaze fixed on those that drew closer, but they inched away when they saw him aim his bow at them.

The intelligent creatures had learned quickly what killed the others of their pack.

"You all want the meat but none are willing to be the butcher," he accused and tensed as one of the larger creatures began to advance. It moved on its knuckles, not its pads like its smaller counterparts. Those darted out of the way, perfectly willing to let the larger monster have its turn at their prey.

The creature was almost as large as he was, Skharr realized, with thick, corded arms in front of shorter, stubby hind legs. Its limbs made it look almost human, but the jaw looked more like a wolf with long, yellow fangs exposed as it approached.

He remembered how the rest appeared to focus their attacks on him when he killed one of the larger monsters, which made it an interesting moment as he studied the pack carefully. All looked hesitant—like they were waiting for something to happen. Perhaps for him to attack first.

Skharr drew the arrow back on the bowstring, ready to take the first step. If they all rushed him, he would only be able to fire so many arrows off before he was swarmed, and it was always better to get the first strike. Especially if it killed the larger of the creatures first.

Suddenly, the massive beast rose on its hind legs, showed its teeth again, and beat its chest once with its right paw before it barked. The others reacted immediately but not in the way he had anticipated. Rather than launch a concerted assault, they all drew back and returned to the rocks.

They weren't running from something and they weren't chasing easier prey. It even looked like a handful were interested in returning to attack him, but another bark from the larger creature scared them back into line.

There was no way to explain the odd behavior, and Skharr held himself ready and waited for an attack as he watched the monsters move away and finally, out of sight of the little enclave he'd been trapped in. It was an unsettling feeling, not knowing why he was being kept alive, but he grasped his bow a little tighter and remained alert and watchful until he was sure that none of the monsters were circling for a different approach.

The barbarian remained entirely baffled until he turned to the wall of stone that he'd been backed up against. Immediately, he noticed that something had changed. It almost seemed impossible but he had begun to doubt that anything was truly impossible in a place like this. Or, at least, anything that couldn't be altered and changed by magical influence.

In this case, he looked through a crack that had appeared in the wall. It was large enough for him to move through and a few flickers of light were visible on the other side.

All this still seemed impossible, but he couldn't help but feel that was the reason why the monsters had moved away. It seemed logical that something inside had scared them off. He pulled his packs off his shoulders and carried them by hand as he slipped through the opening.

It felt like the aperture grew the farther he went through it and soon, he didn't need to shuffle sideways. He started when the wind touched his face as he stepped into the opening that appeared to be covered by vines on the other side. The smells that engulfed him were nothing like those in the cavern.

These were more like flowers with a hint of saffron like he had stepped into a rich, luxuriant garden that had been allowed to grow with only the gentlest guiding touch.

Skharr slipped through the vines that shielded the entrance and smiled when a touch of sunlight warmed his face. It felt impossible but maybe he hadn't been looking correctly. Perhaps this was another way out of the cavern and would lead out into the fresh air. He wouldn't complain about being out of the temple.

"Skharr?"

He peered across the clearing in real surprise. While he hadn't expected to find Cassandra there, perhaps the rest of the group had discovered this welcome space when he was separated from them.

She laughed and ran to where he stood.

"You look about the way we did when we found this," she said and took his hand. "Can you believe it? Just outside that damn temple, you find somewhere like this."

He nodded and tilted his head to survey his surroundings with a critical gaze. Locating Salis and Grakoor in the crowd was easy, but he didn't recognize the others in the group. None of them had been among those they had found, but all wore the same long, gray robes that the acolytes had worn.

He couldn't glean much from that, and he focused his inspection to try to see beyond the obvious. The whole area radiated peace and contentment, which seemed a little odd given the island they had recently left.

"Your mind is not quite sure about what it sees?" a man asked in a deep voice from deeper into the glade. After a moment, Skharr noticed a tall man moving close to him. From his robes and size, he almost thought that it was the high priest, but that was where the similarities ended.

The newcomer was tall, well-built, and clean-shaven. Golden hair rolled down to his shoulders and a pearly-white smile was complemented by a pair of gorgeous blue eyes.

"You can look into minds?" the barbarian asked and watched the man intently—although he didn't miss Cassandra's almost awestruck reaction as the stranger approached.

"I can, but it was not necessary in this instance. You looked confused and it is an expression I have seen on many faces upon entering my glade." The man placed a hand on his shoulder and encouraged him to move forward.

Something like a comforting warmth swept over him as he was drawn farther in, but he caught a flicker of motion from the corner of his eye.

"My followers can be a little…misguided at times, but their intentions are pure," the man said. "This haven is what I have in store for all who enter my temple, no matter what their means. Light and freedom are granted to all."

Something infused the words and made his mind feel like it

might turn to mush, and Skharr nodded agreeably to what the man was saying. But again, something moved and his gaze settled on a figure that was oddly out of place. The old man did not wear the same gray robes as the rest and he led an old donkey.

This was Theros, he realized in an instance. It was almost impossible to forget the man's appearance, even as an older man. A small smile played on his lips as he watched Skharr.

"I know what you are wondering. Not many come into the presence of a god and many are not sure what to expect, but BaroonPatel is more similar to humans than you might think…"

The god's voice trailed off when he caught sight of the old man and he froze as Skharr pulled away from his hands. The barbarian glided to where Cassandra looked a little confused like she wasn't sure what she was looking at.

"What's happening?" she whispered.

The warrior took Salis and Grakoor by the shoulders and made to drag them into the cave they had entered through. With a muttered curse, he paused when he saw that it had disappeared and there was no way back.

"Stinking piles of troll turd on all godsbedammed fucking magic users, gods included." He growled annoyance and turned to look into the glade again. Theros had vanished but his effect had been felt. BaroonPatel seemed to shift from side to side and flickered in and out of sight. His visage changed from that of the heady god he had portrayed to something darker that almost sucked the light from the world around it.

The warrior stood his ground, his hand firm around his weapon as the euphoric effects of whatever was happening around them began to seep away, along with the idyllic vision of the glade they had entered. The sensation of peace disappeared and he realized he could feel the god's focus on him.

The glade was gone and the rocky landscape had returned, darkly illuminated by the tendrils over massive stalactites. But the dark presence remained—not present in the way that the golden-haired image had been, but the god's presence could be felt in the cavern with them. The oppressive sensation felt like it was bearing down on his mind and trying to force it to submit.

This was only a feeling for the moment, but it grew stronger with every second. He drew a deep breath and clutched the nearby rocks with his free hand for balance as the ground shook beneath him.

"You would not find peace in this life!" A booming voice filled the chamber and Skharr saw the high priest approaching them. "You will find it in death instead!"

He held a dagger and an odd glow emanated from his eyes, as well as those of the group that followed him. Twenty of them, by his hasty count, were decked out in full plate armor and a few carried swords while others brandished spears.

One held a staff that radiated magical energy, which he brought down to the earth with a magical word that filled the air and made the ground shake harder.

"He's in my head!" Grakoor screamed and Salis moved to protect him as the quarter-orc dropped to his knees.

The barbarian started to advance but paused as the ground shook violently again and the rocks beneath them began to crack. He hefted his sword and tried not to look into the gap that had suddenly begun to fill with water from the lake.

"Skharr!"

He turned to where Cassandra stood but caught only a glimpse of her before massive boulders shook loose from their positions high above them. In that moment, she slid under the avalanche.

He had no power against this. Skharr was a warrior but standing up to a god needed the power of a paladin who suddenly lay crushed and unmoving beneath the stones.

The god needed to be stopped, however. He had already put his mind to the fact that his task was worth more than his life and he wouldn't stop at anything.

After a moment of consideration during which the shuddering, twisting earth made it difficult to stand or focus on anything else, the barbarian reached back and grasped the silver dagger he wore on his belt.

It was almost a perfect replica of the sword he carried, only smaller with the handle barely large enough to fit in his hand. He wasn't one to throw himself into danger without deep consideration, but there was no time for caution now.

Trusting the word of an elf on the topic of magic felt like the right thing to do. That aside, it was the only option they had left.

Skharr sucked in a deep breath, closed his eyes, and drove the dagger into his own chest.

CHAPTER TWENTY

The earth had ceased its convulsions.

There were many things Skharr assumed dying would feel like. Painful was generally considered the most likely, along with a few other feelings. Elation was one he always thought would come, especially if he found a way to die that was honorable.

Uncomfortable was not one of the feelings he thought would be on his mind but disappointingly, that's exactly what it was. He looked at his chest, where the dagger protruded. A twinge of pain triggered when he moved. He could feel the blade digging into his body but it wasn't quite as painful as he thought it should be.

None of the others were moving. He wondered if he could attack the high priest while they were all standing around, but moving felt a little difficult as any movement from him made the weapon shift inside him.

"My, my, my," said a familiar voice.

Skharr turned to see Theros again. The god was seated on the ground near a small fire and his donkey stood lazily behind him.

"Theros," Skharr grumbled as his attention returned to the dagger in his chest. "It is odd to see you in these circumstances."

"I've been following your actions here," the deity replied with a chuckle. "You all seem to know that you are wildly outmatched and yet are willing to fight all the same. It brings tears to my eyes."

"I see none now."

Theros stood and groaned as if he truly was an old man before he walked closer. "Well, they were there. Interesting, that. It would seem you have more faith in me than your lip service would suggest. Or should I say lack of lip service, eh, DeathEater?"

He realized that the god was talking about the dagger in his chest and chuckled but immediately regretted it as it caused his lungs to brush against the blade.

"I suppose you could say we are all out of options. Faith is all we have left at this point."

"Indeed." Theros looked at the rest of the group with a thoughtful expression. "You have a real party here. The paladin, the high priest, and all the others trying to ignore what's happening in the water."

Skharr looked up and realized that the Lord High God was right. Something crept out of the water and onto the island they stood on.

"I'd rather it wasn't so well attended," he responded caustically. "Especially by whatever the fuck that bottom-spawned shit-ugly bastard is."

"It looks rather like a squid," Theros pointed out. "Almost like what you fought in the other body of water you were trying to get around—although unless I miss my guess, this one will be a few magnitudes greater."

All he could do was agree. At this point, very little of the creature was visible—a handful of tentacles and what looked like the heavy claws of a lobster, but they dug deep into the rock and worked to drag the still hidden body out of the water.

That, he realized, was what caused the ground to shake.

"It's interesting to find you with Tarvis in your hands," the deity continued.

"Tarvis?"

"The dagger protruding from your chest. Did you not know the name?"

"The elf who gave it to me didn't mention a name. She called it a dagger of health whatever the hell that means."

"I suppose she meant that the dagger could be used to save one from death by killing you and bringing you back stronger than ever. That was my brother's intention when he designed it, although he always manages to find a way to screw the recipient of the wish. It is a creative, sadistic idea, playing on the mind of a person who is on their deathbed."

"I need your wisdom," Skharr admitted. He suddenly felt all strength disappear from his legs and almost fell.

Theros was there to catch him. Surprisingly, his old-man frame did not crumple under the weight of the barbarian and he carried him carefully to the fire that he had been seated next to.

"There's a good lad," the god said and set him down gently.

It was an odd feeling to rely on someone else for balance, but Skharr made no mention of it. "Your...your wisdom. As you can see, we are in the midst of a problem and we find ourselves without our paladin. I cannot kill this...this god on my own. I need a miracle from this dagger thrust, the best the blade can provide. I need to ask you...what is the best miracle to ask for?"

Theros chuckled softly as he sat beside him. "My brother will not be pleased. He does enjoy the games he plays with those who use the weapon, as well as the unfortunate circumstances he puts those desperate enough to call for his help through. Of course, that would be mitigated if you were to ask me for the miracle in question."

Skharr nodded. "The god needs to die. I don't know how best to carry it out, and I assumed that you couldn't give it to me yourself."

"For the sake of one of my paladins, I might be able to intervene," the old man told him and looked at the paladin's unmoving body. "However, she would need to ask me for the help herself and I suppose she is in no position to do that. And—good gods, man, what is she wearing?"

The barbarian twisted his head to look. She had discarded the armor that had been collected from the fallen and now wore only the undergarments of chain mail.

"Do you mean the armor or lack thereof?" he asked.

"I gave her a fine suit of plate armor for her to use," Theros muttered and shook his head. "Hmm. What have you been doing with my paladin, DeathEater?"

"Nothing I would speak of unless she is alive." He smiled. "But she did consent to it."

"I suppose that describing your acts together as sensual would be accurate?"

He simply shrugged.

"I see," the god whispered. "Barbarians prefer action over talk, I suppose. Although I would have hoped that the two of you would have had a little more help on this quest."

"We did." Skharr toyed idly with the handle of the dagger. "One is dead and the other two were almost sacrificed. Neither of them is a member of your temple."

"That is a downer on their day."

Skharr grimaced at an odd twitching sensation around the blade buried in his chest.

Theros leaned closer to inspect the weapon carefully. "The point of no return. You can feel it in your chest, yes?"

He nodded, grunting softly.

"It will pierce your heart the moment time resumes," the god informed him.

"Yes."

"You are truly committed to dying so Cassandra might continue the fight?"

"I cannot kill a god. She might have a chance."

"How noble. Or should I say selfish? Do you honestly hope to leave all the duties of dealing with that kraken to her while you flit off to whatever afterlife awaits you?"

All Skharr could offer was a shrug. It had become harder and harder to speak.

"Well, I hate to say it, but you will not leave this battle so easily. She will need you to disconnect the entity controlling the kraken, to destroy the body, and force it back into the plane of gods where it belongs."

"That is good to know," he conceded.

The old man looked a little startled, then clicked his tongue in disapproval. "Oh my. It would appear that I have given up one important aspect of my plan without being prompted. I suppose it means you do not owe me anything for it."

"I'd provide you with treasure, but this dungeon has been surprisingly absent of such riches," the barbarian quipped, his words a little slurred.

"So, one might be able to say that you are doing this for all the right reasons and with no greed in your heart." Theros patted him on the shoulder. "You don't even expect riches in exchange for preventing the world from being subjected to the destruction caused by BaroonPatel."

"Indeed, but I would not turn the prospect of riches down." He shifted uncomfortably on the hard earth.

"So I see." The deity stood quickly and in that moment, Skharr realized that he no longer appeared as an old man. His hair and beard were gray but gone was the frail appearance he assumed. He now seemed almost fifteen feet tall, and for the first time since they had met, appeared as the god he truly was.

"What now?" the barbarian asked.

"Your wish is granted. But you may never know—"

The deity snapped his fingers and suddenly, he vanished. Gone was the donkey as well as the fire where they had been seated. The discomfort in his chest turned into a sharp pain and blood gushed from the wound in his chest.

He sucked in a deep breath but almost felt like his lungs were no longer able to pull the air in. For some reason, he was on his feet again and he realized that he was back where he had been when he first drove the blade into his chest.

The pain struck him like a hammer, and he listed to the left, pressed himself against a large boulder, and felt like he was starting to lose control of his body.

His gaze drifted up and focused on Cassandra, who rushed toward him. Perhaps it was her or it could be someone else. But who else would wear that outfit?

Thinking had become difficult as well and he realized that all he could see was the unyielding rock rising to meet him.

"Wake up!"

The side of Skharr's face stung for the second time and suddenly, everything returned to focus. His lungs sucked air in again and his eyes opened wide as he reached out for something to take hold of.

There was power in her voice and he felt as though the smack was entirely unnecessary. The voice alone carried enough to bring him back to consciousness.

But perhaps Cassandra needed that for herself.

The barbarian looked at his chest and the hole in his armor where the knife had been buried in his heart. No wound remained, although the skin looked a little red and sensitive.

"What the hell was that for?" he asked and put his hand on his cheek.

"It worked, didn't it?" Cassandra snapped in response. Skharr realized that the dagger was no longer in her hand. He turned as the kraken—as Theros had described it—slid back into the water.

She had used the power to heal him and to launch the dagger at the monster. It was an impressive throw and Skharr could see the entity rise out of the beast like the dagger was enough to separate them—or at least partially for the moment.

It wouldn't last, but when it moved sullenly, another idea sprang to mind when he recalled how the tentacled monster had reacted to his sword, which was of the same make.

"How do we kill this?" the surviving mercenary asked. His hands were clenched around his weapons and he looked like his courage was shaken to the core.

The fact that he was still standing his ground despite everything that had gone wrong did say something about his courage, and Skharr could not ask more of a man than to stand firm when all seemed lost.

"I slowed it with that magical dagger but we don't have much time," the paladin said and helped him to his feet. "We need to find a way to destroy it."

"We only need to separate the god that has taken control of the monster," Skharr replied while his fingers probed the place on his chest where the blade had been. "And I think I know of a way to do it."

He lifted his sword and held the handle up for Cassandra to see.

"That is the same design as the dagger," Salis said.

"Yes, and...well, it would be a gamble, but from the way the monster in the other lake reacted, it might be enough to drive the demon from it. I'll need you to distract the monster while I attempt it."

Cassandra nodded and looked at the others. "All right. Grakoor, take Skharr's bow. You'll be able to hit something that large. The rest of us will find other ways to distract the godsbedammed ugly fucker. Skharr...well, I hope you're right."

He grinned, took his bow and quiver from his shoulder, and handed both to the quarter-orc.

"Me too," he admitted, both his hands firmly around his sword.

She patted him on the shoulder in a way that reminded him of how Theros had offered the same gesture. Quickly, he pulled away and circled to where he could see the group of acolytes gathered around the high priest like they were trying to protect him. There would be time to deal with them soon, however, and he rushed toward where the monster now tried to heave itself out of the water.

It was impossibly massive—larger than most houses that Skharr had seen—with heavy carapaces covering its body. Claws held it in place over the island, but the face seemed strangest about it. There was no armor there but hundreds of tentacles extended from where the mouth should have been and dozens of black eyes stared at the acolytes below.

The gray-clad figures had gathered to worship their gods rising from the depths and made no effort to run as the tentacles snatched them one by one to vanish in the swirl where he assumed the mouth was.

The god's presence grew with every feed and it felt as if it somehow beat physically on his psyche. The sensation made it difficult to move, although the effects of the charms he wore to counter the magical effects of the creature allowed him to continue despite the difficulty.

The first reaction from the monster was felt when Grakoor launched his first arrow. It was an impressive shot and struck home from over a hundred paces away. Even a target that large couldn't be an easy shot with an unfamiliar bow.

Skharr felt the beast's displeasure like a smack across the face and it retaliated with a ripple across the land like an earthquake that convulsed in a long line across the whole of the island. He regained his balance, raced forward, and adjusted his sword to hold it more firmly with both hands.

Coming close to the beast made it only that much clearer how truly enormous it was, and Skharr realized that he was screaming while Cassandra used her power to keep it occupied. Perhaps with her armor and with a small group of her fellow paladins, she would have been able to drive the beast back. She knew, however, that this was merely a distraction and so parceled her blows out to sting while she still maintained control of her stamina. Salis and the mercenary raced forward to help pull the acolytes away from the searching tentacles and hacked and slashed at those appendages they encountered.

When he looked up and registered the monster towering over him at an impossible height, Skharr felt his courage falter for a moment—all he wanted to do was turn and run as fast and as far as he could. He could find somewhere to hide, right? Let someone else deal with this...creature. Theros was so invested in seeing it fall. Why didn't he simply do it himself?

He pushed the sensation away with a roar of rage and defiance, lunged at the claw that held the monster anchored in place, and drove his sword into it. The chitinous armor melted away as the blade penetrated easily and smoke streamed from the wound. His jaws clenched, the barbarian continued to cut even when a cloud of the noxious smoke engulfed him. He bellowed another unintelligible battle cry and sliced, hacked, and swung until he was on the other side and the monster's blood coated his skin.

The full weight of the beast's dread gaze settled on him but he was beyond caring.

Another roar rushed through his body and he swung his blade in gleaming arcs that sliced through two tentacles that lunged at him. More smoke issued with the strikes and the pain that the god felt suddenly flared through his body like he was wounding himself.

Despite this, all he could feel was a driving need to deal more damage. "Come on, then, you stinking pile of worthless scum-sucking water snot."

He twisted toward the second claw, stabbed into it as deeply as he could manage, and scowled as the monster came free from the island and began to sink.

The warrior had hoped that it would cause the god to lower itself far enough that he could strike the head, but it moved into the water instead. A retreat was likely to tear into the island from below and he couldn't allow that. He moved as quickly as his body allowed toward the edge, muttered a string of imprecations as the beast slipped slowly under the surface, and without a moment's thought, threw himself into the water.

It was warm almost to the point of pain, but he pushed through it. Desperation propelled him through the water and he managed to find small pockets of air to help him as he pushed forward. The hundreds of tentacles swirled in a malignant dance designed to stop and destroy him. Two latched onto his leg and he twisted to slash them viciously from their stumps.

The black smoke inked out into the water and stung his bare skin. Skharr pushed onward, driven forward by the feeling that he was close. He sensed something akin to fear in the god's shared mind as he swam as hard as he could until he could see the eyes ahead of him. They sucked the light from around him like they were made of darkness. Whether that was the monster or the god, he didn't know and didn't care.

Using the monster's chitin armor, he hauled himself forward and shrieked with the shared pain as he drove his blade into the eye closest to him.

CHAPTER TWENTY-ONE

The feeling was almost physical, although Cassandra knew it to be something a little more psychological. The god exercised a hold over them that enabled them to all feel the pain of the strikes Skharr had dealt the monster with his sword.

She would have to ask him where he got it. But then she watched him dive into the water after the retreating beast and there was suddenly nothing.

No pain, no anguish, and no feeling like a nail scraping over the back of her brain, trying to twist her mind to the control of the beast.

They had saved a few of the acolytes from the monster's tentacles, and those who had survived rose slowly and shook their heads like they were suddenly waking from a dream.

The paladin looked around. Nothing had essentially changed. Well, the rock had stopped shaking beneath their feet but that was all, and yet she almost felt something different about the island they were on. The beauty of the rock formations was suddenly present instead of the dread she had felt upon seeing it.

It was like the world was right again for the first time since she'd set foot in this godsbedammed temple. She scanned the surface of the water, expecting the barbarian to rise up from the depths, but as the seconds passed, doubts began to fill her mind. Even when killing the monster, survival was not a guarantee.

She twisted in search of the others. Those acolytes who had been protecting the high priest still sprawled awkwardly around, not having yet woken from the dream state they had been in, but the man himself was still on his feet.

He stumbled somewhat as he approached, but aside from that, seemed uninjured.

Cassandra felt exhausted and merely watched his progress. His eyes gleamed with hatred.

"He...will rise again!" the man roared, but his voice lacked the booming power it had once held. "Your efforts are for naught, and nothing you can do will stop him from taking his place in this world!"

The priest was armed, and she took a step back as he moved closer. Her feet caught on a few stray pebbles and tripped her, and she landed hard and winced when she felt a stinging pain in her back.

He was an impressive figure, taller and larger than Skharr.

"Your deaths will only serve to bring him to his vessel once more!" The man had a sword in his hand and instead of the white robes he had worn earlier, he'd donned a full suit of armor burnished into a silver gleam. If it had not been for the deranged look in his eyes, Cassandra might have mistaken him for royalty.

Grakoor lunged at him and attacked from the left with his hammer. He struck hard at the breastplate. The high priest staggered back but twisted his body to bring the back of his hand across the quarter-orc's face. The blow was powerful enough to open a cut on his cheek and catapult him a good few yards away.

Salis gripped Cassandra by the arm and dragged her to her feet.

"You're a special kind of mad, aren't you?" the paladin demanded and hefted her sword a little to strengthen her grip.

"What you call my madness is an acceptance of the will of the gods!" The high priest raised his weapon and a grin settled on his face. "And I will show you their will whether you like it or not!"

"I have met a god or two in my time," someone said behind the man, "and they are not pleased with your actions."

The high priest spun and gaped as Skharr approached him from the water. The barbarian was covered in something black—like ink—that coated him from head to toe. Amazingly, the sword in his hands was clean and glowed a bright silver.

"But why tell you?" the warrior asked. "It is better to show you in person."

Skharr looked like he was smirking as the high priest all but frothed at the mouth, and swung his sword in a vicious flurry. However strong he was, though, there was no way to make up for his lack of combat experience and training. His ink-stained adversary stepped closer than the swing could find him and his head jerked forward to hammer into the priest's face. The force of impact shattered the man's nose and broke a few teeth.

The barbarian caught his opponent's wrists and twisted them until he was forced to drop his sword. Without pause, Skharr used the pommel of his sword to crush his eye and turn it into pulp before he drew back and thrust his blade through the man's throat. It emerged on the other side and with a jerk, removed the left side.

Leaving the man with his mangled head almost severed felt fitting, Cassandra thought as the priest fell. The warrior stood, breathing heavily, and attempted to wipe the black ichor from his face.

She laughed and moved toward him until the stench of the black coating reached her and brought her to a sudden halt.

"I would embrace you," she said and took a step back hastily, "but whatever that is...well...I cannot..."

Skharr looked at himself and winced. "I know. I'll likely have to burn these clothes and armor. But for the moment, we need to leave here. The kraken was broken from its host but is by no means dead. In fact, it is quite angry, and will begin ripping through this isle like the mindless monster it is in a moment."

"You mean you didn't kill it?" Salis asked.

"Did you truly think one man with a sword could kill it?" He shook his head.

"I guess all the legends about you aren't true." Grakoor shook his head too. He still cradled his cheek where he had been struck.

"Well, I did tear an old god's entity from the monster it was possessing, but yes, since I failed to kill the creature, I failed to live up to expectations." Skharr rolled his eyes. "We'll return to the boat and consider how large a disappointment I am there."

Cassandra couldn't help a laugh as they complied with his suggestion and retraced their steps. The island had changed a great deal since they had first set foot on it, but the skiff was easy to see. Unfortunately, it had been pushed off the island and now floated freely on the water, which began to grow more and more choppy as time passed.

Skharr hauled it back to shore with help from Grakoor and the group scrambled on board. Cassandra paused and looked back.

She could hear no sound aside from a crack that seemed to echo from the other side of the island. The kraken thrust from the water to a surprising height and plunged onto the island to make the ground shake.

Those acolytes they'd saved from the feeding joined them on the boat so it was almost at capacity. The paladin's gaze settled on the group of acolytes that had been defending the high priest and trying to fight the monster as it rampaged. They would not survive. The fact that they were saving those acolytes who had made it was a saving grace on its own.

Still, she felt a twinge of regret that they couldn't save all those who had been enthralled by the Old God. Even though they had fought at cross-purposes not long before, it had all been at the behest of a mind that controlled theirs. They had no real say in the matter, after all.

Skharr began to row the skiff out. The others in their group picked up the other oars and their combined efforts pushed them farther away from where the released kraken deliberately submerged most of the island in the lake. The ensuing waves made the boat rise and fall precariously. Cassandra didn't like traveling over water, even over the shorter distances, and her stomach churned with each roll and heave of the waves.

None of the others seemed to be similarly affected by the unsettled water, which made it even worse. She held onto the mast like it was her only lifeline as they continued to move away from the rampage, which she refused to watch. Imagining the concept of a monster like that with a deity present in it would have been a disastrous occurrence. Only the monster without a mind would have been terrifying on its own but relatively contained.

The boat shook and she realized that Skharr was dragging their vessel onto the beach with the help of a few others.

"We move!" the barbarian snapped.

She nodded, clambered off, and rushed a little farther from the water's edge, grateful to feel dry ground under her feet since her knees were shaking when she moved.

A powerful hand caught her shoulder and held her on her feet.

"I didn't mean to leave you so...unstable," Skharr said. He still tried to keep his distance as he was covered in the foul-smelling fluid.

"Not to shatter your ego, but that is more from the boat ride than our...shared ride," she whispered as heat touched her cheeks. As much as she liked to consider herself above such things as embarrassment, there was still a hint of her old nature that made her cheeks flush a deep red.

"Noted." He pointed his sword at the door leading into the

temple. "We leave through the way that we entered! And if any of the acolytes still remain to stop us, we'll go through them."

She nodded and saw the agreement among the rest of the survivors, but she doubted that there would be any resistance. The ground vibrated with another thrumming roar from the island they'd left behind and she looked back one more time before she turned and stepped through the door of the temple. She hoped to put this place behind her forever.

Still, she couldn't help the feeling that it would come back to haunt them again. Hopefully, it wouldn't be in her lifetime.

CHAPTER TWENTY-TWO

The foul smell only worsened when the blood began to dry on him. Skharr assumed that the pool he and Cassandra had fallen into likely held some of it as well, but it was nowhere near as rancid as what had coated him as he drove his sword into the kraken's eyes and forced the deity out of the monster.

He would need to burn the clothes when he had a chance. Thankfully, his packs had been spared the treatment, and Horse still carried a few packs of his own that had new clothes for him to wear, although the armor and boots would likely not be recoverable.

Feeling fresh air and proper sunlight on his skin for the first time since they entered the temple—for real this time—was an utter relief. It was as if he had held his breath for hours and was finally allowed to breathe.

The vulnerable feeling left him unsettled, but as he looked around at the rest of the group, it appeared that they were all experiencing the same thing.

"Oy! Stop right there!"

The barbarian turned with his sword already in his hand, drawn and ready for one of the true believers—those who hadn't been brainwashed by the deity—who had likely survived their break from the god's control and were not pleased about it.

He lowered his blade, however, when he realized that he recognized the two men who emerged from the underbrush—the mercenaries who had survived the original onslaught. They had remained in the area, and from the terrified looks on their faces, it looked like they had been contemplating returning to the dungeon to find their friends.

"I thought you two were heading back to civilization." Skharr grumbled and sheathed his weapon.

"We…we were, but we couldn't simply leave our…our friends inside," the one on the left said and tried to force the words from his mouth.

"Adre?" the mercenary survivor asked and took a step forward. "Cres? I thought all the others were killed!"

The friends closed in and exchanged quick embraces. Skharr had thought that the team was merely a group of mercenaries gathered together for the job, but it appeared that they were friends.

"We thought to…go back inside, maybe rescue the survivors or at least avenge those that were fallen," Cres said and shook his head. "We… we ran, but we thought maybe…there was something to be done. It is good that you survived, Gregor."

"I don't blame either of you for running," Gregor admitted and beamed as he placed his hands on the shoulders of his comrades. "The rest of us were trying to run when…when…"

None of them needed to relive the story, and Skharr cleared his throat softly while he focused his gaze on the woodland. It had appeared a little more menacing on their first approach, but that feeling had changed. With the separation of the deity from its host, it appeared that the area would be allowed to settle into its natural condition. The barbarian took a step forward and uttered a loud whistle.

"Horse!" he roared into the trees. "Get out here, you daft bastard! You know I can hear you, yes?"

Sure enough, a few moments later, they could hear the sound of clattering hooves as Horse came out of the trees followed by the other beasts that had been a part of both mercenary groups.

"What kind of troll magic is this?" Gregor asked and regarded Skharr suspiciously. "That he summons the animals out of the forest like they were waiting for us?"

"He talks to horses," Cassandra noted. "No magic. At least, no magic that I know of."

The warrior smirked as the stallion approached him, although the beast paused just short of coming near him, snorted, and shook his head.

"I know, I know," he conceded. "I reek of rotten fucking bottom-feeder fish. That's why I need what's in the saddlebags."

Horse still maintained his distance, and the suspicion of the group was quickly assuaged as they continued to where they could see a few streams of fresh water still flowing from the snow at the top of the mountains. The water was cold, beyond refreshing, and did good work of cleaning the muck from Skharr's skin. Unfortunately, as he suspected, the clothes and armor could not be saved.

It was a pity but necessary to discard them in a pile away from the party and he retrieved a few extra pieces he had brought with him for the journey. He could tell that Cassandra watched him change his clothes and even Salis had managed a few peeks as he pulled the new garments on. None of the others appeared quite as interested, though.

Once he was clothed, Skharr moved to where the paladin stood.

"Verdict?" he asked.

"Nothing I haven't seen before."

"I mean about the smell."

"Oh." She leaned in and sniffed around him. "There is still a hint of the vileness on you but not enough to be repulsive. You should be fine for the moment."

"Right. So, what is our plan?"

"We conferred and none wish to risk going through the city under the mountain again. I might have dealt the monsters residing there a blow, but there would still be enough to cause concern. And now we do not find ourselves constrained by time, we will find our way south to one of the passes that are still open."

Skharr nodded in agreement. "We should not find ourselves involved in any fighting on the way."

"I fear that is a little beyond our control," she said and looked at the group. "But you are right. For now, all those present find themselves weary of fighting."

It seemed fairly obvious, but that would change after a few days. At least in his case.

"We should move," Skharr shouldered his equipment and reclaimed his bow from where Grakoor had left it for him. He had no more arrows and would need to make new ones during their journey, but that did not worry him. There would be time in abundance for it as they took the long way home.

"You've learned your lessons, yes?" the barbarian asked.

"If you mean that attacking a dungeon is generally a bad idea, I will have to agree," Gregor answered, taking a swig from his ale. They were surrounded by a group of folk who had a mind to travel south as well, which made it difficult to hold a conversation, but Skharr was determined to try anyway.

"I was told that dungeons were supposed to be full of treasure," Cres commented. "Well, the legends say that even those that have been taken by someone else tend to have some kind of treasure to be collected by the end, no?"

He shook his head. "This was no ordinary dungeon, for one thing. For another, it was already swarmed with acolytes who likely picked it clean of most of the treasures the dungeon possessed. You were lucky to find what you did at the entrance, where those inside likely hadn't spent much time."

The group exchanged looks, and he knew what they were thinking. They had joined the attack for the coin that was promised, and while surviving a dungeon was a feat in and of itself and would likely result in them acquiring a great deal of paying work in the future, they had hoped that it would result in enough coin where they didn't have to take any work that came their way.

"They had better pay us a hefty amount once we return to the guild," Grakoor growled and shook his head. "That kind of fight is not the kind that should result in a man having to beg for coin afterward."

"They likely will," Skharr assured him and shifted his gaze to where Cassandra carried her drink to the table. She had gone through her first few mugs of ale faster than he had and was already off to draw a few more in as a small group of men approached her.

"Do you think she will go back to being a paladin in that outfit?" he asked.

"I think you like the outfit," Salis snarked with a small grin.

"Obviously," he responded. "What is more surprising, however, is that she appears to like it more. I certainly didn't think I would live to see her using it and only it as we travel."

The fact that she wore only the mail undergarments was interesting, and it was clear at least a half-dozen of the men in the common room of the inn stared at her.

Skharr started to stand, but Salis placed a hand on his shoulder and effectively stopped him.

"She might need help," he growled.

"I doubt it. Watch and learn, DeathEater."

Cassandra seemed surprised that the men approached her. She tilted her head when one pointed at her breasts, laughed, and leaned closer to touch them as the rest of his group cheered him on.

The paladin used her free hand to intercept the man's hand before it could touch her, grasped him by his forefinger and thumb, and twisted them both savagely until a crack was heard from across the room.

Skharr didn't know why he was surprised. Beneath the bubbly and pleasant exterior, there lurked a warrior and a magic-wielder who could beat even him into submission if she truly put her mind to it.

He leaned back in his seat and watched the rest of the group converge on her while the man with the broken fingers screamed in pain. One fell back quickly as she crushed her full mug into the side of his face and used the handle—all that remained of the mug—to batter the skull of another who immediately fell senseless.

The three who remained forced her back a step and tried to engage in a fight, but the woman stepped around them like they were standing still, cocked her elbow to the side, and launched one into one of the tables. He lost a few teeth in his fall.

"I may not be a barbarian by birth but I am by attitude!" she roared at the two men still standing, twisted her body at the hips, and rocketed her fist forward into the nearest drunkard's jaw. He sagged and she left him senseless at her feet as well.

That left one, who appeared to be the least drunk of the group. He immediately turned and raced out the door of the inn to the laughter of the rest of the room.

Cassandra grinned as she took another mug the barkeep had already poured for her and rejoined her group at the table. A trace of blood oozed from her knuckles, but Skharr doubted that she could feel it. Or, if she did, she likely didn't care.

"Those fuckers can kiss my ass," she said as she rejoined their group at the table.

He tilted his head and raised an eyebrow, and the paladin could already see where his mind was going.

"Oh, shut it, that wasn't an offer," she muttered but let a smirk touch her lips. "I'm still a little sore from the last time."

"Last time?" Salis asked and her eyes widened.

Cassandra rolled her eyes. "I should not have said that."

Skharr laughed and took a long swing from his mug. "It's been a long journey, and I must say that it has been an honor to fight and stand alongside you."

The others raised their mugs, assuming that he was making a speech that would end with a cheer. The barbarian shrugged and raised his mug as well.

"To surviving a dungeon," he said as loudly as he could. "That story will have you dining out on it for years!"

"I'll drink to that!" Grakoor roared.

"A low bar indeed," Salis commented. "To Abirat. May he rest well knowing that he helped to defeat a fucking god."

Skharr nodded and raised his mug for that as well. Even though the mercenaries didn't know who she was talking about, he remembered the redhead well and drew a shaky breath.

As the night progressed, the group began to turn in for the night, leaving Skharr and Cassandra alone for the moment.

"We should reach the city in the next couple of days of travel," she said and placed a hand on his shoulder as her voice slurred a little. "And I will likely return to my oath when I do. If this is to be the last time that I am free of the oath, I would want it to be—"

Skharr covered her hand with his. "You don't want to finish that. You are drunk and have no idea what you speak of."

"No, no, I do—"

"Our time together will always be cherished in my mind," he continued and squeezed her hand gently.

"In…in mine as well," she whispered and leaned forward.

Skharr could see where she was going but her head sagged before it could reach him and flopped onto his shoulder instead.

"It's about time for the paladin to sleep," he muttered as she snored gently on his shoulder.

The innkeeper approached to clear the mugs from their table.

"I'll need a room," the barbarian whispered and waved his hand to catch the man's attention.

"For the two of you?" the proprietor asked.

"No, for her."

CHAPTER TWENTY-THREE

I t was odd to see the walls of Ryngold come closer with every step. All told, it had been an interesting journey, and it was coming to an end. There were too many moments when Skharr had thought he would not see the walls again.

And now, finally, the walls were there. There was nothing too important about them and certainly nothing that made them stand out from the other cities he'd seen from a distance. He'd assumed that he might experience a sense of interest upon seeing them.

In the end, they offered nothing but emptiness. He shook his head.

"You know, I remember when you told me that you would not join me as I approached Ryngold," Cassandra said and brought her horse to a walk next to him. "You were headed straight to Skepsis, as I recall."

"I had a mind to simply continue traveling straight to Skepsis," he answered. "But I wanted a bed to sleep in before I headed on my way."

"Why didn't you tell me?"

"I tried, but you wouldn't let me get a word in edgewise," Skharr responded and smirked as he looked at her.

"All right, that's fair enough. You didn't know I was a paladin at that point, I suppose, so you wouldn't have known to not lie to me."

"If I was lying, wouldn't you have been able to see through it?"

"Maybe you didn't know that you were lying in the moment in which you told me, which is an odd loophole in our ability to see to the truth of certain matters. I expect you to take full advantage of it now that you know of it."

He shrugged. "How would I be able to knowingly lie without knowing that I am lying?"

She raised an eyebrow, tilted her head in thought, and shrugged. "You would find a way, I am sure of it."

It was an interesting loophole and one that could be exploited, but it would require more than a little skill and luck to pull it off. Skharr doubted that he would be able to do so himself.

As they moved through the city gates, Cassandra brought her horse to a halt. "I will rejoin my order once I return to the temple, so when next you see me, I will wear more than…"

She didn't need to finish her sentence as he gestured to her lively outfit.

"You mean you'll not forget that you ever traveled with a barbarian?" Skharr asked and tried not to stare.

Cassandra winked at him. "Just because we are back in civilized society, that does not mean that I'll ignore you. Until we meet again, DeathEater."

He bowed his head. "Until we meet again, paladin."

The rest of the group headed off to find accommodations for themselves, mostly around the temples, but Skharr headed directly to where the guilds were situated. There would be time for them to rest, but he wanted to make sure that he would receive some kind of pay for his travels.

Walking Horse through the temples on the way to the guilds attracted more attention than he thought it would, but it didn't seem to matter since he could see a few horses already in the large space. Perhaps they expected him to be riding, or maybe only certain members of certain orders were allowed to ride through it.

The barbarian didn't care either way. Horse would not be tied up outside like some kind of lice-infested nag.

The guildmaster didn't appear to pay Horse any mind either as they approached.

"You truly did it?" the man asked and peered at the scroll the warrior presented him with. "Another dungeon? And killed a god?"

"Banished him," he answered. "Although the dungeon had already been looted bare by the occupants, so there was less treasure mixed in than I would have hoped. That is why I would like to see myself paid for my efforts in that fucking place."

"Ah...well, there might be something of an issue with that."

Skharr narrowed his eyes. He'd assumed there might be difficulty but had hoped it wouldn't come from those who owed him coin.

"An issue?"

"Aye. Whenever the priest of Theros extends a contract to us, it does not fall to me to approve the payment of those who complete the contract."

The scowl deepened on the barbarian's features. If there was any such stipulation, it was because the priest did not want to part with his coin even if the mission was completed. Skharr hoped that folk would know better than to try and fuck him over by this point, but then again, he should have known that there would be a few stragglers in high places.

"Where can I find the high priest to collect my reward?"

"You'll find him in his quarters in the temple. And I do wish you the best of luck, although you should know that the priest-hood in this city are loath to part with their coin. Stickier fingers than the tax collectors, they are."

"I'll simply have to convince them to unstick from what they owe me. I'll return."

"I'm sure you will."

Skharr turned away and his blood started to boil as he gained his bearings quickly and directed himself toward where the Theros temple connected to the guildhall. He shoved through a press of folk who were arriving from another job, or so he assumed.

He froze in place when he felt a hand slide over his belt in search of his coin purse in the press of bodies. The barbarian's hand snapped down to catch the thief when he reached what he was searching for and he squeezed and held on until he heard a soft groan of pain from the boy he had caught trying to pick his pockets.

"That was probably the dumbest thing you've done today," he snapped.

The child was perhaps older than ten years and looked scrawny and ragged as he stared at his captor, unashamed and unafraid.

"And I thought a dumb barbarian wouldn't notice," he all but spat in response. "It's better spent on food for me than for you to stuff your face with our ale!"

He released the boy's hand and swung his quickly to clap it across the youth's mouth. The youngster spun away and fell. It had honestly been a soft, backhanded slap, by Skharr's standards, but was enough to leave the thief with a broken lip as his intended prey settled onto his haunches and loomed over him.

"What did you learn today, boy?" he asked and tilted his head.

The pickpocket didn't answer, still stunned from the strike, and he rubbed his hand over where Skharr hit him. His glare was enough of an answer.

"Nothing? Well, you can learn from a slap, or a stab to the gut, or perhaps someone cutting your hand off when you are caught by another who might be less forgiving than I am. Thieving on the streets is a hard life for any youngster in any city in the world, and you should learn that your food comes not from your hands but from your head."

The barbarian tapped the boy's forehead with his forefinger to drive his point home.

"If you plan to survive in a life of crime, you'll do so by being smarter than the others, not quicker or stronger. Although those might help too, of course."

Skharr straightened again. He hadn't been above thievery in his youth, and in his first few years outside of the clan, he had needed to steal to survive more than once. His survival had depended on him using his brains, and the same lesson could be taught to any child who found himself at cross-purposes with the law.

Hoping that the lesson was taught, Skharr continued to the temple, his determination not diminished by his unexpected encounter with the youth. More than a few people watched him as he entered his destination. He knew his reputation as Theros' barbarian, but the hope was that none would think he was some kind of religious fanatic.

Perhaps they would think that anyway if they found out that he had spoken to the god himself. Then again, why would he ignore it if he had, in fact, met the god?

One of the attendants noticed his approach and jumped quickly in front of him.

"How might I help you?" she asked and peered at him like she wasn't quite sure that what she saw was real.

"I need to speak to the high priest."

"He is retired for the afternoon, and you might want to—"

Skharr shook his head. "I'll speak to him anyway. He is in his chambers, yes?"

"Yes, but—"

She realized that she wouldn't be able to stop him and decided that she could at least move ahead of him to announce his arrival.

"High Priest," she shouted and entered the man's private chambers, "the barbarian—"

"I expected him, Gertrude. Let him in," the older man mumbled and ran his fingers through his beard. "Please leave and close the door behind you."

"Of course."

She did as she was told and left so quickly that Skharr wondered if she had been stung. The two men were now alone and regarded one another in silence.

"I was told by the guildmaster that you needed to approve me being paid for our work," Skharr stated without preamble and folded his arms in front of his chest.

"Well, yes, that is how the work for the temple generally goes. Not that we think you are lying, of course, but you have to understand that we have a few requirements that must be met. How would it look if a barbarian could simply appear before us and demand coin and we approved it merely on his word?"

"It would appear that you are willing to pay a man for his work," he replied bluntly.

"Well, yes."

"Did you know what we were facing in that place?"

"No, and I think—"

"A tentacled beast awaited us in the water of a lake. We emptied half of that enormous body of water to deal with it. And an army of undead ambushed us in an abandoned city under the mountains, and that is not even speaking of the cult that killed their own members to become more powerful. Oh, and there was a kraken imbued with the mind of a god. Need I go on?"

The high priest raised his hands in a vague attempt to stop Skharr from continuing and a sheen of sweat appeared on his forehead.

"I did not mean to push you into anger, DeathEater."

"Trust me, priest, you'll know when I'm angry, and it won't be from the tone of my voice."

The smaller, older man blanched and took a step back.

"I'll expect to hear that I will receive what I am owed from the guild before noon tomorrow," he stated coldly and turned to walk out of the man's private chambers when he was met instead by the sight of a woman as she entered.

It wasn't the younger woman that had announced his arrival. Instead, he was met by the sight of a tall, regal-looking woman who was only too familiar.

She no longer wore only her mail undergarments but long, elegant robes of pure silver. Her hair was shorn to where it barely came down to her shoulders, and her hands were tucked inside her long sleeves. Despite all this, there was no mistaking Cassandra as she entered the chamber.

The young woman quickly burst in behind her and looked flustered.

"The Paladin Cassandra to see you, high priest," she shouted. "She would not wait until you were finished with the barbarian."

"It's for the best," Cassandra noted as she moved to the center of the room. She looked a great deal calmer and more settled than she had before. "My business here has to do with the barbarian."

"Oh…of course." The girl beat another hasty retreat and closed the door behind her.

"Am I to understand that you did not agree to confirm the bounty?" Cassandra asked and looked at the high priest.

Skharr realized that her calm demeanor made the man sweat more than his annoyance with the man had.

"I suppose you are on his side of this discussion?" the high priest asked.

"I am, as I always have been, on the side of truth. I was there when he killed the high priest of the god who possessed the kraken. In fair combat, it should be said. Well, not quite fair once it was clear that the Old God was not filling his limbs with strength, but the fact remains that Skharr killed him."

The high priest sat and dragged a kerchief across his forehead. "Well, yes, but…a barbarian, Paladin Cassandra?"

"I am not the one who suggested we ask a barbarian to assist the temple in its matters," Cassandra answered. "You could ask the High Lord God Theros for his word on it if you wish."

The older man sighed deeply. "I would rather not."

Skharr caught a twitch of annoyance in the woman's features, but it disappeared quickly back and was replaced by the placid expression she wore like a mask.

"It is disappointing that a high priest to Theros would care so much about a person's external appearance when you are expected to be better than that. You will need to seek your own redemption, High Priest."

Instead of moving toward the door, she approached one of the bookshelves. She thumbed over a few leather-bound books and tugged at one. A click sounded and she pulled the bookcase out to reveal a hidden passage, which she slipped through.

From the look of the high priest's surprised features, Skharr could tell that the man hadn't known about the passage himself.

"What…what is she up to?" the man asked aloud.

Skharr tilted his head and shrugged. "I suppose she wanted to show you that she had ways of coming to your private chambers that even you were unaware of. It's something to consider, I suppose. She enacts the will of Theros and would not be stopped by something so trivial as doors or locks in doing so."

The high priest blinked and drew his kerchief over his forehead again as Skharr moved to the door.

"I should hear from the guild before noon tomorrow, yes?" he asked and didn't wait for a reply before he moved out of the inner chamber and closed the door.

The woman he'd once thought was a seamstress certainly

knew what she was doing. When she could look more intimidating than a barbarian without so much as breaking a sweat, that was something to behold.

Skharr smirked and shook his head. It was time to get a drink for himself.

CHAPTER TWENTY-FOUR

I t was not quite the end to the quest that Skharr had hoped it would be, but in the end, they never were. The emptiness had only been slightly helped by the high priest's shenanigans, but not significantly so. Now, he sat for a meal at the same inn he had been in when he first came to Ryngold and listened to a minstrel's soft, lilting voice, and it seemed his meal and evening drink weren't quite what he'd hoped they would be.

Even talking to Horse about his woes with the high priest hadn't been the uplifting experience it usually was, although it was likely because the beast was as tired as he was from the long journey they had taken. Approaching the north again in the dead of winter had not been gentle on either of them.

A night in a cozy stable for Horse and a warm bed for Skharr would do wonders for both of them, and sleep came quickly, despite his troubled mind.

Unfortunately, it did not remain.

Skharr wasn't sure what woke him and he lay motionless and stared at the ceiling of his room for a moment. The door was still closed and latched shut, and he could see no sunlight filtering through the slats placed over the windows.

That didn't mean much, he decided. This deep into winter, the days were much shorter and it could have been morning already for all he knew.

But that was not what woke him. At least, he couldn't hear the cacophony from the kitchens that would indicate that morning had come or was even close.

He straightened on the bed and let his eyes adjust to the darkness while he sneaked his hand toward the sword he kept on the bed with him.

"I don't think you'll need that," said the dark shadow in the corner of the room.

"You never know," he replied and grasped the hilt. He knew the voice, of course. Theros was not forgettable, after all.

The old man's features lit up for a moment as he puffed on a pipe, and the smoke made the room smell of cherries for some reason.

"What are you doing here?" the barbarian asked as his visitor puffed contentedly at the pipe for almost a full minute in complete silence.

"You don't seem particularly happy to see me, Skharr DeathEater."

"I cannot say I am happy with your representatives. An Old God was fighting to drive its return into this realm, and despite the fact that it was stopped, I am apparently to blame for my appearance and origins and not rewarded for what I've accomplished."

Theros waved a dismissive hand at him. "That is a minor hiccup. He will learn, even if I have to teach him myself—although I hope to delegate the task to another should it prove necessary. He is not your challenge to meet."

Skharr narrowed his eyes, which had now acclimated to the darkness in the room. He was able to discern a few lines over the god's features that suggested worry rather than pensive puffing.

"I have to say that for a god, you do not appear to be particularly happy yourself."

"You always were a perceptive one, DeathEater."

The deity stood and in that moment, appeared to fill the room, almost too tall for the ceiling as he paced around the far side of it. It seemed that his preoccupied mind was spent on matters other than keeping his godhood hidden from those who saw him.

"Do you know what a paladin is, Skharr?" Theros asked after a few moments of contemplation.

"Usually…an important representative of whichever temple they have sworn an oath to. They are very high in the hierarchy, as I've come to understand."

The god grunted softly. "Mm, indeed. All that and more. I have found that direct communication with the paladins sworn to me has been necessary when certain tasks need to be implemented."

Skharr straightened even more and his yawn was large enough that he felt his jaw would break in half. "And this concerns me how?"

"Because I cannot have you causing my paladins to run about the world in revealing armor that barely covers their chest and leaves everything visible for you if they happen to bend over or to…climb a wall above you."

"I had no part in encouraging Cassandra into any of that," he retorted. "If you wish to discover your paladin's motives, I suggest you speak to her yourself."

"And your little romp in the dungeon? What am I to think about that episode?"

Skharr shrugged his shoulders. "I don't understand why you're bringing this to me. Is she not an adult, capable of making her own decisions? Am I not a barbarian? I acted no differently than when you appeared to give me that contract in your possession. Do not suggest to me that the contract was all you hoped I would accomplish in your name. Clearing that dungeon out and living for years off the earned treasure? I may be a barbarian but do not mistake me for a fool as well."

The god sneered at him. "Indeed. As evidenced with your ability to consistently remind any you cross as to the size of your...dragon."

"If you think I am alone in that regard, you might not have walked among humans as long as you claim." Skharr felt a heat in his stomach as he pulled his covers away, standing up to face the god boldly. "You would do better to ask a barbarian to drop to all fours and eat grass for the rest of his days than to ask me to ignore the attentions of a beautiful woman."

"And yet your people still take mates and create families."

"Some do, yes," Skharr admitted. "Do you see me so tied down? Do I have little grassgrubs around my feet?"

"Not for lack of trying across the kingdoms you've traveled."

Skharr smirked. "Well, a man must remain in practice."

The god nodded slowly. "She was my most devout paladin."

"On sabbatical."

"And yet in a few months with you, she is parading about in naught but her skin."

"Only in my presence."

Theros eyed him closely before his appearance returned to that of an old man shorter than Skharr, and the barbarian realized that the show was all for his benefit.

"You said all. I am explaining that I am the only one to have seen all and so I speak to you. Thus, I believe there to be justification in your words. Skharr, the man who argues in a court."

"Isn't that what you want this to be?" He gestured to the small inn room that they were in. "Arguing what is and is not appropriate for a paladin to do while on sabbatical from her oath to you? She is her own woman beyond your mere pawn. That she chose to act this way to one who is connected to you and felt safe in doing so is baffling, but she reminded me at every possible juncture that she was on sabbatical, which I feel was more for her benefit than mine."

"What is that supposed to mean?"

Skharr scowled at the god. "You knew me to be a DeathEater, a barbarian in all my ways. Did you truly expect me to be anything else for your benefit?"

Theros glared at him for a moment before the look in his eyes softened. "You are making me young again, Skharr."

It was an oddly soft tone, and not one he expected from the god.

"How is that?"

"Keeping me on my toes. You push things, which is what I expected and indeed wished from you. I merely always assumed that you would extend your propensity for trouble in my brother's direction instead of mine."

"Your brother is—"

"An ass, I know." Theros took his seat and puffed at his pipe again. "That makes me chuckle. I hear that phrase more and more across these lands. Eventually, it will reach his ears and he'll be none too pleased to hear it."

Skharr shrugged. "Send him my way. I'll see if I can add GodKiller to my titles."

The old man shook his head. "You already have, barbarian. Among other things, which includes having a paladin declare herself a barbarian. She has returned to the temple. As she is no longer on sabbatical, do not push her to bed you again."

"I never did," he answered. "I merely did not push her away."

A last puff of smoke hung in the air and Skharr realized that the room was empty. Perhaps Theros hadn't heard his last words and perhaps he had. It didn't matter in the bigger scheme of things.

The warrior rubbed his temples gently. "I need another drink."

He strode to the door and left his boots and most of his clothes behind. Maybe folk would still be downstairs and willing to serve him—or at least not stop him from serving himself.

CHAPTER TWENTY-FIVE

" An actual god this time?"

Skharr shrugged, making sure that there weren't too many people from the various guilds around to hear him talking to the Theros guildmaster.

"A god taking on the form of a kraken," he explained and made every effort to keep his voice down. "It's an odd thing, I have to say, and I wasn't able to kill either of them. What I did manage to do is separate the god from the host creature using a magical sword designed for precisely that purpose."

He drew the blade for the man to see, although the guildmaster seemed less concerned with the blade itself and more with the pair of snakes with emerald eyes on the hilt.

"I've never seen quite the like," the man admitted. "Of course, parting a fucker's spirit from his body would be how I described killing a fucker anyway, so I'll be forgiven for not quite seeing a difference between the two."

"It's... well, not quite—"

Skharr paused in his attempt at explaining how pulling a god from its host was not quite killing it and looked up when the clatter of hooves approached them.

A few mercenaries shouted as they scrambled out of the way of the horses that trotted without slowing as they approached the center of the chamber. All shouts of complaint from those who were forced out of the way were stopped when the mercenaries realized who was riding through the chamber.

Three figures in full plate armor proceeded to where Skharr stood next to the guildmaster's stall. They brought their horses to a sudden halt and climbed lightly from their saddles.

The plate they wore bore Theros' symbol on the breastplates and made it clear who they were representing.

Skharr looked at the sun shining through the stained glass that covered most of the ceiling above them.

"Mid-morning," he noted from where he leaned casually on the stall. The guildmaster's back straightened like a bolt of lightning had streaked through him. "You are a few hours earlier than I anticipated."

The leader of the group advanced sedately and didn't even glance at the barbarian as she removed her helm.

He was not surprised to see that it was Cassandra, although her appearance was wildly changed from how he had seen her before. Her features were severe and her shorter hair was pulled into a rigid braid so it fit better in the helm.

"Guildmaster Korral?" she asked.

The man coughed and glanced around him before he took a step forward.

"Aye, that's…that me."

"In my capacity as Paladin to the High Lord God Theros, I am here to authorize the payment of the contract issued by our High Priest to your mercenary, Skharr DeathEater."

The guildmaster nodded, reached a faintly trembling hand across his desk to retrieve the contract, and fumbled a little before he was able to open the scroll. The paladin, without hesitation, picked up the man's red stamp and pushed it firmly onto the paper to officially close the contract, before she rolled the scroll and handed it to Skharr.

"You may present this to your nearest guildmaster to receive your payment, DeathEater," she said. Her tone was cold, almost like she had never seen him before.

He understood, of course, and was careful to even avoid a tiny smile as he took it from her and handed it to the guildmaster.

"That concludes this contract," she said and turned to the other paladins. At her quick nod, both turned to mount up again.

When their gazes were no longer on her, Skharr allowed himself a trace of fun. His expression utterly neutral, he slid his hand to her ass and gave it a pinch.

She showed no sign that she had even felt it aside from the small, feral grin that appeared on her lips.

"Not all those in armor are stuck up," she whispered and winked at him before she replaced her helm, strode to her horse, and mounted smoothly.

All those present stared as the paladins moved sedately the way they had come along a path that seemed to open automatically for them.

"I suppose I should pay you what you are owed," the guildmaster muttered and wiped his forehead with a cloth. "Minus what the guild is owed in fees, of course."

Skharr nodded. "I expected them to drag their heels on paying me my dues."

"They wouldn't have, not if they intended to send a paladin to certify that you completed the contract. And not simply any paladin either, but one of the Sentinels of this city. I'm surprised she didn't appear with a platoon of her fellow holy warriors in her wake."

"A Sentinel, you say?" he asked. Very few paladins ranked higher than a sentinel—only two whom he knew of, in fact. "Well, that explains why he was angry."

"Who was angry?"

"No one important to this conversation." The barbarian added the last casually but cast a fearful glance in the direction of the temple. "We should complete our business. I mean to leave the city today."

"I'll send for the coin. We'll need to draw it from our coffers. Can you carry a chest with you?"

"I suppose I'll have to."

He wouldn't do it himself, of course. Horse would require many, many apples to do all the work.

Verenvan was a welcome sight. Heading south during the winter was always a pleasant feeling, and after a week on the road, it was comfortable to travel out in the open again without cold winds whipping around him.

The city was as busy as it had been before he left. It felt like he'd been away for years, although it had only been a few months.

Not much had changed. There was still a line at the gate and Skharr remained alert for any who might attempt to lift the chest he had hidden on Horse's saddle.

Few would be stupid enough to rob him, but he'd never thought of the criminals in the region as having an overabundance of brains among them so couldn't be too careful.

One of the guards narrowed his eyes as he approached before recognition dawned on him.

"You're the Barbarian of Theros, are you not?" the man asked and approached the station where the guards were certifying the new arrivals.

"One and the same," the barbarian admitted and glanced around as the other guards heard and immediately turned their attention to him.

"It's difficult to think of you within our walls," the man said, gestured for the other guard behind the desk to move away, and took his place. "Shouldn't you be out and about, setting up emperors and killing dragons, gods, and the like?"

Skharr shook his head. "I haven't killed any dragons."

The man laughed, thinking it was a joke, and handed Skharr a paper of admittance to the city.

"I hope you enjoy your stay, Sir DeathEater."

"I'm no—never mind, thank you."

He entered quickly, not wanting to look the gift horse in the teeth. Let them think whatever they wanted as long as he didn't have to wait out in the heat for any longer than was necessary.

The Swilling Mermaid was certainly a welcome sight, and it appeared as though the feeling was mutual. Not from the mermaid with her tits out carved from wood that was set up on the roof of the place, of course, but from the owner, who recognized him and Horse.

"I thought Horse would be enjoying his time at a farm, siring and eating all day," the man commented as he poured Skharr a tall, frothy mug of ale.

"He lost the taste for it after a few days. We'll try again soon and see if he's willing to spend his waning years fucking mares." He took a sip from the mug.

He paused when he heard a familiar voice speaking loudly. The barbarian turned toward a loud-mouthed patron who shouted indignantly from the stairs.

"You call those lice-riddled piles of hay beds?" the man yelled. "I will not pay for a night on those dung-heaps! In fact, I expect you to provide me with food and drink to sustain the horror of my remaining here for the night."

Skharr tilted his head and looked at the owner.

"How much damage do you estimate?" he asked and took another sip from the flagon.

"Anything more than a table will be paid for from your purse."

He grinned. "Food and beer?"

After a moment of consideration, the man nodded. "One meal."

"Deal," he said quickly before the man had a chance to change his mind. He turned to approach the patron who was still berating the inn's staff. "I haven't had a good brawl in weeks."

AUTHOR NOTES - MICHAEL ANDERLE
JANUARY 8, 2021

WOOT!

Ok, first thank you for joining me on this interesting sword & sorcery effort and reading all of the way to the back, here.

If you have enjoyed Skharr DeathEater (and Horse) all the way through book four, then I figure it is safe to ask you to tell a friend if you know someone who likes these types of stories.

The more fans we can get into the series, the more of them I can do.

I don't expect Skharr to become a best-selling series, but I do hope that we can keep Skharr going as a *solid* selling series. The smaller genre of sword & sorcery (and fanbase) Skharr will resonate with isn't as huge as, say, Urban Fantasy.

But obviously I like it, so I'm happy to be working on this character.

Why Cassandra?

So, I have always been on the outside of the Conan stories (having not read them until after I started Skharr), and even the Red Sonja stories. Although I did look up where Robert E. Howard took his inspiration from for the character.

Having considered the fair world I live in, I assume characters (even paladins) might not be Lawful Good all of the time as even the best aren't always 'on,' and if they are, that usually means there is a problem on the other side.

So I figured a few paladins might want a bit of downtime.

Enter Cassandra, a paladin who is a bit tired of her job. She's on a sabbatical and frankly would like to talk about fashion rather than swords, armor and killing skeletons. She happens upon a barbarian who makes an interesting traveling companion.

She's on leave, she can talk to and do whatever she wants until she takes the mantle of her profession back on her shoulders and has to live appropriately.

I grabbed this idea from a certain religious system here in the United States that has a time for their members called Rumspringa which happens during late teens to (at most) twenty-one.

During Rumspringa, the church rules are relaxed so the youth can experience more of the world and choose to become Amish, or separate from the church.

I figure since Cassandra didn't receive much of a choice when she joined the church, the sabbatical was her opportunity to do the same thing.

Get out, break some rules she finds confining, and basically let her hair down.

And what do you know? She has this virile barbarian just walking along with her, letting her chat and annoyingly NOT trying to bed her.

Dammit!

Further, when she gets pulled back into a church situation, she finds out just who that Barbarian is and hears these wonderful tales about other women working to get under into his loincloth.

It's too good to pass up; she wants to flirt. She's still on sabbatical.

Skharr tries to be a gentleman, then his barbarian attitude kicks in, and he starts giving as good as he gets.

It makes for a fun story as they travel to their potential doom.

Plus, have you ever thought how to create a situation where a female warrior has a *legitimate* reason to wear bikini-chainmail? Further, if they choose to wear such armor, how are they really making sure they are protected?

I have; it's a pain in the ass. So I did the typical author hand-wavium and Cassandra chose to use magic to help her pull off her stunt.

I'm pretty sure I seeded the whole why artists show women warriors wear bikini chainmail question either earlier in this story or an earlier book (I think an earlier book.)

Then, there is the misunderstanding on Cassandra's part about a Barbarian Princess.

As Skharr would say, "Barbarians don't have royalty. There would be no reason for a Barbarian Princess to exist."

They wouldn't wear bikini chainmail either, but Cassandra obviously made that happen.

Ad Aeternitatem,

Michael Anderle

PS – I love to read the reviews (ok, I'll admit I read the 5* for sure most of the time... I can't say I always get back to older books after the first couple of months or the lower stars.)

So, if you enjoyed Cassandra let me know!

No particular reason...

CONNECT WITH THE AUTHOR

Connect with Michael Anderle

Website: http://lmbpn.com

Email List: http://lmbpn.com/email/

Social Media:

https://www.facebook.com/LMBPNPublishing

https://twitter.com/MichaelAnderle

https://www.instagram.com/lmbpn_publishing/

https://www.bookbub.com/authors/michael-anderle

Made in the USA
Las Vegas, NV
18 May 2022

49038819R00164